Self-thinning and Growth Modelling for Even-aged Chinese Fir (*Cunninghamia Lanceolata* (Lamb.) Hook.) Stands

杉木自然稀疏与生长模拟

Zhang Jianguo   Duan Aiguo

Sun Honggang   Fu Lihua

Science Press

Beijing

Brief introduction of content

Based on long-term re-measurement data obtained from permanent plots representing different planting densities of chinese fir plantations, dominant height growth model, basal area growth model, diameter distribution model and self-thinning rule were systematically built and discussed, and some new modelling technologies were put forward and used. This book includes nine chapters, and can be used and referred for those working toward the healthy management of fast-growing and high-yielding plantation.

ISBN: 978-7-03-032020-9

© 2011 Science Press Beijing
16 Donghuangchenggen North Str.
Beijing, China

Preface

Forest managers, planners and policy makers forecast the outcomes of different forest management measurement in order to make wise decisions for the biggest benefit. Efficient and readily understandable models of growth and yield can become invaluable tools. With suitable inventory and other resource data, growth models provide a reliable way to examine silvicultural and harvesting options, to determine the sustainable timber yield, and examine the impacts of forest management and harvesting on other values of the forest.

In stand growth model system, dominant height growth model, basal area growth model, diameter distribution model are the three nuclear components. The self-thinning rule describes a density-dependent upper boundary of stand biomass for even-aged pure plant stands in a given environment, so far, the debate about it has not been adequately resolved. Therefore, the building of dominant height, basal area and diameter distribution models and self-thinning rule were considered as main research fields in this book.

However, growth models are of limited use on their own, and need long-term experimental data to testify, also require ancillary data to provide useful information. chinese fir is one of the most important coniferous species for timber production in southern China, with 9.21 million ha of single species or mixed stands occurring in both artificial plantations and natural forests. Long-term re-measurement data obtained from permanent plots representing different planting densities of chinese fir plantations were used to fit different models with different modelling technologies.

In our studies, algebraic difference method and generalized algebraic difference method were provided to build polymorphic dominant height model and polymorphic site index equations. A new high-performance diameter distribution function and Fuzzy functions were innovatively introduced and applied to model stand diameter distributions, and reason for differing simulation accuracies among growth equations was revealed. Self-thinning rule was testified and discussed for chinese fir plantations, the selection methods of data points and regression methods were compared and analyzed to estimate the self-thinning boundary line.

This book was researched and written over a period of several years, and many people and several institutions have supported this work in various ways. We are grateful for the long-term support of Subtropical Forest Experiment Centre of Chinese Academy of Forestry, Weimin State-owned Forest Farm in Shaowu City of Fujian province. Very thanks to Professor Tong Shuzhen for experiment design and selfless support.

Zhang Jianguo, Duan Aiguo, Sun Honggang, Fu Lihua

05. May. 2011.

Contents

Preface

CHAPTER ONE: Modelling of dominant height growth and building of
polymorphic site index equations of chinese fir plantations 1

   1 Introduction 1

   2 Material and methods 3

   3 Results and analysis...8

   4 Conclusions 18

CHAPTER TWO: A review of stand basal area growth models...................... 20

   1 Introduction 20

   2 Features of stand basal area growth models 24

   3 Types of models...25

   4 Early work on stand basal area models..28

   5 Recent progress and future directions...30

   6 Conclusions 32

CHAPTER THREE: Individual tree basal area growth dynamics of chinese fir
plantations 38

   1 Introduction 38

   2 Materials and methods...39

   3 Results and discussion...42

   4 Conclusion...45

CHAPTER FOUR: Application of theoretical growth equations for stand
diameter structure simulation of chinese fir plantations 47

   1 Introduction 47

   2 Materials and methods...49

   3 Results and analysis...53

   4 Conclusions 61

CHAPTER FIVE: A new high-performance diameter distribution function for
unthinned chinese fir (*Cunninghamia lanceolata*) Plantations in southern
China 63

   1 Introduction 63

   2 MATERIALS AND METHODS 65

   3 RESULTS AND DISCUSSION 70

4 Conclusions 78

CHAPTER SIX: Application of fuzzy functions in stand diameter distributions
of chinese fir (*Cunninghamia lanceolata*) plantations 81

1 Introduction 81

2 Data and Methods..83

3 Results and Discussion...86

4 Conclusion..93

CHAPTER SEVEN: Testing the self-thinning rule in chinese fir (*Cunninghamia
lanceolata*) plantations 96

1 Introduction 96

2 Materials and methods..99

3 Results 102

4 Discussion 106

CHAPTER EIGHT: Estimation of the self-thinning boundary line within even-
aged chinese fir (*Cunninghamia lanceolata* (Lamb.) Hook.) stands: Onset
of self-thinning 114

1 Introduction 114

2 Materials and Methods 116

3 Results 118

4 Discussion 122

5 Conclusions 125

CHAPTER NINE: A comparison of methods for estimating the self-thinning
boundary line: selecting data points and fitting coefficients 128

1 Introduction 128

2 Material and Methods..133

3 Results and Discussion..135

4 Conclusions 140

CHAPTER ONE:
Modelling of dominant height growth and building of polymorphic site index equations of chinese fir plantations

Abstract Difference methods based on six growth equations such as Richards, Weibull, Korf, Logistic, Schumacher and Sloboda were adopted to build polymorphic dominant height and site index equations for chinese fir plantations in southern China. Data from stem analysis of 157 trees were used for model construction. The performance of fifteen equations including ten kinds of difference equations was compared under different conditions. Effects on modeling precision caused by the variation of fitting data sets, site index, stands age and freedom parameter were analyzed and discussed. Results showed that the attributes of inflection points of the biological growth equations had very important effects on their precision while modeling dominant height. Difference equations had a better modeling precision for regional data sets than the prototypes of equations. The polymorphic dominant height equations, such as the two-parameter polymorphic forms of Korf, Richards, Weibull and three-parameter polymorphic form of Sloboda, showed higher precision. The two-parameter polymorphic form of Korf equation was selected to build polymorphic site index equation for chinese fir plantations.

Key words Dominant height modeling; polymorphic site index model; Difference method

1
Introduction

Dominant height model and site index curve plays an important role in the stand growth and management model system (Clutter *et al.*, 1983; Avery and Burkhart, 1994). Currently, two kinds of methods are often adopted for building dominant height model. One method is to directly apply the prototype of a theoretical equation, many single-variable functions, having the asymptotic value and inflection point, can be used for modelling stand dominant height growth(Zeide, 1993; Garcia, 1997); the other is using the differential form of theoretical equation(Border *et al.*, 1988; Amaro *et al.*, 1998). The latter approach is more flexible, and has increasingly become main research methods, but there is not a few specific applications of such method. For the development of site index curve, 3 ways usually are selected as follows: ① parameter estimation method (Mark and Nick, 1998); ② guide curve method (Newberry and Pienaar, 1978; Lee and Hong, 1999); ③ difference equation (Border *et al.*, 1984; Lee, 1999; Kalle, 2002). Generally, polymorphic dominant height model can explain and describe the phenomenon that a site index curve decides a dominant height curve, better simulate dominant height growth than the simplex model, and has good theoretical explain (Devan and Burkhart, 1982 ; Mark and Nick, 1998).

For the building of polymorphic site index equation of chinese fir plantation, the methods ①, ② are used to be selected. The method ① expresses all or some equation parameters as a function of site index (Scientific research coordination group for chinese fir cultivation in southern China, 1982; Luo *et al.*, 1989; Liu and Tong, 1996), the advantages of this method is clearly expressing the polymorphic meaning of site index equation, but often having the problems that the dominant height of standard age is inconsistent with the value of site index and the site index is not easily given when the dominant height and stand age are known; the method ② directly applies the theoretical growth equation with polymorphic meaning, such as sloboda equation that is applied many times at present (Gadow and Hui, 1998), but still lacks of the studies of polymorphic expression form of other common theoretical growth equation. When differential equations are developed to build site index equations, since the freedom of choice or operation parameters are different in different ways, and the resulting site index equations may produce two forms including single form and polymorphic form. It is worth to make clear that the application of guide curve method and differential equation method both can get site index curve with the characteristics of single or polymorphic form while building site index curve.

In summary, although the dominant high model and polymorphic site index equation have been studied widely in the world, a large number of single and polymorphic dominant hight equations are still lacking of systematic comparison studies, and failed to specify the inherent reasons that cause high or low precision for different dominant height model. The lack of deeply understanding and exploration for the polymorphic forms of many theoretical equations virtually restricts application of theoretical equations in this aspect, and thus has affected the development of dominant high model and polymorphic site index equation for many tree species.

Based on several common dominant hight equations, the polymorphic expressions were built by adopting differential equation method, and the polymorphic expression mechanism and the advantages and disadvantages of polymorphic dominant hight equations was comprehensively discussed and analyzed. In order to provide good theoretical and practical basis for the establishment of advantages of dominant high models and site index equations of chinese fir and other tree species plantations.

2
Material and methods

2.1
Material

Data used in this article were collected from 157 analytical stems of chinese fir dominant trees in southern China. The standard sites located in Huitong county of Hunan province, Damiao Mountain of Guangxi province, Liping county of Guizhou province and Nanping and Sanyuan county of Fujian province, these regions all belonged to the central districts for chinese fir. The survey years was 1981, 1954, 1955 and 1956 respectively, the number of analytical stems were 31, 35, 43, 48 respectively, the total stems were 157.

The area of standard site of Huitong county of Hunan province was 300~500 m², other provinces were 1000 m². The stands in Fujian province originated from cutting seedlings, other provinces from seedlings.

The age of dominant trees all arrived at or near the index age (20a) for chinese fir. For trees whose age exceeded the index age, we directly used tree height at 20a to determine site index classes, for trees whose age were lower than 20a, the national site index table was applied to get respective site index class. The statistical data of standard sites in different provinces were shown as Table 1.

Table 1   Statistical table of stem analysis data of chinese fir

Standard sites	Age/a			Height/m		
	Min.	Max.	Mean	Min.	Max.	Mean
Huitong county of Hunan province	5	63	19	2.80	28.21	14.37
Damiao mountain of Guangxi province	5	43	21	2.65	27.00	17.32
Liping county of Guizhou province	5	46	23	2.33	27.65	16.18
Nanping and Sanyuan county of Fujian province	5	36	21	3.30	30.70	15.95
Total	5	63	21	2.33	30.70	15.79

2.2
Methods

2.2.1
Dominant height growth equation

Five theoretical growth equations, Richards equation, Weibull equation, Korf equation, Logistic equation and Schumacher equation, were selected as candidate equations for modelling dominant height growth process. these equations were widely used for the simulation of tree growth, especially for the Richards Equation, (Rennolls, 1995; Li, 1996; Amaro et al., 1998; Gadow and Hui, 1998; Li *et al.*, 1999). Mathematical expression of the equations were shown as Table 2.

Table 2   The mathematical expression of five theoretical growth equations

Equation	Expression	Inflection point		Parameter
		Abscissa	Ordinate	
Richards	$y = a(1 - \exp(-bx))^c$	$1/(b \ln c)$	$a(1 - 1/c)^c$	$a, b > 0$
Weibull	$y = a(1 - \exp(-bx^c))$	$((c-1)/bc)^{1/c}$	$a(1 - \exp(1-c)/c)$	$a, b, c > 0$
Korf	$y = a\exp(-b/x^c)$	$((c+1)/bc)^{-1/c}$	$a\exp((c-1)/c)$	$a, b, c > 0$
Logistic	$y = a/(1 + \exp(b - cx))$	b/c	$a/2$	$a, c > 0$
Schumacher	$y = a\exp(-b/x)$	$b/2$	ae^{-2}	$a, b > 0$

The five above-mentioned equations were all S-shaped growth equations with inflection points and asymptotic lines. In which, equations, such as Richards, Weibull and Korf equation, had the charateristics that the coordinates of inflection points were variable multiples of asymptotic values, while Logistic equation and Schumacher equation presented a fixed multiple. The meanings of parameters and their complex relationship of these equations were explained by Duan *et al.* (2003).

2.2.2
Difference equation

For any equation that can reflect the relationship between tree height and age, the differential form always can be gotten by using the differential method, and the differential equations can simulate the height growth process of stand dominant trees. The data for fitting differential equation can be derived from the permanent plots, interval plots and temporary plots. When the data comes from long-term observation data or analytical stem materials, the use of differential equations is more appropriate (Amaro et al., 1998).

Differential method was used for five theoretical growth equations, and their differential forms were gotten. Through viewing parameter *b* as freedom parameter, retaining asymptotic parameter *a* and shape parameter *c*, four two-parameter differential equations and one one-parameter differential equation were gotten after differential elimination method.

Through differential but no elimination method, three-parameter Richards and Weibull differential equations were obtained. In order to compare the simulation effects of differential equations with different freedom parameters, two differential equations, respectively with parameter a or c as freedom parameter, were gotten from Richards function. Korf equation was taken as an example to elaborate the basic form process of every differential equation.

Through selecting any two pairs of stem analysis data of dominants and heights (t_1, H_1) and (t_2, H_2), and substituting them into Korf equation, formula (1) and (2) could be obtained as follows:

$$H_1 = a\exp(-b/t_1^c) \tag{1}$$

$$H_2 = a\exp(-b/t_2^c) \tag{2}$$

and convert to:

$$\ln H_1 - \ln a = -b/t_1^c \tag{3}$$

$$\ln H_2 - \ln a = -b/t_2^c \tag{4}$$

After divided formula (3) by (4), the difference equation of Korf could be gotten as follows.

$$H_2 = H_1^{t_1^c/t_2^c} \cdot a^{1-t_1^c/t_2^c} \tag{5}$$

The difference forms of other equations could be obtained like Korf equation (Table 3). In order to comprehensively introduce good dominant height growth equations and compare the fitting characteristics of three-parameter difference equations, the difference form of Sloboda equation was also listed (Gadow and Hui, 1998).

If letting $H = H_2$, $t = t_2$; $SI = H_1$, $T = t_1$, where SI and T respectively stand for site index and index age, and substituting into all difference equations in Table 3, the site index equations originated from corresponding difference equations could be gotten (Table 4). The site index equation of Korf was built as follows.

$$H = SI^{T^c/t^c} \cdot a^{1-T^c/t^c}$$

The dominant growth curves of different site indices (e.g. 16, 18, 20) could be obtained through above-mentioned formula. When dominant height H and stem age t were known, the stand site index could be calculated through this formula.

Table 3   The expression of every difference equation

Prototype of equation	Difference equation	Freedom parameter	Designation
Korf	$H_2 = H_1^{t_1^c/t_2^c} \cdot a^{1-t_1^c/t_2^c}$	b	(5)
Richards	$H_2 = a(1-(1-(H_1/a)^{1/c})^{t_2/t_1})^c$	b	(6a)
	$H_2 = a \cdot \exp(\ln(H_1/a) \cdot \ln(1-e^{-bt_2})/\ln(1-e^{-bt_1}))$	c	(6b)
	$H_2 = H_1((1-\exp(-bt_2))/(1-\exp(-bt_1)))^c$	a	(6c)
	$H_2 = a(1-(1-a^{-1/c}H_1^{1/c}) \cdot \exp(-b(t_2-t_1)))^c$		(6d)
Weibull	$H_2 = a-a((a-H_1)/a)^{t_2^c/t_1^c}$	b	(7a)
	$H_2 = a+(H_1-a) \cdot \exp(-bt_2^c + bt_1^c)$		(7b)
Logistic	$H_2 = a/((a/H_1-1) \cdot \exp(ct_1-ct_2)+1)$	b	(8)
Schumacher	$H_2 = a \cdot \exp(t_1/t_2 \cdot \ln(H_1/a))$	b	(9)
Sloboda	$H_2 = a(H_1/a)^{\exp(-b/((c-1) \cdot t_1^{c-1})+b/((c-1) \cdot t_2^{c-1}))}$	d	(10)

Table 4   Ten kinds of site index equations and their expressions of inflection point[①]

Prototype of equation	Site index equation	Expression of inflection point	Number
Korf	$H = SI^{T^c/t^c} \cdot a^{1-T^c/t^c}$	$t = T(\ln(a/SI)/(1+1/c))^{1/c}$	(5)
Richards	$H = a(1-(1-(SI/a)^{1/c})^{t/T})^c$	$t = -T\ln(c+1)/\ln(1-(SI/a)^{1/c})$	(6a)
	$H = a \cdot \exp(\ln(SI/a) \cdot \ln(1-e^{-bt})/\ln(1-e^{-bT}))$	$t = \dfrac{1}{b} \cdot \ln\dfrac{\ln(SI/a)}{\ln(1-\exp(-bT))}$	(6b)
	$H = SI((1-\exp(-bt))/(1-\exp(-bT)))^c$	$t = \ln c/b$	(6c)
	$H = a(1-(1-a^{-1/c}SI^{1/c}) \cdot \exp(-b(t-T)))^c$	$t = T+1/b \cdot \ln(c \cdot (1-a^{-1/c}SI^{1/c}))$	(6d)
Weibull	$H = a-a((a-SI)/a)^{t^c/T^c}$	$t = T((1/c-1)/\ln(1-SI/a))^{1/c}$	(7a)
	$H = a+(SI-a) \cdot \exp(-bt^c + bT^c)$	$t = ((c-1)/(bc))^{1/c}$	(7b)
Logistic	$H = a/((a/SI-1) \cdot \exp(cT-ct)+1)$	$t = T+1/c \cdot \ln(a/SI-1)$	(8)
Schumacher	$H = a \cdot \exp(T/t \cdot \ln(SI/a))$	$t = -T\ln(SI/a)/2$	(9)
Sloboda	$H = a(SI/a)^{\exp(-c/((d-1) \cdot T^{D-1})+c/((d-1) \cdot t^{d-1}))}$	$c\ln\dfrac{SI}{a} \cdot \exp(m+\dfrac{c}{(d-1)t^{d-1}})+dt^{d-1}+c=0$	(10)

① The expression of inflection point is the abscissa.

2.2.3
Polymorphic site index equation

For the purpose of obtaining the polymorphic expression forms of many theoretical equations, difference method was used and ten difference equations were produced (Table 3). Based on analysis for inflection points of difference equations, the characteristics of single or polymorphic form of the ten equations was discussed, and ten corresponding site index equations were conducted (Table 4).

For all site index equations in Table 4, if $t = T$, then there is $y = SI$. This means that these site index equations, obtained by the difference method, will not produce the contradiction that the value of tree height at index age is inconsistent with the site index value. From the variation of inflection points of every equation in Table 4, the abscissa of inflection points of those equations numbered 5, 6a, 6b, 6d, 7a, 8, 9, 10 are correlative to site index, which indicates that the obtained site index equations can ensure that different site index has a different height growth curve, that is, the eight site index equations are all polymorphic. Then there is another question to be answerd that if these polymorphic site index equations can guarantee the biological significance of inflection points? Which needs a further exploration. For the inflection points of equation 5, 6a, 6d, 8, 9, when SI increases, t decreases; for equation 6b, due to $\ln(1-\exp(-bT)) < 0$, the age t at inflection point decreases with the increasing of SI; for equation 7a, the relationship between t and SI is correlative to parameter c; for equation 10, originated from Sloboda, the variation of t at inflection point is not obvious with SI.

Thus, at least the six equations numbered 5, 6a, 6b, 6d, 8, 9 have good biological sense, that is, the better the site condition (SI) is, the earlier the inflection point occurs, on the contrary, the worse the site condition is, the later the inflection point occurs, which fully reflects the biological law that trees arrive fast-growing year earlier in the better site.

2.2.4
Parameter estimation

The data collected was organized into two forms. One was the pair data of dominant heights and ages, which was used to fit the prototype of five theoretical growth equations. The other is double pairs data of dominant heights and ages for fitting ten difference equations. While fitting, all the data were divided into three levels including site indices, provinces and districts, to compare simulation accuracy of the candidate equations at three levels. As the candidate equations all are nonlinear, so the nonlinear regression method of SAS software was adopted for parameter estimation.

2.2.5
Test statistics

Generally, the methods for model test often include two points, one is the biological meaning of models and its parameters, and the other is characterized by the statistical indices that describe the actual fitting effect of models, but often a compromise between the two is considered (Amaro et al., 1998). The statistical variables used here are average residual (*MR*), absolute mean residual (*AMR*), relative absolute residual (*RAR*), residual sum of squares (*RSS*), standard residual (*SR*) and coefficient of determination (R^2), in which, *AMR, RAR , RSS, SE* are the index for the accuracy of the model, *AMR* and R^2, respectively, stand for the model bias and efficiency. The calculation formula of these statistics were listed in Table 5.

Table 5   The statistics used for test of models[1]

Statistics index	Symbol	Formula	Ideal value
Mean residual	*MR*	$\sum_{i=1}^{n} \dfrac{(obs_i - est_i)}{n}$	0
Absolute mean residual	*AMR*	$\sum_{i=1}^{n} \dfrac{\|obs_i - est_i\|}{n}$	0
Relative absolute residual	*RAR*	$\dfrac{1}{n}\sum_{i=1}^{n} \dfrac{\|obs_i - est_i\|}{obs_i}$	0
Residual sum of square	*RSS*	$\sum_{i=1}^{n} (obs_i - est_i)^2$	0
Standard residual	*SR*	$\sqrt{\dfrac{\sum_{i=1}^{n}(obs_i - est_i)^2}{n}}$	0
Coefficient of determination	R^2	$1 - \dfrac{\sum_{i=1}^{n}(obs_i - est_i)^2}{\sum_{i=1}^{n}(obs_i - \overline{obs}_i)^2}$	1

① *obs_i, est_i, n* respectively stand for the *i*th observed value, the *i*th estimated value, number of observations.

3
Results and analysis

3.1
Comparison of modelling precision of dominant growth models

Table 6 showed the values of parameters and modelling precision indices of five theoretical growth equations and ten difference equations while modelling dominant height growth.

3.1.1
Factors for difference of modelling precision

When the data originated from the stands with same site index of same district, the selected statistics all showed that the size sequence of modelling precision for five theoretical growth equations was Korf> Richards> Weibull> Schumacher> Logistic. Through substituting evaluated parameters into formula of inflection points of five equations, the values of inflection points of five equations were obtained while modelling stands dominant height growth. Then it could be found that the relative location of inflection points, namely the rates of coordinates of inflection points to asymptote values of five equations, were 0.0001~0.1786, 0.0498~0.3103, 0.0303~ 0.3940, 0.1353 and 0.5 respectively.

In the view of modelling precision of equations, it could be found that the relative position of inflection point of equations had close correlation with modelling precision of equations for stand dominant height. For the equations with fixed inflection points, the equation that had a smaller fixed inflection point had a higher simulation accuracy, and this phenomenon had nothing to do with the number of parameters of equation (such as the two-parameter Schumacher equation and three-parameter Logistic equation). Which showed that the inflection point of stand dominant height growth curve occurred early, and meant that the fast-growth period of stand dominant height already appeared at the young years.

In fact, for many tree species, due to the rapid growth in early time, the inflection point of stand dominant height growth curve does not exist, the growth pattern is more accordant with a convex-shape curve, which may be the factor that Logistic equation is not suitable for modelling dominant height growth. From the occurrence time of age of inflection point of Korf equation, the fast-growth period of stand dominant height of chinese fir plantation occurred at 2 or 8 years old for collected data.

3.1.2
Modelling precision of difference equations

3.1.2.1
Effect of fitting data

From Table 6, it could be found that AMR of equations was less than 0.5 m or a little higher, and RAR is less than 0.05 when the fitting data based on the site level. Which indicated that the selected equations all can well simulate the dominant height growth process. Statistical variables *AMR*, *RAR*, *SR* showed that the size sequence of modelling precision of selected equations was Korf, 7b, Richards, 6d, 10, Weibull, 5, 6a, 7a, Schumacher, Logistic, 9 and 8. The results showed that the equations with fixed inflection points, such as Schumacher and Logistic, had relative low modelling precision than other equations with floating inflection points regardless of whether the equations were difference equations or not, the equations with three parameters (excepting Logistic equation) had more higher modelling precision than equations with two parameters, the prototype of every theoretical growth equation had more higher modelling precision than its difference form that only had one parameter. For two-parameter difference form of Weibull equation (7a), the prediction values of parameter *c* were all greater than 1, which indicated that equation 7a was a polymorphic equation. Obviously, when the fitting data based on the site level, the modelling precision of polymorphic equations were not more higher than the single-form equations. The *MR* of 6a, Richards, Korf were relatively small, indicating that the errors distribution of these three equations were more symmetrical nearby *x* axis.

Table 6   Dominant height fitting results for site index-level data set

Equation	Parameters			MR	AMR	RAR	RSS	SR	R^2
	a	*b*	*c*						
Korf	15.6990~87.4769	5.0164~16.4066	0.1200~1.3844	0.0022	0.2389	0.0199	27.6038	0.2662	0.9930~0.9997
Richards	12.5186~59.5427	0.0130~0.2132	1.0633~3.6214	−0.0035	0.2697	0.0209	35.2862	0.2900	0.9879~0.9994
Weibull	11.8894~51.3291	0.0063~0.0533	1.0318~2.0038	−0.0087	0.2935	0.0236	42.2420	0.3104	0.9863~0.9994
Schumacher	16.4651~43.9068	8.2336~24.7520		0.0438	0.3902	0.0433	77.4831	0.4807	0.9739~0.9989
Logistic	11.6704~31.3989	1.5846~3.0959	0.0980~0.3840	−0.0258	0.5034	0.0455	117.7375	0.5495	0.9689~0.9993
(5)	15.1023~70.5481		0.0760~1.4662	0.0077	0.3069	0.0206	41.5303	0.3422	0.9606~0.9979
(6a)	12.2659~34.7447		1.1344~4.0557	−0.0005	0.3224	0.0205	45.1675	0.3554	0.9338~0.9981
(6d)	14.9681~39.4285	0.0009~0.1352	0.3151~3.8750	−0.0141	0.2729	0.0193	31.1026	0.2926	0.9724~0.9999
(7a)	11.5729~32.9764		1.1284~2.1800	−0.0077	0.3455	0.0218	53.7170	0.3839	0.9041~0.9979
(7b)	14.0592~40.1788	0.0025~1.7257	0.0873~2.1717	0.0120	0.2549	0.0158	31.3702	0.2849	0.9721~0.9991
(8)	11.5692~30.2524		0.1003~0.4059	0.0391	0.5548	0.0373	130.7375	0.6200	0.9040~0.9990
(9)	15.3130~41.0334			0.0726	0.4532	0.0354	98.1112	0.5499	0.9340~0.9969
(10)	14.6754~58.7902	0.1059~2.7311	0~1.6081	0.0164	0.2559	0.0161	32.6364	0.2948	0.9642~0.9986

When fitting data based on district level, the maximum *SR* and *AMR* of eight selected difference equations were respectively 1.7032, 1.0087, far less than the minimum values 11.6877 and 2.6360 of the prototype of equations (Table 7). The coefficients of determination R^2 of difference equations were all above 0.95, obviously higher than the prototypes of equations those coefficients of determination were 0.6241~0.8652. This indicated that the modeling precision of difference equations was much higher than the prototypes of equations, and polymorphic equations were prior to single-form equations while modeling district-level data. In polymorphic height equations, the two-parameter polymorphic forms of Korf, Richards, Weibull equations and three-parameter polymorphic form of Sloboda equation had high modeling precision, their AMR were all below 0.55, the relative errors were all less than 0.05, the distribution of residuals were relatively uniform, which showed that these four polymorphic equations could well simulate stands dominant height growth of chinese fir plantations in different district.

Table 7   Dominant height fitting results for district-level data set

Equation	The range of parameters			MR	AMR	RAR	RSS	SR	R^2
	a	b	c						
Korf	29.7826~44.9120	6.6616~8.7804	0.6815~0.9149	0.0091	2.6611	0.1963	757.4266	3.4515	0.6256~0.8648
Richards	22.7054~29.1024	0.0601~0.0927	1.3787~1.6735	0.0001	2.6377	0.1953	749.5918	3.4222	0.6288~0.8652
Weibull	22.2845~28.3397	0.0186~0.0292	1.2286~1.3572	0.0043	2.6360	0.1953	749.0169	3.4202	0.6295~0.8651
Schumacher	28.2801~34.1850	10.1664~13.5230		0.0657	2.6828	0.2018	771.3482	3.4680	0.6241~0.8491
Logistic	21.4865~26.8332	1.9073~2.0490	0.1293~0.1744	−0.0300	2.6883	0.2077	767.4136	3.4263	0.6284~0.8580
(5)	37.3666~83.9088		0.4244~0.7693	−0.0781	0.5062	0.0364	25.4128	0.7030	0.9820~0.9954
(6a)	26.6448~32.2117		1.1977~1.6179	−0.0872	0.5297	0.0354	27.8310	0.7423	0.9790~0.9955
(6d)	28.9271~54.4855	0.0113~0.0522	0.7666~1.2005	0.0090	0.7583	0.0547	63.0167	1.1308	0.9513~0.9931
(7a)	26.6000~31.8248		1.1291~1.3258	−0.0863	0.5489	0.0366	30.1205	0.7762	0.9758~0.9953
(7b)	98.0553~29276.4	0.0006~1.6657	0.0007~1.1333	0.0463	0.5941	0.0462	39.9226	0.8871	0.9724~0.9936
(8)	24.7615~27.9540		0.1059~0.1788	0.0828	1.0087	0.0722	105.2357	1.4693	0.9273~0.9900
(9)	27.8398~30.6511			0.0141	0.6758	0.0538	50.8875	0.9981	0.9784~0.9954
(10)	43.6792~418 048.9	0.2653~1.2449	1.0236~1.6323	−0.0019	0.4557	0.0320	19.9005	0.6094	0.9830~0.9954

When fitting data based on production region level, from Table 8, it could be found that difference equations and polymorphic equations were respectively prior to the prototypes of equations and single-form equations, this phenomenon was same as results from district-level data. The most statistical indices indicated two-parameter polymorphic forms of Korf, Richards equations and three-parameter polymorphic form of Sloboda equation had relative high modeling precision, their AMR, RAR, SR were respectively below 0.55, 0.05 and 0.5. Which showed that these three polymorphic equations could well simulate stands dominant height growth of chinese fir plantations at level of production region. The two-parameter polymorphic form of Weibull equation had the smallest *MR* (−0.3181), indicating that the deviation of the equation was negative and large. Regardless of the numbers of parameters, two-parameter forms of Richards and Weibull equations had higher modeling precision than three-parameter polymorphic forms of them.

Table 8   Dominant height fitting results for production region-level data set

Equation	The range of parameters			*MR*	*AMR*	*RAR*	*RSS*	*SR*	*R²*
	a	*b*	*c*						
Korf	38.7003	7.5231	0.7431	0.0091	2.7092	0.2007	3251.4264	3.4574	0.7584
Richards	25.9004	0.0706	1.4557	−0.0112	2.7260	0.2030	3250.8078	3.4571	0.7585
Weibull	25.3907	0.0264	1.2549	−0.0129	2.7336	0.2045	3257.7093	3.4608	0.7580
Schumacher	31.1111	11.5025		0.0671	2.7573	0.2054	3300.7397	3.4835	0.7554
Logistic	23.4847	1.9721	0.1516	−0.0352	2.8028	0.2156	3362.6082	3.5160	0.7504
(5)	48.9420		0.5916	−0.0491	0.5147	0.0371	114.0247	0.6475	0.9879
(6a)	28.3463		1.3784	−0.0729	0.5335	0.0363	124.3379	0.6761	0.9867
(6d)	33.2889	0.0302	0.8560	0.0162	0.7528	0.0558	281.6568	1.0176	0.9700
(7a)	30.6000		1.2620	−0.3181	0.6239	0.0415	156.9861	0.7597	0.9865
(7b)	165.1728	9.7603	0.0056	0.1223	0.5928	0.0481	178.5193	0.8101	0.9824
(8)	25.7048		0.1273	0.1111	0.9886	0.0714	468.5967	1.3125	0.9525
(9)	25.8967			0.0208	0.6572	0.0529	206.3156	0.8709	0.9846
(10)	1382.5028	0.6097	1.5165	0.0208	0.4696	0.0332	92.5651	0.5834	0.9903

Generally, the modelling precision of every equation decreased with the expansion of data unit, the modelling precision for data of site index level was obviously higher than district level and production region level, and the modelling precision for data of district level was higher than production region level.

When the modelling precision of equations for different district data was analyzed respectively, the statistical indices showed that the difference equations were prior to their prototypes. The mean absolute errors of five prototypes are all above 2.4 m, not being suitably used for district-level dominant height growth models.

However, eight difference equations had relatively stable modelling precision for district-level dominant height growth. Excepting for three-parameter polymorphic form of Sloboda equation, the *SR* values of other difference equations for Fujian province were all bigger than the values of the other three districts (Table 9). Because the stands in Fujian province originated from cutting seedlings and other provinces from seedlings, the result might mean that most models were more appropriate for stands originated from seedlings, not from cutting seedlings.

Table 9   The statistics (SR) of every equation in different district

District	Equation												
	10	5	6a	7a	7b	9	6d	8	Richards	Weibull	Korf	Schumacher	Logistic
Fujian	0.5329	0.7332	0.7690	0.7803	1.0175	1.2582	1.3452	1.6928	4.3438	4.3396	4.3623	4.3739	4.3461
Guizhou	0.5921	0.6787	0.7594	0.7688	0.7801	0.8172	0.9786	1.3640	2.4269	2.4280	2.4305	2.4903	2.4925
Guangxi	0.7066	0.7274	0.7384	0.7665	0.9090	1.0121	1.1421	1.4567	3.5070	3.5093	3.5177	3.5200	3.5404
Hunan	0.6061	0.6727	0.7024	0.7893	0.8417	0.9048	1.0572	1.3636	3.4073	3.4110	3.4077	3.4334	3.4654

3.1.2.2
Effect of site index and age

Fig. 1 and Fig. 2 showed the distribution condition of residuals with age and site index for thirteen kinds of dominant height growth equations. The residuals distribution visually verified the sequence of modelling precision of these equations for fitting the data of production region level. The residuals distribution with age for different equations was not consistent, the difference between the prototypes of five theoretical growth equations and their polymorphic forms was great. The residuals of different age intervals for high-precision equation 5, 6a and 10 had no obvious change with the increase of age, the middle values of residuals were always close to 0. For the equation 6a (two-parameter polymorphic form of Richards equation), the residuals distribution showed that the dominant height was slightly underestimated in the early and latter growth stage, while in the medium stage about 15 to 40 years, a little over-estimated. On the whole, the maximum absolute error of five theoretical equations first increased and then decreased with the increase of age, and almost all of the difference equations presented gradually decreased.

Excepting three-parameter polymorphic form of Sloboda equation, the residuals of dominant height growth equations all increased with the increase of site index. The selected growth models had a higher estimation for dominant height growth of low site indices, and a lower estimation for high site indices. The deviation first decreased and then increased with the increase of site index. Comparing with their prototypes, the residuals of all the difference equations or polymorphic forms had a relatively flat increase trend with the increase of site index, which showed that the difference equations or polymorphic equations had more stable modelling performance than their prototypes for dominant height growth of stands with different site indices. From Fig. 1, it could be found that different equations had different critical values of site indices when the dominant height was estimated from under-estimated to over- estimated.

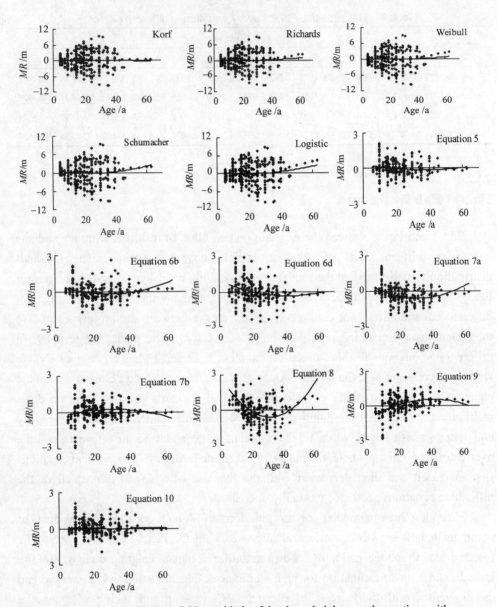

Fig. 1   The residual distribution of thirteen kinds of dominant height growth equations with age

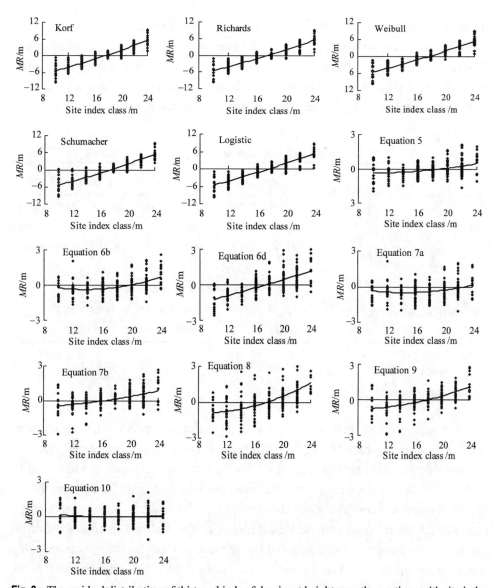

Fig. 2 The residual distribution of thirteen kinds of dominant height growth equations with site index

3.1.2.3
Effect of freedom parameter

The statistical result of three difference forms of Richards equation was laid out when modelling dominant height growth at district and production region level (Table 10). It could be found that the difference form with parameter c being free had the lowest MR, and Amaro et al. (1998) had thought this form was better, but other statistical variables showed this form didn't simulate well in our studies, and the difference equation with parameter *a* or *b* being free had satisfied modelling effect. However, Because the difference equation originated from Richards with freedom parameter *a* was single-form function, the difference equation with freedom parameters *b* was obviously the only choice for the building of polymorphic site index curve families.

Table 10   The statistical results of difference forms of Richards

Data	Freedom parameter	*MR*	*AMR*	*RAR*	*RSS*	*SR*	R^2
	a	0.0831	0.4974	0.0323	24.4914	0.3808	0.9776~0.9959
District level	*b*	−0.0872	0.5297	0.0354	27.831	0.4396	0.9790~0.9955
	c	−0.0373	0.6549	0.0447	45.0952	0.7231	0.9693~0.9942
	a	0.0959	0.491	0.0327	108.9995	0.6577	0.9887
Production region level	*b*	−0.0729	0.5335	0.0363	124.3379	0.7024	0.9867
	c	−0.0148	0.6602	0.0462	208.2557	0.9091	0.978

3.1.3
Asymptotic parameter

When modelling data based on district and production region level, the asymptotic parameters of two-parameter polymorphic Weibull equation (7b) and three-parameter polymorphic Sloboda equation (equation 10) were unusually large, the estimates lost its biological meanings what the asymptotic parameter had. Excepting for equation 7b and 10, the asymptotic parameter *a* of the other equations all had a more reasonable range, basically guaranteeing its own biological meaning. The factors that caused abnormal values of asymptotic parameter included two aspects, one was the fitting data, the other was selected equations, when the factor came from the latter, it might mean that the selected equations like equation 7b and equation 10 were not suitable for long-term forecasts.

3.2
Building of polymorphic site index equation

Good dominant height growth model was the solid foundation for the construction of polymorphic site index equations. From above studies, it could be found that the polymorphic dominant height models, obtained by difference method, had good biological interpretation basis and very high simulation accuracy, in which, the two-parameter polymorphic forms of Korf, Richards, Weibull and three-parameter polymorphic form of Sloboda had relatively high precision, these equations all could be used to build polymorphic site index equation for chinese fir plantations. Considering relatively brief expression form, high precision and good theoretical meaning, the two-parameter polymorphic form of Korf equation was selected to build polymorphic site index equation for chinese fir plantations in central production region.

$$H = SI^{20^{0.5916}/t^{0.5916}} \times 48.9420^{1-20^{0.5916}/t^{0.5916}} \tag{11}$$

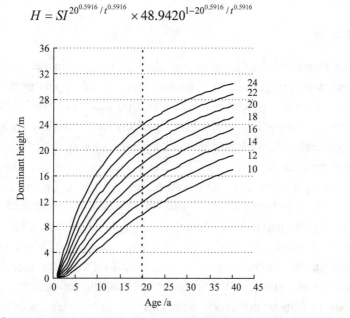

Fig. 3   The polymorphic site index curves of chinese fir plantations

Substituting the values of site index such as 10, 12, 14, 16, 18, 20, 22, 24 into formula 11, the polymorphic site index curve families of chinese fir plantations could be obtained as shown in Fig. 3. Dotted line in Fig. 2 described the theoretical values of stands dominant height of different site index at the age of site index. It was clear that the polymorphic site index equation for chinese fir plantations (formula 11) did not produce the problem that the dominant height at standard age was inconsistent with the value of site index, and according to, the site index could be calculated easily by formula 11 when dominant height and stands age were known.

Table 11 listed the abscissas of inflection points of the dominant height growth curves under the condition of different site indices. It could be found that abscissas of inflection points showed a decreasing trend with increasing of site index. This phenomenon reflected the biological properties that the fast-growth age of dominant height came more earlier for stands with higher site indices. Which further testified the polymorphic quality of formula 17.

Table 11   The variation of inflection point of dominant height growth curve with site index

Inflection point/a	Site index/m							
	10	12	14	16	18	20	22	24
Abscissa	8.20	6.68	5.49	4.53	3.76	3.11	2.57	2.12

4
Conclusions

The construction of polymorphic dominant height model and polymorphic site index equation always was the important and difficult aspect in the research field of forest growth model system. In this studies, the usual parameter prediction method and guide curves were abandoned, while based on six theoretical growth equations, the difference method was adopted to build several polymorphic site index equations, then their polymorphic meaning was discussed, and the modelling precision of thirteen dominant height models was comprehensively analyzed, five main conclusions were obtained. ① Based on theoretical growth equation, the difference method could be used to build polymorphic dominant height equation with good biological interpretation basis and very high simulation accuracy. ② The variation range of inflection points of growth equations had critical effect on the modelling precision for dominant height growth. ③ For fitting data at site index level, the prototypes of equations and their difference equations all had better modelling precision for dominant height growth, and the former had more higher precision, but for a wider range of fitting data, such as district-level and production-region-level data, the difference equations obviously had better performance. ④ The polymorphic dominant height models had relatively high simulation accuracy, in which, the two-parameter polymorphic forms of Korf, Richards, Weibull and three-parameter polymorphic Sloboda equation were found better and suitable to be used for dominant height growth models. ⑤ The reasonable polymorphic site index equations could be built by good polymorphic dominant height growth models.

Reference

Amaro A, David R, Margarida T, *et al*. 1998. Modelling dominant height growth: Eucalyptus plantations in Portugal. For Sci, 44(1): 37~46
Avery T E, Burkhart H E. 1994. Forest measurement. New York: McGraw–Hill Book Co. 408
Borders B E, Bailey R L, Clutter M L. 1988. Forest growth models: Parameter estimation using real

growth data series. pp. 660~667 in Forest Growth Modelling and Prediction. Volume 2. USDA For Serv Gen Tech Rep, NC~120

Borders B E, Bailey R L, Ware K D. 1984. Slash pine site index from a polymorphic model by joining (splining) non-polynomial segments with an algebraic difference method. For Sci, 30:411~423

Clutter J L, Forsion J C, Pienaar L V, et al. 1983. Timber management. New York: John Wiley and Sons. 333

Devan J S, Burkhart H E. 1982. Polymorphic site index equations for loblolly pine based on a segmented polynomial model. For Sci, 28: 544~555

Duan A G, Zhang J G, Tong S Z. 2003. Application of six growth equations on stands diameter structure of Chinese fir plantation. Forest Research, 16(4): 423~429

Gadow K V, Hui G Y.1998. Modelling Forest Development. Goettingen: Cuvillier Verlag

Garcia O. 1997. Another look at growth equations. Working paper, Royal Veterinary and Agricultural University, Copenhagen

Kalle E. 2002. A site dependent simultaneous growth projection model for Pinus kesiya plantations in Zambia and Zimbabwe. For Sci, 48(3): 518~529

Lee S H. 1999. Developing and comparing site index curves using polymorphic and anamorphic equations for Douglas-fir. Jour. Korean. For Soc, 88(2): 142~148

Lee Y J, Hong S C. 1999. Estimation of site index curves for Slash Pine (Pinus elliottii Engelm.) Plantations. Jour. Korean. For Soc, 88(3): 285~291

Li J X. 1996. Studies on adaptation of three growth models to Chamaecyparis formosensis Matsum plantation. Seasonal Journal of Taiwan Forest, 29(2): 3~14

Li X F, Wang M L, Huang W Z. 1999. Using linear model to testify the adaptation of site index model for different Chinese fir provenances. Forest Research, 12(5): 505~509

Liu J F, Tong S Z. 1996, New technology of Chinese fir plantation management. Word Forestry Research, 9(Special): 46~80

Luo Q B, Wu Z D, Jiang J S. 1989. Studies on building polymorphic site index model by using Richards function. Forest Research, 2(6): 534~539

Mark O K, Nick J L. 1998. Site index curves for Pinus nigra grown in the south island high country, New Zealand. New Zealand Journal of Forestry Science, 28(3): 389~399

Newberry J D, Pienaar L V. 1978. Dominant height growth models and site index curves for site-prepared slash pine plantations in the lower coastal plain of Georgia and North Florida. Univ of Ga Plantation Mgt Res Coop Res

Rennolls K. 1995. Forest height growth modelling. For Ecol Manage, 71: 217~225

Zeide B. 1993. Analysis of growth equations. For Sci, 39(3): 594~616

CHAPTER TWO:
A review of stand basal area growth models

Abstract   Growth and yield modelling has a long history in forestry. The methods of measuring the growth of stand basal area have evolved from those developed in the U.S.A. and Germany during the 20 century. Stand basal area modelling has progressed rapidly since the first widely used model was published by the U.S. Forest Service. Over the years, a variety of models have been developed for predicting the growth and yield of uneven/even-aged stands using stand-level approaches. The modelling methodology has not only moved from an empirical approach to a more ecological process-based approach but also accommodated a variety of techniques such as: ①simultaneous equation methods, ②difference models, ③artificial neural network techniques, ④linear/nonlinear regression models and ⑤matrix models. Empirical models using statistical methods were developed to reproduce accurately and precisely field observations. In contrast, process models have shorter histories, developed originally as research and education tools with the aim of increasing the understanding of cause and effect relationships. Empirical and process models can be married into hybrid models in which the shortcomings of both component approaches can, to some extent, be overcome. Algebraic difference forms of stand basal area models which consist of stand age, stand density and site quality can fully describe stand growth dynamics. This paper reviews the current literature regarding stand basal area models, discusses the basic types of models and their merits and outlines recent progress in modelling growth and dynamics of stand basal area. Future trends involving algebraic difference forms, good fitting variables and model types into stand basal area modelling strategies are discussed.

Key word   Basal area growth; Modelling methods; Review

1

Introduction

Forest managers monitor stand growth and prescribe silvicultural treatments at increasing stand ages due to the potential value of their plantations. Yet, the effective stand management is hindered when accurate models of stand dynamics are unavailable. Basal area growth prediction is an essential factor and the foundation of model systems of stand and yield prediction (Tang and Du, 1999). Basal area growth prediction describes forest dynamics over time (i.e. growth, mortality, reproduction and associated changes at the stand level) and is hence widely used in forest management for its ability to update inventories, predict future yield and to explore management alternatives. Compared with such measures as stand diameter, tree height or crown diameter, basal area possesses a high degree of exactness in measurement or prediction; as a concept, it is applicable to a wide range of conditions and at times points to the true causes and effects of underlying superficial appearances. Basal area is interesting for forest inventories because it is highly correlated with volume and growth of forest stands. Many silvicultural and forest management considerations, such as thinning intensity, are based on basal area ground measurements. In addition, the mean annual increment curve of basal area is a useful tool for the correct management of forest stands and contributes to estimate the timing of intermediate and final cuts.

Growth and yield modelling has a long history in forestry. As early as the early 1920s, the U.S. Forest Service published its first widely used yield tables for southern pines. Similar tables, based on a considerably more restricted sample, were also prepared by Meyer (1942). However, these methods were not used for predicting growth projection purpose. Gevorkiantz (1934) discussed an approach to improve predicting precision based on yield tables and showed the existence of significant correlations between the percentage growth of basal area and age, stand density as measured by a stand density index (Reineke, 1933) and initial basal area. MachKinney *et al.* (1939) further generalized the normal yield table procedure for loblolly pine (*Pinus taeda*). These tables were developed from sample plots with a wide range of stocking, using multiple regression techniques in place of the earlier developed graphic methods. Wellwood (1943) employed a similar procedure to reanalyzed the same data using regression rather than graphic techniques. Sullivan and Clutter (1972) refined and extended Clutter's (1963) models by simultaneously estimating yield and cumulative growth as a function of initial stand age, initial basal area, site index and predicted stand age. It has been 25 years since the first IUFRO meeting on forest growth and yield modelling and 35 years since compatible growth and yield models have been developed. Furthermore, the proceedings of Ek *et al.* (1988) documented worldwide efforts in these areas during the 1970s and 1980s. In the last two decades, along with the rapid development of advanced mathematical statistics and computing technologies, basal area modelling methodology and technology at the stand level have progressed enormously and many mathematics-based basal area models such as simultaneous equation methods (Eerikäinen, 2002), difference models (Carson and Garcia, 1999; Corona *et al.*, 2002, García and Rui, 2003; Andrés *et al.*, 2004), artificial neural network techniques (Liu *et al.*, 2003), linear/nonlinear regression models (Ralph *et al.*, 2000; Fang *et al.*, 2001; Sharma *et al.*, 2002; Wang *et al.*, 2003) and matrix models (Stanton, 2001; Hao *et al.*, 2005a, 2005b; Zhao *et al.*, 2005) have been established and used in forest management (Table 1 shows a simple comparison of these types of models). As well, process-based models and hybrid models have been developed for simulating stand basal area dynamics (Kimmins *et al.*, 1999; Wang and Kimmins, 2002;

Table 1 Advantages and disadvantages with five mathematic-based basal area models

Comparison items	Difference models	Linear/nonlinear regression models	Artificial neural network matrix models techniques		Simultaneous equation method
Example	Zhang et al. (2004)	Fang et al.(2001)	Liu et al. (2003)	Hao et al. (2005a)	Eerikäinen (2000)
Driving variables	Initial basal area; initial stand age	Stand dominant height (m); tree per hectare (stem/hm²); stand age	Note (3)[a]; Note (3)[b]	Basal area (m²/hm²); volume (m³/hm²); trees (stem/hm²); mean basal area (m²/hm²)	Note (5)[a]
Equations	$H_2 = H_1^{f_1/f_2} \cdot a^{1-f_1/f_2}\left(\dfrac{1-e^{-b_2}}{1-e^{-b_1}}\right)^c$ Note (1)[a]	$\ln(BA) = \beta_{2,0} + \beta_{2,1}/t$ $+\beta_{2,2}\ln(HD)$ $+\beta_{2,3}\ln(TPH)+\varepsilon_B$ Note (2)[a]	$g_i = a_i + \sum_{i=1}^{n_2} b_{ij} x_i$ $h_i = 1/(1+e^{-g_i})$ $q_k = c_k + \sum_{j=1}^{m_h} d_{ij} h_k$ Note (3)[c]	$Y_{t+\theta} = G_t(y_t - h_t) + W_1$ $G_t = \begin{bmatrix} a_{1t} & & & \\ b_{1t} & a_{2t} & & \\ & b_{2t} & \ddots & \\ & & b_{(n-1)t} & a_{nt} \end{bmatrix}_{m \times n}$ $W_1 = \begin{bmatrix} I_t \\ 0 \\ 0 \\ \vdots \\ 0 \end{bmatrix}$ Note (4)[a]	$H_{dom} = f(T,T_{SI},SI)$ $N = f(T)$ $D_{GM} = f(T,H_{dom},N)$ $G = f(T,N,D_{GM})$ $V = f(G,H_{dom},T)$ Note (5)[b]
Advantages	Compatibility step - invariance; biological capacities, good simulating flexibilities.	Compatibility; highly simulating precision; Univariate prediction; the more information on variation available, the more simulating precision.	Have the ability to learn complex patterns and trends; more tolerant of imperfect data.	Relative simple and useful for predicting stand dynamics.	Driving variables take advantage of biological conditions; highly simulating precision.

Continued

Comparison items	Difference models	Linear/nonlinear regression models	Artificial neural network matrix models techniques		Simultaneous equation method
Disadvantages	Weakly understood with stand future conditions; inherently descriptive nature.	Strongly contemporaneous correlation.	The input features may be misclassified.	Inherently correlations with many driving variables.	The statistically significant isn't obvious; the precision is influenced strongly by stand density and site quality.

Note (1)[a]: H_1 is the basal area at the stand age of t_1; H_2 is the basal area at the stand age of t_2; a, b and c are parameters to be estimated from empirical data.

Note (2)[a]: BA=basal area per hectare (m²/hm²); HD=dominant height (m); TPH=tree per hectare (stem/hm²); t=stand age (year); $\beta_{20}, \beta_{2.1}, \beta_{2.2}$ and $\beta_{2.3}$ are parameters; ε_B = error terms.

Note (3)[a]: An example is Multi-layer Perception (MLP).

Note (3)[b]: 1 overstory species composition; 2 understory species composition; 3 stand total basal area (m²/hm²); 4 hardwood basal area percentage (%) of live overstory trees; 5 total net volume of live trees (m³/hm²); 6 acceptable growing stock (%); 7 elevation (m); 8 current FIA forest type assigned by the USFS's algorithm; 9 tree standard size; 10 slope (%); 11 aspect (degree); 12 physiographic class (soil moisture) as estimated by FIA personnel; 13 organic depth; 14 rooting depth; 15 mottling depth; 16 bedrock depth; 17 subsoil texture; 18 parent material; 19 moisture class.

Note (3)[c]: g_i is the net input to the hidden nodes; a_i is the weight (i.e., coefficient); n_x is the number of input features (x_i); n_h is the number of the hidden nodes; c_k is a bias (i.e., intercept); d_{jk} is the weight from the hidden layer to the output layer.

Note(4)[a]: Y_t =a column of vector representing the state of the stand at time t; G_t = growth matrix that defines transition probabilities by species and diameter classes; θ =period interval between inventories; I_t =number of ingrowth at time $t+\theta$; y_t =a vector representing the number of trees in each diameter class, at time t; h_t =a vector representing the number of trees harvested in each diameter class, at time t; W_1 =a vector of constants; a_{ii} =a probability of staying to the next diameter class $i+1$ from diameter class i, over time t to $t+\theta$.

Note(5)[a]: 1 stand dominant height (m); 2 stand age from planting (year); 3 index age (a); 4 stems per hectare; 5 basal area median diameter (cm); 6 stand basal area (m²/hm²); 7 total stand volume over bark (m³/hm²).

Note(5)[b]: H_{dom}=stand dominant height (m); T =stand age from planting (a); T_{SI} =index age (a); SI =site index (m); N =stems per hectare; D_{GM} =basal area median diameter (cm); G =stand basal area (m²/hm²); V =total stand volume over bark (m³/hm²).

Wei *et al.*, 2003).

In these models, the scale ranges from the whole stand to the forest ecosystem and the objective extends from stand basal area prediction to ecological description. Moreover, most of these models continue to evolve with new data, modified design objectives and advances in mathematical and computational procedures. However, the first relatively comprehensive summary of research trends and modelling approaches for stand basal area is now more than 20 years old (Bailey and Ware, 1983; Pienaar and Shiver, 1986). There are only a few reviews available in this research field, such as, the essence of the simulating precision of theoretical growth equations (Zhang and Duan, 2004) and the necessity for creating hybrid models. Therefore, a summary of more recent advances in this field is obviously needed. For this purpose, our objective of this paper is to review the published growth and yield models for uneven/even-aged stands. From the historical development and recent progress, we will state our opinions on the future directions of alternative modelling approaches for growth and dynamics of stand basal area.

2
Features of stand basal area growth models

There are two basic stand structures—even-aged and uneven-aged—in silvicultural systems, although Smith *et al.* (1996) pointed out that under natural forest conditions gradations exist between the two. An even-aged stand is a group of trees composed of a single age class which originated within a short period of time. An uneven-aged stand consists of trees of many ages, and has varied crown canopy of trees and irregular stand profile in the vertical dimension (Peng, 2000). Because the biological growth of trees depends on interactions of constructive metabolism (anabolism) and destructive metabolism (catabolism), the catabolism embodies the restraints by external (competition, limited resources and stress) and internal (aging and self-regulatory) factors as well as their combinations (respiration). Therefore, postulates in growth equation are often formulated in pairs to reflect the multiplicative and limiting components imposed by finite spaces (Li *et al.*, 2000). As a result, the growth and yield of stand basal area, whether even-aged or uneven-aged stands, will monotonously increase with stand age and, eventually, approach a relatively stable maximum. In this respect, the Schumacher equation was applied to predicting basal area growth in thinned slash pine plantations (Pienaar and Shiver, 1986) and two forms of the basal area increment function, the Richards model and the Gompertz function, were used to simulate stand dynamics (Candy, 1989). Both of these have been cast as generalized linear models and a quasi-likelihood approach was adopted in the modelling of the random component of each model. The step-invariance is extensively applied to un-even/even-aged stands (Du and Tang, 1997). However, Ochi and Cao (2003) pointed out that the constraints placed by the compatibility on the system of equations might reduce the accuracy of the model. So they developed an annual growth model that predicted basal area based on information from the previous year. The asymptotic value is a decreasing function of the basal area in accordance with the self-thinning rule (Somers and Farrar, 1991). Pienaar and Turnbull (1973) concluded that the same asymptotic basal area is attainable over a wide range of initial densities. The lowest initial densities tend to have the lowest estimates of the asymptotic value. The asymptotic value is a function of trees per unit area that also changes over time. Heavy mortality can cause a large enough decline in the asymptotic value so that a decrease in basal area is predicted, as would be biologically reasonable (Somers and Farrar, 1991).

3
Types of models

The growth model is a tool to provide better information for forest management. Most discussed approaches for forest modelling are grouped into three types: empirical, process-based and hybrid models.

3.1
Empirical models

Over the past decades, empirical models experienced considerable success in forest growth and yield prediction. Empirical models are derived from large amounts of field data and describe growth rate as a regression function of variables such as site index, age, stem density and basal area. Empirical models rely on a process of production, in which a set of simulation system inputs and outputs are observed, recorded and measured and some or all of the mathematical models are inferred. These empirical models are based on massive experimentation or inventory where available input and output data are accepted as the most appropriate. The major strength of the empirical approach is in describing the best-suited relationship between the measured data and the growth-determining variables using a specified mathematical function of curve. In implementation, empirical models require only simple inputs and are easily constructed. They are also easily incorporated into diversified management analyses and silvicultural treatments and are able to achieve greater efficiency and accuracy in providing quantitative information for management. They may be an appropriate method for predicting short-term yield for time scales over which historical growth conditions are not expected to change significantly.

On the other hand, each forest presents a nearly unique condition that cannot be readily observed elsewhere in space or time. Forest models generally require that a model can be applied to a situation that has never or rarely existed before. In this regard, empirical modelling approaches are limited because data must be measured directly from the condition for prediction. These models provide a means of interpolating and extrapolating knowledge from weakly understood conditions. The reliability of the model prediction is proportional to the generality of the mechanisms and/or relationships on which the model is based. If a specific mechanism or relationship operates only under the condition in which the model was found, the relationship is normally invalid in subsequent modelling efforts because the assumed conditions are not likely to occur elsewhere in space or time. Fortunately, several good improvements with respect to the models have been proposed (Talkkari *et al.*, 1999; Pinkard and Battaglia, 2001; Peng *et al.*, 2002; Zhou *et al.*, 2005; Sampson *et al.*, 2006). For instance, Hély *et al.* (2003) and Kjell and Lennart (2005) incorporated physiological and/or ecological processes into their empirical models that are potentially capable of overcoming the shortcomings of the techniques mentioned above.

3.2
Process-based models

Process-based modelling is defined as a procedure by which the behavior of a system is derived from a set of functional components and their interactions with each other and with the system environment through physical and mechanistic processes occurring over time (Bossel, 1994). Unlike empirical models, process models generally are developed after a certain amount of knowledge has been accumulated using empirical models and may describe a key ecosystem process or simulate the dependence of growth on a number of interacting processes, such as photosynthesis, respiration, decomposition and nutrient cycling. These models offer a framework for testing and generating alternative hypotheses and have the potential to help to describe accurately how these processes will interact under given environmental changes. Consequently, their main contributions include the use of eco-physiological principles in deriving the model and specification and a long-term forecasting applicability within a changing environment. A number of process-based growth and yield models have been developed to help predict forest growth and yield under changing conditions. However, the process-based models need to be as accurate as the empirical models over decades of rotation lengths commonly considered in forest management (Peng, 2000).

Table 2 briefly lists the advantages and disadvantages of empirical and process models. Generally, a weakness of growth and yield models is the strength of process models and vice versa. It is almost always possible to find an empirical model that provides a better fit for a given set of data due to the constraints imposed by the assumptions of process models.

Table 2　Comparison of major features of growth and yield models (empirical vs. process)

Items	Empirical models	Process models
Research intensity	Intermediate	High
Extension service	High	Low
Prediction rotation	Short-term	Long-term
Complexity	Low to high	High
Flexibility	Intermediate to high	Low
Model parameters	Few to many	Many
Field measurements plots	Many	Few to many
Environmental measured factors	Site index, site characteristics	Temperature, light, water, nutrients and disturbance
Inherent nature	Descriptive	Predictive
Simulating advantage	Precision	General
Scale	small	Small to large

3.3
Hybrid models

Empirical and process models can be married into hybrid models in which the shortcomings of both component approaches can, to some extent, be overcome. Specifically, incorporating key elements of the empirical and process approaches into a hybrid ecosystem modelling approach can result in a model that can be used to predict forest growth and production for both the short and long term. Kimmins (1990) developed a framework for hybrid simulation yield modelling that uses historical growth patterns as a baseline estimate for future forest growth under unchanged conditions and then simulates the changes in future forest growth modified by the expected changes in the growth-determining processes (Peng, 2000). Battaglia et al. (1999) appear to have been among the first to hybridize a process-based site productivity model with an empirical growth projection model developed for *E. niten* plantations to allow the prediction of height and basal area growth over time.

Annikki *et al.* (2000) proposed that the implementation of process-based models and more generally, the causal thinking behind them, would be accelerated if it were accepted that hybrid models could improve on the predictions of both process-based models and empirical models. Korzukhin *et al.* (1996) argued that all empirical models have causal elements and all causal models have empirical elements. The need for empirical system-level information in process-based models arises when some parameters cannot be reasonably estimated from their definition. If this is the case, the hybrid characteristics of the models has to be reflected in the methods of parameter estimation and model evaluation, which have usually been defined separately for the two extreme types of the model. Methods of dealing with the mixed characteristics of process-based models include Monte Carlo methods (Hornberger and Cosby, 1985), simultaneous parameter fitting (Sievänen and Burk, 1993), as well as the more recent Bayesian techniques of parameter estimation (Gertner *et al.*, 1999; Green *et al.*, 2000). The basic idea behind all these methods is that some of the parameter values can be determined exactly on the basis of a *prior* information, others can be given intervals of likely variation and some cannot be determined at all on the basis of our current knowledge.

4
Early work on stand basal area models

The origin of modern forest simulation systems lies in the development of yield tables in the late 18th century. Extensive collection of forest biomass data and estimates of existing timber volumes had led to the development of growth and yield models as powerful prediction tools for forest management since the last century (Peng, 2000). MacKinney, Chaiken and Schumacher (1937) generalized these earlier normal yield tables by including a measure of stand density as a third independent variable in addition to age and site index. An important contribution in the evolution of this type of stand-level yield prediction methodology was made by Clutter (1963) who derived yield equations from growth rate equations by integration, thus ensuring compatibility between growth and yield equations. He pointed out that a set of multiple regression equations can be used to describe the relationship between basal area growth and age, site and stand density.

A similar result was published by Clutter and Jones (1980), who derived a single basal area projection equation for old-field slash pine (*Pinus elliottii* Engelm.) plantations based on age and basal area at the beginning of the projection period. Burkhart and Sprinz (1984) used simultaneous estimation to derive compatible volume and basal area projection equations and invariance for projection length was applied. A more general compatible basal area growth and yield model was proposed by Bailey and Ware (1983) whose model reflected the biological process of stand dynamics and proved step-invariance in detail. Because age, stand density and site quality were found to be related to each other, Pienaar and Shiver (1984) used the Chapman–Richards growth model to generate a set of yield curves that have been "harmonized" with respect to differences in planting density. The approach used here is different from the parameter estimates that would have been obtained for each planting density independently. That is, all parameters are estimated simultaneously from the entire data set, thus ensuring estimates for which the sum of squared deviations from observed basal area for models of similar form is at a minimum. Matney and Sullivan (1982) chose compatible stand level projection equations similar to those presented by Clutter (1963), later refined by Sullivan and Clutter (1972) because of their demonstrated applicability. In these basic yield tables, an asymptotic model is often preferred on the assumption that mature stands achieve a relatively stable maximum basal area stocking density determined by site. The model may also be devised to include the expression of a single inflection point in the growth curve (Pienaar and Turnbull, 1973). Somers and Farrar (1991) defined and proved a compatible basal area model with the derivation of the Chapman–Richard function. Their work showed that a general sigmoid-shaped function could be derived by considering the growth rate of any population as the difference between the anabolic (constructive metabolism) and catabolic rates (destructive metabolism).

To improve the shortcomings of empirical statistical models, a number of process-based models have been developed (Running and Coughlan, 1988; Kimmins, 1993; Korol et al., 1994; Kimmins et al., 1995) for describing complex interacting processes in forest ecosystems. The first process-based approach in tropical rain forest modelling was established by Bossel (1991, 1994) and Glauner et al. (2003). Mäkelä and Hari (1986) appear to have been among the first to recognize the need of developing process-based growth and yield models simultaneously with the more traditional statistical ones. They concluded that stem height, stand volume and population density were all determined by physiological processes, but that tree growth development over time was based on tree geometry and an empirical competition index. Kimmins (1990) further pointed out that process-based models could provide quantitative estimates of the potential growth of plantations in new areas and developed his FORCYTE model. This model is immensely complicated and undoubtedly represents an excellent summary of current knowledge about forest ecosystems; but a considerable amount of input information and the complexity of the model makes it difficult to envisage how it could be rigorously tested in any quantitative sense. Bossel (1991) and Kimmins (1993) have reviewed the historical development of process-based models. Korol *et al.* (1996) noted that they obtained a reasonable estimate of net primary productivity available for growth and a correlation between the measured and modeled stand volume increment and basal area increment.

5
Recent progress and future directions

Presently, one trend in growth and yield research is the development of a flexible growth theory with broad and general validity, with emphasis on its application to specific situations. This constitutes a shift from a purely empirical and inductive approach towards a deductive approach.

Long-term spacing studies in plantations have demonstrated that the basal area per acre increases asymptotically with age, that the asymptote varies with site quality and that at any given age, basal area is positively correlated with the number of trees per acre and with site quality. The efforts in modelling increased the scope of model applications and the complexity of the models (Li, 1995; Li *et al.*, 1997; Sun *et al.*, 1998; Wu and Hong, 1998; Wu *et al.*, 1999; Li *et al.*, 2000; Snowdon, 2002; Hu, 2003; Zhang and Duan, 2004).

On the other hand, the algebraic difference forms of the empirical models were applied in order to improve the simulating precision of stand basal area dynamics (Pienaar and Rheney, 1990; Zhang and Duan, 2004). Du and Tang (1997) and Ochi and Cao (2003) discussed the step-invariance with algebraic difference forms, which ensures obtaining consistent results when forest managers consider various alternatives in managing their stands. This method has the great advantage of using the least amount of knowledge of stand growth dynamics, so that one can predict the stand conditions accurately at any given point in time in accordance with the biological characteristics of the stand.

Meanwhile, there are about a dozen of empirical functions (such as the Richards, Bertalanffy, Gompertz, Logistic and Mitscherlich equations) used for description of the size of an organism. They are valued for pragmatic reasons of goodness of fit and convenience of calculation. The parameters of these equations are computed to minimize the deviations from the data and have obvious biological meaning except for serving practical purpose (Zeide, 2003). By predicting the high simulating precision under the full array of different independent variables and comparing the expected outcomes, researchers can decide the independent variables and/or the correspondingly best-suited combinations. Based on the stand basal diameter dynamics of artificial plantations, a significant simulating precision theory was published by Zhang and Duan (2004): ① generally, the simulating precision with empirical models is not strongly affected by the stand age, site quality, stand density and thinning intensity; compared with that of empirical models the attribute of the stand itself is weak; ② the inflection point values of empirical models are strongly correlated with the corresponding model simulating precision and the simulating precision of existing inflection points is higher than that of non-existing inflection points; ③ the more the maximum inflection point intervals fit the curves of the empirical models, the more precise the inflection point values. Because the stand basal area is strongly correlated with the stand basal diameter, it is entirely possible to estimate parameter distribution intervals and to illustrate the validity of empirical models for simulating stand basal area dynamics. Du (1996) further discussed the importance of stand age, stand density and site quality for improving the precision of empirical models when simulating stand basal area dynamics. As a result, to improve the simulating precision with stand basal area and forecast stand dynamics, it is essential to bring stand age, stand density and site quality into the empirical models.

More recently, process-based models and their theory have developed considerably. Mäkelä et al. (2000) argued that the future lies in the development of mixed or hybrid models that combine bio-physical processes and relationships based on tree-evel and stand-level measurements. In their review of the application of process-based models to the forest management, Battaglia and Sands (1998) made the same point and asserted that the process of determining an appropriate model structure must start with the end user. This was restated more strongly by Sands et al. (2000), who argued that process-based models have potentially a valuable role in forest management, but the fulfillment of this potential would be greatly enhanced if the developers of a model were to involve prospective clients in model development and work closely with them in developing applications. 3–PG (Landsberg and Waring, 1997) is a generalized stand model applicable to plantations or even-aged, relatively homogeneous forests that were developed in a deliberate attempt to bridge the gap between the mensuration-based growth and yield and the process carbon-balance models. Output variables of the 3–PG model include monthly or annual values of leaf area indices, stem mass and volume, stem growth rate, mean annual increment, stem basal area and number of stems. Pennanen *et al.* (2004) tracked the basal area and volume of each tree species in each forest patch through integrating a sub-model of stand development with a landscape simulator. This new modelling approach allows addressing various theoretical questions and developing, as well as testing, alternative silvicultural and forest management scenarios. A statistical model has been developed as a decision-support tool for stand-level analysis in forest management planning (Matala *et al.*, 2005). This model showed that tree volume is a function of tree diameter and height. The relationship between tree volume and basal area has been discussed by many investigators (Edgar and Burk, 2001; Dean, 2004; Maltamo *et al.*, 2006; Jensen *et al.*, 2006). It is possible to predict stand basal area by a statistical model. A dynamic whole stand model for Scots pine (*Pinus sylvestris* L.) plantations has been developed by Ulises *et al.* (2006). The model uses three transition functions expressed as algebraic difference forms of the three corresponding state variables (the number of trees per hectare, stand basal area and dominant height) to project the stand state at any given point in time. In addition, the model incorporates a transition function for predicting the initial stand basal area, which can be used to establish the starting point for the simulation.

Models of any sort should encapsulate the essential features of the simulated system, although they very seldom provide unequivocal answers. Empirical and process approaches (models) can be married into hybrid models in which the shortcomings of both component approaches can, to some extent, be overcome. However, it does not mean that one can treat plants as consisting of elementary units and then a computer program takes care of all the elements and integrates their activities to the functioning of the whole plant. Conversely, this framework neglects the most essential thing about trees—they are living beings (Zeide, 2003). In other words, the tree or the stand is more than the sum of its finite parts. When we choose a model to simulate stand basal area dynamics, accuracy, generality and broad utility should be considered. The most important thing is that the biological characteristics must be fully embodied by the chosen model.

6
Conclusions

The discussion about stand basal area growth models can be concluded as follows:
Algebraic difference forms of empirical models can adequately describe stand growth dynamics and meet the step-invariance, good simulating flexibilities and

compatibility demands.

Stand age, stand density and site quality are the most important determinants for spatial and temporal development of stand characteristics such as basal area; algebraic difference forms of empirical models can be fully reflected in the relationship of stand basal area, stand age, stand density and site quality.

Hybrid models that incorporate the physiological and ecological processes into empirical models are potentially capable of overcoming the shortcomings of predicting stand dynamics at any given point in time.

References

Andrés B O, Miren D R, Gregorio M. 2004. Site index curves and growth model for Mediterranean maritime pine (*Pinus pinaster* Ait.) in Spain. For Ecol Manag, 201: 187~197

Annikki M, Joe L, Alan R, *et al.* 2000. Process-based models for forest ecosystem management: current state of the art and challenges for practical implementation. Tree Physiol, 20: 289~298

Bailey R L, Ware K D. 1983. Compatible basal-area growth and yield model for thinned and unthinned stands. Can J For Res, 13: 563~571

Battaglia M, Sands P J, Candy S G. 1999. Hybrid growth model to predict height and volume growth in young *Eucalyptus globules* plantations. For Ecol Manag, 120: 193~201

Battaglia M, Sands P J. 1998. Process-based forest productivity models and their application in forest management. For Ecol Manag, 102: 13~32

Bossel H. 1991. Modelling forest dynamics: moving from description to explanation. For Ecol Manag, 42: 129~142

Bossel H. 1994. Modelling and simulation. Wellesley, MA: A K Peters Ltd., 484

Burkhart E, Sprinz T. 1984. Compatible cubic volume and basal area projection equations for thinned old-field loblolly pine plantations. For Sci, 30: 86~93

Candy S G. 1989. Growth and yield models for *Pinus radiate* in Tasmania. New Zealand J For Sci, 19(1): 112~133

Carson D, Garcia H. 1999. Realized gain and prediction of yield with genetically improved *Pinus radiate* in New Zealand. For Sci, 45(2): 186~200

Clutter J L, Jones E P. 1980. Predicting of growth after thinning in old-field slash pine plantations. USDA Forest Serv Res Pap SE, 14

Clutter J L. 1963. Compatible growth and yield models for loblolly pine. For Sci, 9(3): 354~371

Corona P, Antonio M P, Scotti R. 2002. Top-down growth modelling: a prototype for poplar plantations in Italy. For Ecol Manag, 161: 65~73

Dean J T. 2004. Basal area increment and growth efficiency as functions of canopy dynamics and stem mechanics. For Sci, 50(11): 106~116

Du J S, Tang S Z. 1997. The review of studies on stand basal area growth mode. For Res, 10(6): 599~606 (in Chinese with an English abstract)

Du J S. 1996. Model Studies of Effects on Stand Growth by Thinning. Ph. D. Thesis. Beijing: Beijing Forestry University (in Chinese)

Edgar C B, Burk T E. 2001. Productivity of aspen forests in northeastern Minnesota, U.S.A., as related to stand composition and canopy structure. Can J For Res, 11: 1019~1029

Eerikäinen K. 2002. A site dependent simultaneous growth projection model for *Pinus kesiya* plantations in Zambia and Zimbabwe. For Sci, 48 (3): 518~529

Ek A R, Shifley S R, Burk T E. 1988. Forest growth modelling and prediction. In: USDA For Gen Tech Rep NC, 1,149

Fang Z, Bailey R L, Shiver B D. 2001. A multivariate simultaneous prediction system for stand growth and yield with fixed and random effects. For Sci, 47(4): 550~562

García O, Rui F. 2003. A growth model for eucalypt in Galicia, Spain For Ecol Manag, 173: 49~62

Gertner G Z, Fang S, Skovsgaard J P. 1999. A Bayesian approach for estimating the parameters of a forest process model based on long-term growth data. Ecol Model, 119: 249~265

Gevorkiantz S R. 1934. The approach of under-stocked stands to normality. J For, 32: 487~488

Glauner R, Ditzer T, Huth A. 2003. Growth and yield of tropical moist forest for forest planning: an inquiry through modelling. Can J For Res, 33: 521~535

Green E J, McFarlane D W, Valentine H T. 2000. Bayesian synthesis for quantifying uncertainty in predictions from process models. Tree Physiol, 20: 415~538

Hao Q Y, Meng F R, Zhou Y P, *et al.* 2005a. A transition matrix growth model for uneven-aged mixed-species forests in the Changbai Mountains, northern China New For, 29: 221~231

Hao Q Y, Meng F R, Zhou, Y P, *et al.* 2005b. Determining the optimal selective harvest strategy for mixed-species stands with a transition matrix growth model. New For, 29: 207~219

Hély C, Flannigan M, Bergeron Y. 2003. Modelling tree mortality following wildfire in the southeastern Canadian mixed-wood boreal forest. For Sci, 49(4): 566~576

Hornberger G M, Cosby B J. 1985. Selection of parameter values in environmental models using sparse data: a case study. Appl Math Comput, 17: 335~355

Hu X L. 2003. Studies of basal area growth models of *Larix olgensis* stands. For Res, 16(4): 449~452 (in Chinese with an English abstract)

Jensen J L, Humes K S, Conner T, *et al.* 2006. Estimation of biophysical characteristics for highly variable mixed-conifer stands using small-footprint lidar Can J For Res, 36: 1,129~1,138

Kimmins J P, Brunner A, Mailly D. 1995. Modelling the sustainability of managed forest: hybrid ecosystem simulation modelling from individual tree to landscape. In: Forest Ecosystem Working Group Session. Portland, Maine

Kimmins J P, Mailly D, Seely B. 1999. Modelling forest ecosystem net primary production: the hybrid simulation approach used in FORECAST. Ecol Model, 122: 195~224

Kimmins J P. 1993. Scientific foundations for the simulation of ecosystem function and management in FORCYTE-11. Northwest region, Forestry Canada, Information Report NOR-X-328, 88

Kimmins. 1990. Modelling the sustainability of forest production and yield for a changing and uncertain future. For Chron, 6: 271~280

Kjell K, Lennart N. 2005. Modelling survival probability of individual trees in Norway spruce stands under different thinning regimes. Can J For Res, 35: 113~121

Korol R L, Milner K S, Running S W. 1996. Testing a mechanistic model for predicting stand and tree growth. For Sci, 42: 139~153

Korol R L, Running S W, Milner K S. 1994. Incorporating inter-tree competition into an ecosystem model. Can J For Res, 25: 413~424

Korzukhin M D, Mikaelian M T, Wagner R T. 1996. Process versus empirical models: which approach for forest ecosystem management? Can J For Res, 26: 879~887

Landsberg J J, Waring R H. 1997. A generalized model of forest productivity using simplified concepts of radiation-use efficiency, carbon balance and partitioning. For Ecol Manage, 95: 209~228

Li F R, Wang Y H, Hou L J. 1997. Comparison of the Chap-man–Richards function with the Schnute model in stand growth. J For Res, 8(3): 137~143 (in Chinese with an English abstract)

Li F R, Zhao B, Su G. 2000. A derivation of the generalized Korf growth equation and its application. J For Res, 11(2): 81~88 (in Chinese with an English abstract)

Li F R. 1995. A Simulation System of Stand Dynamics for larch Plantation. Ph. D. Thesis. Beijing: Beijing Forestry University (in Chinese)

Liu C, Zhang L, Davis C J, et al. 2003. Comparison of neural networks and statistical methods in classification of ecological habitats using FIA data. For Sci, 49(4): 619~631

MacKinney A L, Schumacher F, Chaiken L. 1937. Construction of yield tables for non-normal loblolly pine stands. J Agric Res, 54: 531~545

Mäkelä A, Hari P. 1986. Stand growth model based on carbon uptake and allocation in individual trees. Ecol Model, 33: 205~229

Mäkelä A, Landsberg J J, Ek A R, et al. 2000. Process-based models for forest ecosystem management: current state of the art and challenge for practical implementation. Tree Physiol, 20: 289~298

Maltamo M, Eerikäinen K, Packalén P, et al. 2006. Estimation of stem volume using laser scanning-based canopy height metrics. Forestry, 79(13): 217~229

Matala J, Ojansuu R, Peltola H, et al. 2005. Introducing effects of temperature and CO_2 elevation on tree growth into a statistical growth and yield model. Ecol Model, 181: 173~190

Matney T G, Sullivan A D. 1982. Compatible stand and stock tables for thinned and unthinned loblolly pine stands. For Sci, 28: 161~171

Meyer W H. 1942. Yields of even-aged stands of loblolly pine in northern Louisiana. Yale Univ School For Bull, 51, 58

Ochi N, Cao Q V. 2003. A comparison of compatible and annual growth models. For Sci, 49(2): 285~290

Peng C H, Liu J X, Dang Q L, et al. 2002. TRIPLEX: a generic hybrid model for predicting forest growth and carbon and nitrogen dynamics. Ecol Model, 153: 109~130

Peng C H. 2000. Growth and yield models for uneven-aged stands: past, present, and future. For Ecol Manage, 132: 259~279

Pennanen J, David F G, Marie–Josée F, et al. 2004. Spatially explicit simulation of long-term boreal forest landscape dynamics: incorporating quantitative stand attributes. Ecol Model, 180: 188~195

Pienaar L V, Shiver B D. 1984. An analysis and model of basal area growth in 45–year-old unthinned and thinned slash pine plantation plots. For Sci, 30: 933~942

Pienaar L V, Shiver B D. 1986. Basal area prediction and projection equations for pine plantations. For Sci, 32(3): 626~633

Pienaar V, Rheney W. 1990. Yield prediction for mechanically site-prepared slash pine plantations. South J Appl For, 14: 104~109

Pienaar V, Turnbull J. 1973. The Chapman–Richards generalization of von bertalanffy's growth model for basal growth and yield in even-aged stands. For Sci, 19(1): 2~22

Pinkard E, Battaglia M. 2001. Using hybrid model to develop silvicultural prescriptions for Eucalyptus nitens. For Ecol Manage, 154: 337~345

Ralph D N, David G R, Ruth D Y, et al. 2000. Early cohort development following even-aged reproduction method cuttings in New York northern hardwoods. Can J For Res, 30: 67~75

Reineke L H. 1933. Perfecting a stand-density index for even-aged forests. J Agric Res, 46: 627~638

Running S W, Coughlan J C. 1988. A general model of forest ecosystem processes for regional applications. I. hydrological balance, canopy gas exchange and primary production processes.

Ecol Model, 42: 125~154

Sampson D A, Waring R H, Maier C A, *et al*. 2006. Fertilization effects on forest carbon storage and exchange, and net primary production: A new hybrid process model for stand management. For Ecol Manag, 221: 91~109

Sands P J, Battaglia M, Mummery D. 2000. Application of process-based models to forest management: experience with PROMOD, A sample plantation productivity model. Tree Physiol, 20: 383~392

Schumacher. 1939. A new growth curve and its application to timber-yield studies. J For, 37: 819~820

Sharma M, Oderwald R G, Amateis R L. 2002. A consistent system of equations for tree and stand volume. For Ecol Manag, 165: 183~191

Sievänen R, Burk T E. 1993. A process-based model for the dimensional growth of even-aged stands. Scand. J For Res, 8: 28~48

Smith D M, Larson B C, Kelty M J, *et al*. 1996. The Practice of Silviculture: Applied Forest Ecology. New York: Wiley

Snowdon P. 2002. Modelling type 1 and type 2 growth responses in plantations after application of fertilizer or other silvicultural treatments. For Ecol Manag, 163(1): 229~244

Somers L, Farrar M. 1991. Biomathematical growth equations for natural longleaf pine stand. For Sci, 37(1): 227~244

Stanton B J. 2001. Clonal variation in basal area growth patterns during stand development in hybrid poplar. Can J For Res, 31: 2059~2066

Sullivan A D, Clutter J L. 1972. A simultaneous growth and yield model for loblolly pine. For Sci, 18(1): 76~86

Sun X M, Li F R, Niu S, *et al*. 1998. A study on growth model for *Larix olgensis* plantation. For Res, 11(3): 306~312 (in Chinese with an English abstract)

Talkkari A, Kellomaki S, Peltola H. 1999. Bridging a gap between a gap model and physiological model for calculating the effect of temperature on forest growth under boreal conditions. For Ecol Manag, 119: 137~150

Tang S Z, Du J S. 1999. Determining basal area growth process of thinned even-aged stands by crown competition factor. Sci Silv Sin, 35 (6): 35~41 (in Chinese with English abstract)

Ulises D A, Fernando C D, Juan G Á G, *et al*. 2006. Dynamic growth model for Scots pine (*Pinus sylvestris* L.) plantations in Galica (north-western Spain). Ecol Model, 191: 225~242

Wang J R, Kimmins J P. 2002. Height growth and competitive relationship between paper birch and Douglas-fir in coast and interior of British Columbia. For Ecol Manag, 165: 285~293

Wang J R, Letchford T, Comeau P G. 2003. Influences of paper birch competition on growth of understory white spruce and subalpine fir following spacing. Can J For Res, 33: 1,962~1,973

Wei X, Kimmins J P, Zhou G. 2003. Disturbances and the sustainability of long-term site productivity in lodgepole pine forests in the central interior of British Columbia—an ecosystem modelling approach. Ecol Model, 164: 239~256

Wellwood R W. 1943. Trend towards normality of stocking for second-growth loblolly pine stands. J For, 41: 202~209

Wu C Z, Hong W. 1998. Study on quantitative dynamics of *pinus taiwanensis* population. J. Zhejiang For Coll, 15(3): 274~259 (in Chinese with an English abstract)

Wu X F, Deng B L, Hu Y. 1999. Study on dynamics models of forest growth and nutrition IV. Stand section area equation of Chinese fir forest. Life Sci Res, 3(3): 256~261 (in Chinese with an English abstract)

Zeide B. 2003. The U-approach to forest modelling. Can J For Res, 33: 480~489

Zhang J G, Duan A G. 2004. Study on Theoretical Growth Equation and Diameter Structure Model. Beijing:Life Science Press, 2~7

Zhao D H, Borders B, Wilson M. 2005. A density-dependent matrix model for bottomland hardwood stands in the lower Mississippi alluvial valley. Ecol Model, 184: 381~395

Zhou X L, Peng C H, Dang Q L, et al. 2005. Predicting forest growth and yield in northeastern Ontario using the process-based model of TRIPLEX1.0. Can J For Res, 35: 2268~2280

CHAPTER THREE:
Individual tree basal area growth dynamics of chinese fir plantations

Abstract   The fixed-effect model for individual tree basal area growth modelling for chinese fir (*Cunninghamia lanceolata*) in spacing plantations was developed using panel data. The heterogeneity of individual increment basal area among the different blocks was analyzed with independent variables [diameter of breast height (DBH) and live crown ratio (LCR)], dummy variables with stand planting density, competition indices, and site and stand age effects. The result indicates that there is a strong relationship between stand planting density and competition indices, but both of them are important factors impacting individual tree basal area increment growth. The impact of site condition and stand age varies with different stand density. The fitting deviation of the individual tree basal area increment increases along with site indices and stand ages.

Key words   Fixed-effect regression model; Individual tree basal area; chinese fir

1
Introduction

Chinese fir is one of the most important fast-growing coniferous tree species in the subtropical zone in China (Lei, 2005). The key to solve timber supply-demand conflict is to silviculture fast-growing, high-yield, good-quality plantations. Insight into tree species' growth dynamics is basically a precondition to manage plantations.

Recently, individual tree basal area growth modelling was used to simulate and predict growth and yield in pure even-aged stands (Wykoff, 1990; Monserud and Sterba, 1996; Mailly *et al.*, 2003), which can reflect tree growth trends precisely (Hökkä and Groot, 1999; Zhang *et al.*, 2004). So, tree basal area is seen as a promising approach. The theoretical growth equations and composite models were used to simulate tree basal area growth trends. The theoretical growth equations can reflect good biological growth characters (e.g., inflection points) but potential growth can not be reliably estimated. Thus the composite model was chosen. A composite model incorporates tree (e.g., tree size, LCR) and stand (e.g., age, site, stand density) characteristics in a single equation and can reflect inter-tree competition.

We analyzed individual tree basal area growth dynamics with panel data fixed-effect model. This study was undertaken to test the hypothesis that competition indices that more explicitly take into account the spatial distribution of trees in even-aged stands would be better correlated with tree growth increment than non-spatial indices. A second objective was to identify DBH and LCR that in combination with other independent variables, best describes basal area increment in even-aged chinese fir stands.

2
Materials and methods

2.1
Experimental sites

The chinese fir stands located in Fenyi County (27°34′N, 117°29′E), Jiangxi province, in central China were established in 1982. The area lies in the middle of Qingshiwan Mountain's southern face, at an elevation of 250 m. The soil type is red soil. Average annual precipitation is about 1591 mm. Most of the precipitation lies in between April and September as rain. Annual mean maximum temperature is 28.8 ℃ and minimum temperature −5.3℃。Annual mean frost-free season is 265 days.

The plots were planted in a random block arrangement with the following tree spacing: 2m×3m (A, 1667 stems/ha), 2m×1.5m (B, 3333 stems/ha), 2m×1m (C, 5000 stems/ha), 1m×1.5m (D, 6667 stems/ha) and 1m×1m (E, 10 000 stems/ha). Each spacing level was replicated three times. Each plot comprised an area of 20m×30m and a buffer zone consisting of similarly treated trees. Sampling was performed in each winter from 1983 to 1990 and then every other year until 2006. Six dominant trees were selected to compute site index with 20 reference age. The measurements comprised the total tree height (m), diameter at breast height (cm), crown width within and between rows (m) and height to the base of the lowest live branch (m). Live crown ratio (LCR) is obtained by live crown length dividing into total tree height. The individual tree basal area (m^2) was estimated using the experimental formulae:

$$TBA = \frac{\pi d^2}{40\ 000} \tag{1}$$

π -the ratio of circumference of a circle to its diameter; d -diameter at breast height (cm).

A summary of the statistics for the plots is presented in Table 1.

Table 1   Summary of the chinese fir stands

Stand attributes features	Mean	S.D.[①]	Minimum	Maximum
Age/a	16	6	2	26
Density/(stems/ha)	4143	1130	1500	10 000
Diameter at breast height/cm	10.78	3.45	7.91	19.62
Mean crown length/m	0.0095	0.05	0.0021	0.0227
Average tree basal area/dm^2	0.07	0.0156	0.01	0.32
Live crown ratio	0.3251	0.2269	0.1917	0.8103

① S.D.: standard deviation.

2.2
Analysis approach

As for the different plot blocks, the model's intercepts are different from each other, so the regression parameters can be obtained when the dummy variables were added to regression model. In the present study, the three kinds of fixed effects regression model were used to simulate tree basal area growth dynamics.

I: Regression slope coefficients are identical, and intercepts are not. In this paper, we presume that site index is a constant in some a plot all the time, but intercepts changes among the different plots. The fixed-effect model emphasizes relationship between tree basal area increment growth and site.

$$y_{it} = \alpha_i + \beta X_{it} + \varepsilon_{it}, \quad i = 1,\cdots,N; t = 1,\cdots,T \tag{2}$$

y_{it} denotes plots observations of characteristics of N individuals over T time periods; α_i and β are 1×1 and $1 \times K$ vectors of constants that vary across i and t, respectively; $X_{it} = (x_{1it},\cdots,x_{kit})'$ is a $1 \times K$ vectors of exogenous variables{DBH, LCR}, and ε_{it} is the error term. In this paper, α_i means random variables and can explain $X_{it} = (x_{1it},\cdots,x_{kit})'$ variation;

II: Regression intercepts are the same, and slope coefficients are not. Stand ages are always changing in any plots all the time, and intercepts changes among the different plots. So, this fixed-effect model emphasizes relationship between tree basal area and stand ages.

$$y_{it} = \gamma_t + \beta X_{it} + \varepsilon_{it}, \quad i = 1,\cdots,N; t = 1,\cdots,T \tag{3}$$

γ_t denotes 1×1 vector of variables that vary across i.

III: Both slope and intercepts coefficient are the variables. In this paper, we assume that site and stand ages are changing all the time. That is, this fixed-effect model emphasizes relationship between tree basal area and site and stand ages. So intercepts include α_i and γ_t.

$$y_{it} = \alpha_i + \gamma_t + \beta X_{it} + \varepsilon_{it}, \quad i = 1, \cdots, N; t = 1, \cdots, T \qquad (4)$$

We also use dummy variables to explain relationship between tree basal area and the initial stand density. The four dummy variables denote

$$B = \begin{cases} 1, 2m \times 1.5m \\ 0, otherwise \end{cases}, \quad C = \begin{cases} 1, 2m \times 1m \\ 0, otherwise \end{cases}, \quad D = \begin{cases} 1, 1m \times 1.5m \\ 0, otherwise \end{cases}, \quad E = \begin{cases} 1, 1m \times 1m \\ 0, otherwise \end{cases}.$$

If dummy variable B equals 1, then C, D and E equals 0, respectively.

A selection of five competition indices was tested for inclusion in a predictive model of basal area increment. These ranged from simple indices such as density and basal area of competitor trees to more complex indices such Hegyi's competition index (Table 2). The search radius (R) for inclusion of competitor trees was set to 2.0 times the mean crown radius of canopy trees in these stands. A tree was considered to be a potential competitor when its DBH was found to be equal or greater than two thirds of the DBH of the subject tree.

Table 2   List of competition indices

Index	Name	Definition[①]	References
Distance-independent indices			
1	Nn	Number of neighbors j (trees situated at less than R meters, on a per-hectare basis)	
2	SBA	Sum of the basal areas of the neighbors j situated at less than R meters, on a per-hectare basis: $SBA = \sum_{j=1}^{n} BA$	Steneker and Javis (1963)
3	$C18$	Sum of DBH_j of the neighbors j situated at less than R meters, divided by the subject tree DBH_i : $C18 = \sum_{j=1}^{n} D_j / D_i$	Lorimer (1983)
Distance-dependent indices			
4	$C14$	Sum of the ratios between the competitor j and subject tree i DBH, divided by the square root of the ratio between the distance separating the competitor j with subject tree i and the search radius: $C14 = \sum_{j=1}^{n} \dfrac{D_j/D_i}{\sqrt{DIST_{ij}/R}}$	Lorimer (1983)
5	DCI	Hegyi's diameter-distance competition index, for neighbors j situated at less than R meters: $DCI = \sum_{j=1}^{n} \left(\dfrac{D_j}{D_i} \times \dfrac{1}{DIST_{ij}} \right)$	Hegyi (1974)

① BA_j, basal area of competitor tree j; D_j, diameter at breast height of competitor tree j; D_i, diameter at breast height of subject tree i; $DIST_{ij}$, distance between subject tree i and competitor j; R, search radius.

The growth model used in this study is a least-squares dummy-variable (LSDV) regression model between basal area increment ($m^2 \cdot a^{-1}$, in transformed) and nine kinds independent variables combinations (Table 3). SAS mixed procedure (SAS V.9.0, 2004) was used for estimation models parameters and obtained standard deviation (S.D.) and coefficient of determination (R^2).

Table 3   List of nine kinds of the independent variables combinations

Name	Regressions	Fixed-effects
1	DBH, LCR	
2	DBH, LCR	site index, stand age
3	DBH, LCR, stand density	
4	DBH, LCR, stand density	site index, stand age
5	DBH, LCR, stand density, *Nn*	site index, stand age
6	DBH, LCR, stand density, *SBA*	site index, stand age
7	DBH, LCR, stand density, *C14*	site index, stand age
8	DBH, LCR, stand density, *C18*	site index, stand age
9	DBH, LCR, stand density, *DCI*	site index, stand age

3
Results and discussion

Least Squares method was used to estimate DBH and LCR parameters and the estimated results are very significant at 1% level indicated at the column (1) (Table 4). This result indicates that growth of DBH can lead to basal area increment augment and LCR is positive correlated with tree basal area increment. However, the result at the column (2) shows that the omission variables including site index and stand age result in the larger model parameters. That is, when the fixed-effect with site index and stand age was includes in regression models, the goodness of fitting (R^2) increases from 0.2440 to 0.9865. Meanwhile, parameter of LCR decreases from 1.8358 to 0.7611 and DBH from 0.3210 to 0.0505, which means that separate site and stand age effects from DBH and LCR variables. Therefore, site index and stand age simultaneously are added regression models from column (4) to (9).

The regression model at the column (3) adds stand density factors at the base of column (1). The positive regression parameters with stand density blocks increase when stand density becomes large. The regression result at the column (4) shows that stand density parameters become gradually negative when regression model adds site and stand age effect. Compared with the column (2) results, the goodness of fitting with column (4) decreases to 8 percent.   As a result, site conditions affect tree basal area increment growth more important than that of stand density.

Table 4　Individual tree basal area growth models regression with the independent variables[①]

Regressions	Individual tree basal area growth models								
	(1)	(2)	(3)	(4)	(5)	(6)	(7)	(8)	(9)
DBH	0.3210 (0.0063) ***	0.0505 (0.0111) ***	0.2917 (0.0024) ***	0.1235 (0.0085) ***	0.1026 (0.0063) ***	0.1260 (0.0072) ***	0.1115 (0.0064) ***	0.1094 (0.0060) ***	0.1079 (0.0063) ***
LCR	1.8358 (0.1392) ***	0.7611 (0.0980) ***	1.1958 (0.0521) ***	0.5356 (0.1064) ***	0.1108 (0.1959)	0.2126 (0.1226) *	0.1551 (0.0976)	0.1734 (0.0877) **	0.0889 (0.0917)
B density (2m×1.5m)			0.6466 (0.039) ***	0.0031 (0.0361)	−0.0535 (0.0269)	0.0164 (0.0303)	−0.0794 (0.0276) ***	−0.0514 (0.0264) *	−0.1155 (0.0276) ***
C density (2m×1m)			0.8956 (0.0381) ***	−0.0687 (0.0499)	−0.1121 (0.0365) ***	−0.052 (0.0418)	−0.2024 (0.0378) ***	−0.2097 (0.0371) ***	−0.0243 (0.0372) ***
D density (1m×1.5m)			1.0205 (0.0372) ***	−0.1531 (0.0594) **	−0.1525 (0.0437) ***	−0.1339 (0.0497) ***	−0.0867 (0.0454) *	−0.3499 (0.0464) ***	−0.1657 (0.0433) ***
E density (1m×1m)			1.0702 (0.0366) ***	−0.1686 (0.0627) ***	−0.1242 (0.0465) ***	−0.1515 (0.0521) ***	−0.0961 (0.0477) **	−0.1328 (0.0127) ***	−0.0904 (0.0469) *
Site effect	No	Yes	No	Yes	Yes	Yes	Yes	Yes	Yes
Age effect	No	Yes	No	Yes	Yes	Yes	Yes	Yes	Yes
Nn				−0.1854 (0.020) ***					
SBA						−0.0800 (0.0298) ***			
C14							−0.1171 (0.0169) ***		
C18								−0.1328 (0.0127) ***	
DCI									−0.1389 (0.0163) ***
Adjust−R^2	0.2440	0.9865	0.9063	0.9809	0.9863	0.9810	0.9872	0.9891	0.9873
F value	62.287	506.592	376.369	553.236	738.561	597.761	789.982	924.327	795.113
S.D.	0.5567	0.0743	0.1955	0.0884	0.0696	0.1079	0.0673	0.0618	0.0669

① S. E. including parentheses under coefficients, significance of statistics with ***1%, **5%, *10% levels.

Inter-tree competition indices were added to individual tree basal area increment growth model from column (5) to (9). The goodness of fitting can be increased when inter-tree competitor indices were added into regression models. Parameters of competition indices are all negative, which means that inter-tree competition is negative correlated with tree basal area increment. Parameters of the distance-independent indices (e.g., SBA, Nn) are inconsistent. When SBA and Nn parameters increase one unit, tree basal area decreases 0.0800 and 0.1854 units, respectively. Parameters of the distance-independent indices ($C14$, DCI) increase one unit, and then tree basal area decreases 0.1300 units accordingly.

Parameters with DBH fluctuate between 0.1000 and 0.1300. That is, when DBH increases one unit, tree basal area increment increases 13%. Parameters with LCR are all positive but change in the different regression models. That means LCR is positive correlated with tree basal area increment.

Parameters with stand density dummy variables become larger, when competition indices were added into regression model. This is because inter-tree competition begins after stand canopy grow close. The denser stand density, the less tree basal area increment grows.

Tree basal area increment fitting derivation at the different initial stand density is inconsistent, which tree basal area increment derivation is positive correlated with site (Table 5). The tree basal area increment derivation increases 0.1593 units, when site index increases one unit (Table 6). The tree basal area fitting derivation at the different stand age is also inconsistent (Table 7), which explains tree basal area derivation 85.99% (Table 6). Tree basal area derivation is positive correlated with stand age. When stand age increases one unit, tree basal area increment derivation increases 0.0245 units. Compared with site index, stand age is little effect on tree basal area derivation.

Table 5   Individual tree basal area derivation at the different site conditions

Plot No.	Site index/m	Fitting derivation	Plot No.	Site index/m	Fitting derivation
A_1	17.52	0.405 467	C_3	15.66	−0.010 052
A_2	18.12	0.201 743	D_1	14.4	−0.228 297
A_3	16.84	0.421 436	D_2	14.24	−0.227 550
B_1	16.18	0.233 582	D_3	14.34	−0.168 851
B_2	15.32	−0.016 129	E_1	14.74	−0.248 257
B_3	15.98	0.219 883	E_2	15.82	−0.236 119
C_1	14.94	0.006 720	E_3	16.02	−0.226 191
C_2	15.42	−0.127 385		15.66	−0.010 052

Table 6   Fitting derivation of individual tree basal area

Stand factors	Parameters		Correlation coefficient
	Slopes	Intercept	
Site index	−2.5016 (−4.2085)	0.1593 (4.2189)	0.7385
Stand age	−0.3371 (−5.0008)	0.0245 (5.5863)	0.8599

Table 7   The estimated values of the individual basal area at the different age

Stand age/a	Fitting derivation	Stand age/a	Fitting derivation
5	−0.443 692	15	0.116 344
6	−0.274 285	17	0.146 638
7	−0.153 190	19	0.146 467
8	−0.088 244	21	0.153 643
9	−0.041 187	23	0.149 438
11	0.031 952	25	0.176 570
13	0.079 548		

4
Conclusion

DBH and LCR were inferior to explain individual tree basal area increment growth, whose goodness of fitting is only 0.2440. Adding site and stand age effects, goodness of fitting increases rapidly from 0.2440 to 0.9865, which means site and stand age have a great impact on the tree basal area increment growth. However, site and stand age can increase tree basal area increment fitting derivation. The initial stand density is negative correlated with tree basal area increment. That is, the more the initial stand density, the less individual tree basal area is. The distance-dependent indices can prove superior to better distance-independent indices based on their goodness of fitting with tree basal area increment. Especially, distance-independent indices with $C14$ and Hegyi's are strictly positive correlated with tree basal area increment. Computing the distance-independent indices with SBA into the fixed-effect growth models, the initial stand density are more correlated with tree basal area increment.

References

Hegyi F. 1974. A simulation model for managing jack – pine stands //In Proceedings, Growth Models for Tree and Stand Simulation, IUFRO S4.01– 4.Edited by Fries, j., Stockholm, Sweden: Department of Forest Yield, Royal College of Forestry, 74~ 87

Hökkä H, Groot A. 1999. An individual-tree basal area growth model for black spruce in second-growth peatland stands. Can J For Res, 29: 621 ~ 629

Lei J. 2005. Forest Resource in China. China Forestry Publishing House, Beijing, China, 172p (in Chinese)

Lorimer C G. 1983. Tests of age-independent competition indices for individual trees in natural trees hardwood stands. For Ecol Manag, 6: 343~360

Mailly D, Turbis S, Pothier D. 2003. Predicting basal area increment in a spatially explicit, individual tree mode: a test of competition measure with black spruce. Can J For Res, 33: 435~443

Monserud R A, Sterba H. 1996. A basal area increment model for individual tree growing in even and uneven-aged forest stands in Austria. For Ecol Manag, 80: 57~80

Steneker G A, Jarvis J M. 1963. A preliminary study to assess competition in a white – spruce trembling aspen stand. For Chron, 39: 334~336

Wykoff W R. 1990. A basal area increment models for individual conifer in the northern Rocky mountains. For Sci, 36:1077~1104

Zhang L, Peng C, Dang Q. 2004. Individual tree basal area growth models for jack pine and black spruce in northern Ontario. The For Chron, 80: 366~374

CHAPTER FOUR:
Application of theoretical growth equations for stand diameter structure simulation of chinese fir plantations

Abstract   Theoretical growth equations are important tools in research into both the theoretical and practical application of stand diameter structure simulation. This study investigated the influence of stand characteristics and equation composition on the simulation performance of theoretical growth equations, to assist with the selection and application of theoretical growth equations. The results showed that stand age, site, planting density, and thinning intensity have a weak influence on the simulation accuracy of six growth equations including the Richards equation. Thus, stand attributes contributed little to the differences in simulation accuracy among the different growth equations. The inflection points of the stand diameter cumulative percentage distribution curve had a main distribution interval of (0.4, 0.6), showing a 1/2 close rule. The inflection point attributes of the growth equations were strongly related to simulation accuracy of each equation. The equations with an inflection point showed much higher simulation accuracy than the Mitscherlich equation, which has no inflection point. With regard to the equations with floating inflection points, the larger the inflection point distribution range of the fitting curvesis, the higher the simulation accuracy of the growth equation has. With respect to the equations with fixed inflection points, the simulation accuracy of the equation could be measured by the position of the equation inflection point relative to the main interval of stand inflection points. For these equations, the closer the equation inflection point was to the center of the main interval of stand inflection points, the higher the simulation precision of the equation was. The larger the effective inflection point interval of the theoretical growth equation was, and the closer the inflection point was to 0.5, the more effective the equation inflection point was and the higher simulation precision the equation had. The discovery of this phenomenon provides a scientific basis for selection of a stand diameter structure model for Chinese fir plantations and other tree species.

Key words   Theoretical growth equations; Diameter distribution; Modeling precision; Inflection point

1
Introduction

A theoretical growth equation, as a model to describe the size change of an organism or a population with age, reflects the regularity of an organism's growth or population dynamics (Zeide,1989; 1993). The overall growth process of trees typically exhibits a sigmoid curve. Thus, in a specific stand, the growth of a single tree theoretically exhibits a S curve and the whole stand growth shows a 'slow-quick-slow' pattern. The accumulative percentage distribution of trees' diameter class in the stand caused by differentiation is also S-shaped. Therefore, a theoretical growth equation representing a S-shaped or similarly shaped curve can be applied to simulation of forest growth or distribution at the single tree, stand and diameter-class levels.

Simulation of stand diameter structure is at the core of stand growth simulation research. From an applied research perspective, research on stand diameter structure modelling can be generally categorized into two kinds, namely dominant parametric and non-dominant nonparametric approaches, including the relative diameter method, probability density functions, theoretical growth equations, percentile prediction, *k*-nearest neighbor estimation, as well as other fitting methods. Before the mid–1990s, theoretical growth equations were mainly applied to the construction of stand or tree-level growth models. More recently, their advantages for researching and constructing stand diameter structure models have gradually become apparent. Applied theoretical growth equations mainly include population dynamics models (such as Logistic) and the Richards equation (Gadow and Hui, 1998; Ishikawa, 1998). The Gompertz and Logistic equations were proposed relatively early and were both initially applied to the description of population growth and distribution. The Gompertz equation was first described by Gompertz (1825) to describe population decline and age distribution. Wu (1988) applied this equation to study the diameter distribution structure of chinese fir plantations and the result showed good compatibility. The Logistic equation was pioneered by the Belgian mathematician Verhulst (1838) to describe the population increase rule. It is arguably the most famous equation in ecology because, during the 170 years since its origin, it has been widely used by scholars worldwide. Hui and Sheng (1995) were the first author to apply the Logistic equation to research stand structure in China. According to Richards equation, Ishikawa once applied it to the description of forest diameter distribution, but failed to propose the theoretical basis for application of this equation to studying stand diameter distribution. When analyzing the source and mathematical analyticity of growth equation, Duan (2003) found that '*S*' equations, such as the Richards, Weibull, Mitscherlich and Korf equations, including the Gompertz, Logistic and other equations similar to '*S*', can all be applied to simulation of stand diameter structure under certain assumptions and performed a comparative analysis of the simulated accuracy of these equations.

Stand management measures and growth equations used for simulation are two main factors influencing stand diameter structure simulation accuracy. Stand management measures, such as different site indices, planting density and thinning intensity, can all influence the formation of stand diameter structure and thus might affect the simulation accuracy of growth equations. However, limited research on this aspect has been published. With regard to selection of a growth equation, usually one or two growth equations are selected for data fitting, but systematic comparative research on different growth equations is lacking, and consequently there is still a poor understanding of the reason for high or low accuracy of theoretical growth equations when simulating stand diameter structure. This study utilized permanent observation data for chinese fir plantations in the subtropical region of southern China, and studied the influence degree of stand management measures and inflection point differences on the simulation accuracy of theoretical growth equations, with the aim of elucidating the reason for differences in simulation accuracy among different theoretical growth equations.

2
Materials and methods

2.1
Material for experiment

Chinese fir (*Cunninghamia lanceolata*) stands located in Fenyi city, Jiangxi Province, China, experience a subtropical climate. The altitude is 114°33′E, latitude 27°34′N. Mean annual temperature, rainfall and evaporation are 16.8 °C, 1656 mm, and 1503 mm, respectively.

The unthinned stands of chinese fir were established in 1981. Planting density was limited within an optimum range according to managerial purposes. The series of stand planting densities was 1667 (A), 3333 (B), 5000 (C), 6667 (D), 10 000 (E) stems /ha. Every planting density had 3 designed replications. Each plot area was 0.06 ha and two adjacent plots were separated by buffer zone. All trees in each plot were marked for continuous measurement. Stem diameter at breast height (DBH) was measured after tree height reached 1.3 m. All stands were measured every year before reaching 10 years old, and every two years after reaching 10 years old; all stands were measured 10 times. Self-thinning occurred in all stands during the experimental period. The basic information of 150 unthinned stands is described in Table 1. The database obtained from these unthinned stands was used to build models of diameter distribution.

Another database comprised of 159 diameter frequency distributions was used to test the models. The data came from a thinning study of chinese fir plantations established in the same environment as the above-mentioned unthinned stands. Among the 159 diameter distributions, 63 distributions came from unthinned stands, the remaining came from thinned stands. All thinning was from below. Each plot area was 0.05 ha. The basic information of used stands data for model evaluation is described in Table 2.

Table 1   Description of the data used for model development

Planting density/(stems/ ha)	Stands density/(stems/ ha)	Numbers of stands	Age/a	Site index /m[①]	DBH/cm	Height/m
1667(A)	1633~1667	30	6~20	12.52~16.42	7.90~18.35	5.50~15.50
3333(B)	3200~3333	30	6~20	14.52~16.92	6.59~14.07	5.10~15.2
5000(C)	4267~5000	30	6~20	14.07~14.47	5.59~12.27	4.65~13.70
6667(D)	5450~6667	30	6~20	12.88~13.25	5.16~10.89	4.60~12.60
10 000(E)	5783~10 000	30	6~20	13.85~14.23	4.97~10.75	4.40~13.20

① The value of site index is equal to the average dominant height of actual stand of chinese fir plantation at the reference age of 20. Dbh means diameter at breast height.

Table 2   Description of the data used for model evaluation

Plots	Stands density/ (stems/ ha)	Numbers of stands	Age/a	Site index /m[①]	DBH/cm	Height/m
Un-thinned stands	1680~4800	63	9~20	13.98~17.85	6.40~16.90	5.10~15.80
Thinned plot	1000~5380	96	9~27	13.35~18.93	5.30~20.00	4.40~17.20

① The value of site index is equal to the average dominant height of actual stand of chinese fir plantation at the reference age of 20. Dbh means diameter at breast height.

2.2
Research method

2.2.1
Mathematical properties and interrelationship of six theoretical growth equations

The Weibull distribution function (Beiley, 1973), most commonly applied in diameter distribution simulation, and five theoretical growth equations comprising the Gompertz (Gompertz, 1825), Mitscherlich (Mitscherlich, 1919), Logistic (Verhulst, 1838), Richards (Richards, 1959) and Korf (Kiviste, 1988) equations, were adopted to simulate the forest diameter cumulative percentage distribution. The basic form of each growth equation is shown in Table 1. There is a compact mutual transformation relationship between the growth equations. Regarding the Richards equation, the following five situations apply. ① When $m < 1$, the equation can be written as $y = A(1 - be^{-kx})^{\frac{1}{1-m}}$. In the formula, A, b, $k > 0$, which is the form of the Richards equation that is usually applied.② When $m > 1$, the equation can be written as $y = A(1 + be^{-kx})^{\frac{1}{m-1}}$. In the formula, A, b, $k > 0$, and the equation is called Logistic. ③ When $m = 0$, it is the Mitscherlich growth equation, i.e. $y = A(1 - Be^{-kx})$. In the formula, A, b, $k > 0$. ④ When $m = 2$, it becomes the Logistic equation, i.e. $y = A(1 + be^{-kx})^{-1}$. In the formula, A, b, $k > 0$. This can be explicitly seen when observing the differential expression of the Richards and Logistic equations, which also shows a subtle relationship between the two equations. ⑤ When $m \rightarrow 1$, the equation becomes the Gompertz growth equation, i.e. $y = Ae^{-be^{-kx}}$. In the formula, A, b, $k > 0$. When the parameter $c = 1$ in the Korf equation, this formula becomes the Schumacher equation. If $c \rightarrow \infty$, it becomes the Gompertz equation. Regarding the Weibull function, when the parameter $c = 1$, this formula becomes the Mitscherlich equation.

The existence of an equation asymptote and a good monotonic relationship equips the six theoretical growth equations with a mathematical basis for simulating stand diameter cumulative distribution. By using accumulation operation or data normalization the original stand diameter data is changed to a (0, 1) series. Subsequently, the upper asymptotic value of each equation when simulating stand diameter distribution can be set as 1.

2.2.2
Theoretical basis of applying a growth equation to stand diameter structure

When investigating the diameter's accumulative frequency y, the increase in diameter accumulative frequency can be compared to population growth in nature. Therefore, the increase in diameter accumulative frequency dy/dx is positively correlated to accumulative frequency and is constrained by maximum frequency. Differential expression of each equation can then be written as:

$$dy / dx = rf(y) \cdot g(y)$$

In this formula, r is the mathematical combination of each equation's parameters and can be taken as the intrinsic growth rate in each equation. The factor $f(y)$ and y are positively correlated, $g(y)$ is constrained by the upper asymptotic value of y and is negatively correlated to y. The calculation of r, $f(y)$ and $g(y)$ in each growth equation is listed in Table 3.

In Table 3, the positive correlations of Gompertz, Mitscherlich, Logistic, Richards and Korf equation, $f(y)$, is obvious (the positive correlation of Mitscherlich is taken as constants 1). In the Weibull equation, when $c > 1$, $f(y)$ increases with increasing y. When $c = 1$, the Weibull equation becomes the Mitscherlich equation. When $0 < c < 1$, there is no inflection point in the equation. In this situation, $f(y)$ and $g(y)$ together compose a differential expression negative correlation. The negative correlation of the differential expression of the Gompertz, Mitscherlich, Logistic, Korf and Weibull equations is obvious. For the Richards equation, $g(y)$ of the differential expression increases with decreasing y, if $0 < m < 1$. When $m > 1$, the negative correlation $1/[1/(1-(y/A)^{1-m})-1]$ is positively correlated to y. However, because the value of r also becomes negative, after transferring the minus, $g(y)$ of the differential expression becomes $1/[1/(1-(y/A)^{1-m})-1]$. The value of this formula decreases with increasing y and forms a negative correlation. Generally speaking, in nature the restriction of environmental volume is simplified to linear restriction. However, in fact this can be linear (such as the Logistic equation), as well as nonlinear (such as the Richards equation). It is a special case that the parameter c of the Mitscherlich and Weibull formulas ranges between (0, 1). Zeide (1993) excluded the Weibull equation when he categorized each equation into two kinds: LT and logarithm of time-decline. This study simplified the growth equation to the product of positive correlation and negative correlation. Subsequently, it is possible to understand the equation structure based on a theoretical explanation.

Table 3   Basal forms and mathematical analysis of six theoretical growth equations

Equation	Expression formula	Ordinate of inflection point	r	$f(y)$	$g(y)$	Parameter range
Mitscherlich	$y = 1 - le^{-mx}$	No	m	1	$A-y$	$l, m > 0$
Gompertz	$y = \exp(-e^{a-bx})$	$1/e$	b	y	$\ln K - \ln y$	$a, b > 0$
Logistic	$y = 1/(1+e^{p-qx})$	$1/2$	q	y	$1 - \dfrac{y}{C}$	$p, q > 0$
Richards	$y = (1 - be^{-kx})^{\frac{1}{1-m}}$	$m^{\frac{1}{1-m}}$	$\dfrac{k}{1-m}$	y	$\dfrac{1}{1/(1-(y/A)^{1-m})-1}$	$b, k, m > 0$
Korf	$y = \exp(-b/x^c)$	$\exp(-1-1/c)$	$b^{-\frac{1}{c}}(c+2)$	y	$(\ln A - \ln y)^{\frac{c+1}{c}}$	$b, c > 0$
Weibull	$y = 1 - \exp[-(x/b)^c]$	$1 - \exp(1/c-1)$	$\dfrac{Ac}{b}$	$[\ln A - \ln(A-y)]^{\frac{c-1}{c}}$	$1 - \dfrac{y}{A}$	$b, c > 0$

2.2.3
Methods of parameter prediction

Since the six growth equations are all nonlinear equations, their parameters are first estimated from empirical values and stand diameter distribution curves, and then solved using the non-linear regression procedure of SAS software (SAS Institute, Cary, North Carolina, USA). The residual standard error (S) is used to compare the simulation accuracy of each equation. Intuitive analysis and graphical exploration were used to examine the influence of stand characteristics, such as, age, site, density and thinning intensity, and the influence of different growth equations on simulation accuracy.

$$S=\sqrt{\frac{1}{n-2}\sum_{k=1}^{n}(obs_k - est_k)^2}$$

In the above formula, S is residual standard deviation, n is sample number, and obs_k and est_k are the kth observation value and the kth estimated value, respectively.

3
Results and analysis

3.1
Comparison of simulation accuracy of the theoretical growth equations

The simulation results of each theoretical growth equation are listed in Table 4. The rank order of the six theoretical growth equations based on simulation accuracy (from highest to lowest) was Richards > Logistic > Weibull > Gompertz > Korf > Mitscherlich.

Table 4　Total residual standard deviation (S) of six theoretical growth equations

Logistic	Gompertz	Richards	Korf	Weibull	Mitscherlich	Rank order of precision[①]
10.5174	18.1300	6.8795	28.7844	10.8341	65.6401	R>L>W>G>K>M

① R, L, W, G, K and M represent the Richards, Logistic, Weibull, Gompertz, Korf and Mitscherlich equations, respectively.

3.2

Influence of stand characteristics on simulation accuracy of growth equations

To evaluate the influence of different stand characteristics and growth equations on simulation accuracy, the stands were categorized according to age, site, planting density and thinning intensity and the respective simulation accuracy of each equation was calculated. The data presented in Table 5 is sum of residual standard errors when age and planting density are different. However, since the number of stands is different, the average residual standard errors at different sites and at different thinning intensities is presented.

Table 5   Modelling precision of six theoretical growth equations under different stand characteristics

Stand characteristic[①]		Logistic	Gompertz	Richards	Korf	Weibull	Mitscherlich
	6	0.2740	0.4320	0.2148	0.7023	0.2625	1.8219
Age[*]/a	12	0.2798	0.6355	0.1888	0.9323	0.2374	2.5255
	20	0.3051	0.6620	0.1823	0.8620	0.2661	2.4450
	12	0.0154	0.0301	0.0098	0.0508	0.0163	0.1179
	14	0.0212	0.0382	0.0140	0.0625	0.0212	0.1308
Site index[**]/m	16	0.0239	0.0389	0.0153	0.0568	0.0257	0.1484
	18	0.0232	0.0303	0.0162	0.0485	0.0237	0.1217
	100	0.6258	1.0908	0.5307	1.4077	0.6336	5.9662
	200	0.5864	1.3116	0.3545	1.7326	0.5147	5.2613
Planting density[*] /(stems/600m^2)	300	0.6535	1.3501	0.4458	1.9830	0.5078	4.6627
	400	0.5017	1.2405	0.3511	1.9199	0.4253	4.3470
	600	0.5195	1.0509	0.3477	1.7787	0.4385	3.5560
	Contrast	0.0209	0.0328	0.0178	0.0581	0.0153	0.1152
	Weak	0.0200	0.0312	0.0173	0.0540	0.0182	0.1171
Thinning density	Medium	0.0204	0.0299	0.0171	0.0532	0.0200	0.1035
	Strong	0.0248	0.0308	0.0171	0.0491	0.0261	0.1162

① Asterisks * and ** indicate the data were sum of residual standard errors and average residual standard error, respectively.

From Table 5, it is apparent that, in general for all of the growth equations, some differences existed in the diameter structure simulation accuracy for different stand ages, sites, planting densities and thinning intensities as a result of differences in the simulated object, i.e. the specific stand. However, the influence of these stand attributes was weak. With regard to stands of the same age, site, planting density or thinning intensity, differences in the simulation accuracy of the different growth equations were obvious. Two-factor analysis of variance showed that only site index significantly influenced the simulation accuracy among the different growth equations ($P < 0.05$). Age, planting density, and thinning intensity did not significantly influence the simulation accuracy of the equations ($P > 0.05$). However, the simulation accuracy of different growth equations differed significantly ($P < 0.01$). Therefore, the contribution of characteristics of the stand itself to differences in simulation accuracy among the growth equations was very weak, and site had the greatest influence on simulation accuracy.

3.3
Reason for different simulation accuracies among the growth equations

In theoretical growth equations, the equation inflection point is crucial and has definite biological meaning. On one hand, the inflection point is the concave–convex demarcation point of the growth equation curve, which decides the equation shape. On the other hand, the cumulative percentage distribution of trees' diameter class within the stand caused by differentiation also shows a S-shaped distribution. When modelling diameter distribution, the inflection point presents at the time of maximum cumulative frequency variation., it can be estimated that the properties of the inflection point of the growth equation will greatly influence simulation accuracy. Therefore, when researching the reason for differences in simulation accuracy among the growth equations, differences in the inflection point of the equation necessarily becomes the focus of investigation.

3.3.1
Inflection point range of experimental stand diameter cumulative distribution curve

Regarding a single stand, the equation with the highest simulation accuracy most precisely reflects the actual diameter distribution of the stand. Therefore, the diameter distribution represented by the equation with the highest simulation accuracy was selected as the experimental distribution of stand diameter and its inflection point was taken as the actual inflection point of the stand diameter distribution. Thus, 491 inflection points were obtained for the 491 stands. Table 6 summarizes the distribution of inflection point of the 491 stands. The inflection point of the stand experimental diameter cumulative percentage distribution curve had a distribution range, mainly between (0.4, 0.6). The percentage of stand inflection points within this range was as high as 82.28%. This indicates that the inflection point of the stand diameter cumulative percentage distribution curve is not a fixed value but is floating, and the inflection point of most experimental samples was 0.4~0.6.

Table 6   Distribution of ordinates of stand inflection points

			Ordinates of stand inflection points			
Range			0.2621~0.7643			
Interval	0.2~0.3	0.3~0.4	0.4~0.5	0.5~0.6	0.6~0.7	0.7~0.8
Proportion	0.2%	5.91%	31.36%	50.92%	11.41%	0.2%

3.3.2
Distribution of inflection points of each growth equation

The distributions of inflection points for the six theoretical growth equations are shown in Table 7. The inflection point of the fitting curve of the Richards, Korf and Weibull equations also had a floating range, not a fixed value, and each equation had a unique main distribution interval. Among the equations, the inflection point distribution range of the Richards equation best approached the actual inflection point distribution range of the stand diameter distribution curve. Its inflection point distribution interval was also (0.4, 0.6) within which 82.29% of inflection points were distributed, which was almost identical to the actual stand inflection point distribution. The inflection points of the Weibull equation were mainly distributed in the interval (0.5, 0.6), which included 77.19% of the inflection points, which was higher than the proportion of actual stand inflection points distributed in this interval. The inflection point of the Korf equation mainly lay in the range (0.2, 0.4). The Logistic and Gompertz equations had fixed inflection points, respectively 0.5 and 0.7. The Mitscherlich equation has no inflection point.

Table 7   Distribution of ordinates of inflection points for each theoretical growth equation[1]

Equation	Mitscherlich	Gompertz	Logistic	Weibull				
Range	No	≈0.37	0.5	0.2455~0.6001				
Interval	—	≈0.37	0.5	0.2~0.3	0.3~0.4	0.4~0.5	0.5~0.6	0.6~0.7
Proportion	—	100%	100%	0.41%	3.46%	18.74%	77.19%	0.2%

Equation	Korf			Richards					
Range	0.1906~0.3489			0.2621~0.7643					
Interval	0.1~0.2	0.2~0.3	0.3~0.4	0.2~0.3	0.3~0.4	0.4~0.5	0.5~0.6	0.6~0.7	0.7~0.8
Proportion	0.2%	55.6%	44.2%	0.2%	5.5%	38.7%	43.59%	11.81%	0.2%

① The total of the diameter distribution curve inflection point depicted by optimum simulating equation of all single stand is taken as actual inflection point range of stand diameter distribution.

3.3.3
Comparison of simulation accuracy of growth equations with or without inflection point

All of the growth equations listed in Table 5 have an inflection point except for the Mitscherlich equation. In combination with the data from Table 2, the simulation accuracy of the Richards, Logistic, Weibull, Gompertz, and Korf equations was, respectively, 74.7, 36.2, 33.4, 12.9, and 5.5 times that of the Mitscherlich equation. The theoretical and experimental values for the Richards, Korf and Mitscherlich equations are compared in Fig. 1. The theoretical and experimental values corresponded well for the Richards and Korf equations, whereas the fitting curve of the Mitscherlich equation (lacking an inflection point) obviously deviated from the experimental values. These results led to an obvious conclusion: the simulation accuracy of a growth equation with an inflection point is higher than that of a growth equation without an inflection point.

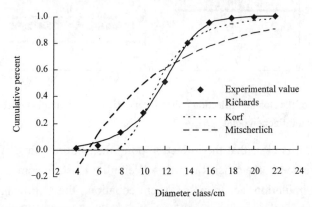

Fig. 1   Comparison of theoretical and experimental values among three growth equations

3.3.4
Comparison of simulation accuracy of growth equations with floating inflection point

Since the inflection point of the stand experimental diameter cumulative percentage distribution curve has a certain floating range, the growth equation showing the highest simulation accuracy should be the equation with a floating inflection point. The inflection point of the fitting curve of the Richards, Korf and Weibull growth equations all have a floating range. The fitting curve inflection point distribution of the three equations and the stand experimental inflection point distribution are shown in Fig. 2.

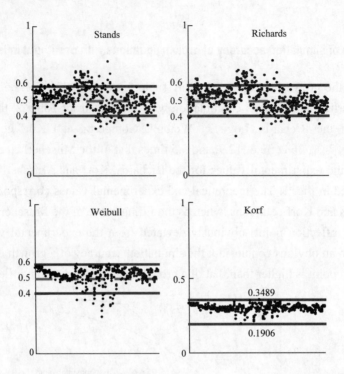

Fig. 2 Distribution of the floating inflection points for the Richards, Weibull and Korf equations and the stand experimental inflection point

From Fig. 2, it is clear that the inflection point distribution range of the optimum fitting curve decreased in the order Richards > Weibull > Korf. In combination with the comparison of simulation accuracy of each equation, the following preliminary conclusion was drawn: as for the growth equations with floating inflection points, the higher the inflection point distribution range of its fitting was, the higher the simulation accuracy of the growth was. The inflection point range of the most accurate (Richards) equation was almost identical to that of the stand experimental data. In addition, the inflection point distribution in the main distribution interval (0.4, 0.6) was also identical. Obviously, it is strongly related to the more accurate fitting of the Richards equation to the stand diameter distribution. Weibull equation was previously recognized as mainly taking the form of a probability density function. Because an inflection point exists when the shape parameter $c > 1$, this study considered the Weibull equation as a growth equation. The fitting results showed that the inflection point distribution ratio of the Weibull equation in the range (0.4, 0.6) was 95.93%, similar to the main inflection point distribution range of the stand, and thus showed high simulation accuracy. The inflection point floating range of the fitting curve of the

Korf equation was 0.1906~0.3489, and its simulation accuracy was much lower than that of the Richards and Weibull equations. This was mainly because the inflection point floating range was not within the main distribution interval of the stand inflection point. To better explain this phenomenon, the concept of an equation effective inflection point interval is proposed here. The effective inflection point interval for an equation is related to the general distribution range and main distribution interval is. The larger the effective inflection point interval is, the higher the effectiveness of the equation inflection point is, and thus the simulation accuracy of equation is increased. The Richards equation has a wide inflection point distribution range, its main distribution interval is in line with the main existing interval of the stand inflection point, and its effective inflection point interval is large, therefore it has high simulation accuracy. The inflection point floating range of the Weibull equation is slightly narrower, so the effective inflection point interval is slightly smaller, thus its simulation accuracy is lower than that of the Richards equation. Although the inflection point of the Korf equation has a floating range, the distribution range is too narrow and its inflection point is mainly beyond the main existing interval of the stand inflection point (0.4, 0.6). Therefore, its effective inflection point interval is small and the simulation accuracy is much lower than that of former two equations.

3.3.5
Comparison of simulation accuracy of growth equations with fixed inflection point

The Gompertz and Logistic equations have a fixed inflection point. The position of the inflection points of the two equations relative to those of the stand diameter cumulative percentage distribution curve are shown in Fig. 3. What must be noted is that the inflection point path of the Logistic equation is parallel to the x-axis, and the equation inflection point (0.5) lies within the main distribution interval (0.4~0.6) of the stand inflection point, and in particular is located at its center. Therefore, this equation showed good fitting performance. The Gompertz equation also performed well, but its inflection point deviated from the main existing interval of the stand cumulative distribution curve, thus it showed lower simulation accuracy than the Logistic equation. These results showed that, with regard to equations with a fixed inflection point, the degree of simulation accuracy of the equation can be measured by the relative position of the equation inflection point in the main existing interval of stand inflection points. The closer the stand inflection point to the center of the main interval of stand inflection points (i.e. the more accurate the inflection point), the more accurate is the equation simulation.

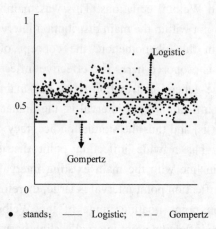

Fig. 3   The distribution of the fixed inflection points for the Gompertz and Logistic equations relative to the inflection points of the stand experimental data

3.3.6
Comparison of simulation accuracy of growth equations with fixed inflection point and floated inflection point

As outlined earlier, the rank order of the overall accuracy of the six growth equations (from highest to lowest) was Richards > Logistic > Weibull > Gompertz > Korf > Mitscherlich. Thus, it cannot be concluded that the simulation accuracy of equations with a floating inflection point is higher than those with a fixed inflection point or vice versa. It can be found that the higher the proportion of equation inflection points in the main distribution interval of inflection points of the stand diameter cumulative percentage distribution curve, the more accurate the equation simulation, as was the case for the Richards, Logistic and Weibull equations. Equations whose inflection points fall beyond the main distribution interval of inflection points of the stand diameter cumulative percentage distribution curve showed lower simulation accuracy, such as the Gompertz and Korf equations. Therefore, it is considered that the larger the equation effective inflection point interval, and closer the inflection point position to the center of the main interval of stand inflection points, the more accurate the equation simulation. It is noteworthy that the Logistic equation, which has a fixed inflection point, showed very similar simulation accuracy to the Weibull equation, which has a floating inflection point. The Korf equation, which has a floating inflection point, showed less effective inflection points and lower simulation accuracy than the

Gompertz equation because the upper limit of its inflection point distribution range was lower than the inflection point value of the Gompertz equation, which has a fixed inflection point. These findings show that besides the main distribution interval (0.4, 0.6), the inflection point of the stand diameter cumulative percentage distribution curve also obeys a '1/2' close rule.

4
Conclusions

Theoretical growth equations show good performance in the simulation of stand diameter structure, but simulation accuracy differs among different growth equations. In this study, the reason for this phenomenon was examined from the perspective of stand characteristics and inflection points of equations, and the following conclusions were drawn.① Generally, stand factors such as age, site, tree density and thinning intensity have no significant effect on the simulation accuracy of the six growth equations compared. Therefore, differences in simulation accuracy of the growth equations caused by stand characteristics are very weak, with site showing the greatest influence. ② The inflection point of the stand diameter cumulative distribution curve of chinese fir plantations has a distribution range. The dereferencing of the growth equation inflection point is strongly related to the degree of simulation accuracy of each equation. Equations with an inflection point show much higher simulation accuracy than equations without an inflection point. ③ The inflection point of the stand diameter cumulative percentage distribution curve has a main distribution interval (0.4, 0.6), and shows a '1/2' close rule. The larger the effective inflection point interval of the fitting curve of the theoretical growth equationis, and the closer the inflection point is to 0.5, the more effective the equation inflection point and more accurate the equation simulationis. The discovery of this phenomenon provides a scientific basis for selection of growth equation for simulation of forest stand diameter structure.

Reference

Bailey R L, T R Dell. 1973. Quantifying diameter distribution with the Weibull function. For Sci, 19:97~104

Charles P Winsor. 1932. The Gompertz curve as a growth curve. Proceedings of The National academy of Sciences, 18(1): 1~9

Duan AG, Zhang JG, Tong S Z. 2003. Application of six growth equations on stands diameter structure of Chinese fir Plantation. Sci Sil Sin, 16: 423~429

Gompertz B. 1825. On the nature of the function expressive of human mortality, and on a new mode of determining the value of life contingencies. Phil. Transac Roy Soci London, 115: 513~585

Hui G Y, Sheng W T. 1995. Study on stand diameter structure model [J]. Forest Research, 8(2): 127~131

Ishikawa, Y. 1998. Analysis of the diameter distribution using the RICHARDS distribution function (III). Relationship between mean diameter or diameter variance and parameter m or k of uniform and even –aged stands. J Plann, (31): 15~18

Kiviste A K. 1988. Mathematical functions of forest growth. Russion: Estonian Agricultural Academy

Mitscherlich E A. 1919. Problems of plant growth. Landwirt schaftli che jahrbucher Berlin，53: 167~182

Ricker W E. 1979. Growth rates and models. Fish Physiol, 8: 677~743

Richards F J. 1959. A flexible growth function for empirical use. J Exp Bot, 10(29): 290~300

Verhulst P F. 1838. Correspondence Mathe-matique et Physiques [French], 10:113~121

Wu C Z, Hong W. 1998. Study on diameter structure model of Chinese fir plantation. Journal of Fujian College of Forestry, 18(2): 110~113

Zeide B. 1989. Accuracy of equations describing diameter growth [J]. Can J For Res, 19: 1283~1286

Zeide B. 1993. Analysis of growth equations. For Sci, 39(3): 594~616

CHAPTER FIVE:
A new high-performance diameter distribution function for unthinned chinese fir (*Cunninghamia lanceolata*) Plantations in southern China

Abstract   The objective of this study was to introduce a new high-performance diameter distribution function. Long-term repeated measurement data sets, comprised of 309 diameter frequency distributions from chinese fir (*Cunninghamia lanceolata*) plantations in southern China, were used. Of these, 150 plots were used as fitting data, and the other 159 plots were used for testing. Nonlinear regression method (NRM) or maximum likelihood estimates method (MLE) were applied to estimate the parameters of models, and the parameter prediction method (PPM) and parameter recovery method (PRM) were used to predict the diameter distributions of unknown stands. Four main conclusions were obtained: ① R distribution presented a more accurate simulation than three-parametric Weibull function, ② the parameters p, q and r of R distribution proved to be its scale, location and shape parameters, and have a deep relationship with stand-level variables, which means the parameters of R distribution have good biological interpretation, ③ the main distribution range of inflection points for the cumulative diameter distribution of chinese fir plantations was 0.4~0.6, ④ the goodness-of-fit test showed diameter distributions of unknown stands can be estimated by applying R distribution. Furthermore, the non-rejection rate of methods A, B and C was 80.50%, 73.58% and 79.87%, respectively. These results are all higher than the 72.33% non-rejection rate of method D, which was based on three-parametric Weibull function. From the viewpoint of modelling precision and biological interpretation, method B may be most suitable because of its good convergence, high precision and multiple stand variables.

Key words R distribution; Three-parametric Weibull distribution; Theoretical meaning; distribution parameters; Modelling precision; Inflection points

1
Introduction

Applications of diameter distributions to describe forest stand structure are well known and numerous (Gove and Patil, 1998; Burgess *et al.*, 2005). Accurate quantification of tree characteristics permits study of the interaction among physical and physiological processes and growth. Quantification of diameter distributions over time allows the manager to relate the parameters of the distribution to stand age or stand density (Schreuder and Swank, 1974). The stand volume characteristics are calculated using diameter distribution and tree height and volume models (Bailey and Dell, 1973). Growth and yield prediction based on the diameter distribution approach has also been widely used (Clutter *et al.*, 1983).

Over the last 30 years various probability density functions (PDF) such as normal, log-normal, gamma, beta, Johnson's S_B, and Weibull have been widely used to describe the diameter frequency distributions of forest stands (Bailey and Dell, 1973; Burkhart and Strub, 1974; Hafley and Schreuder, 1977; Little, 1983; Kilkki and Paivinen, 1986; Brooks and Borders, 1992). Additionally, in studies of cumulative diameter distribution, different theoretical growth equations such as Logistic, Gompertz, Mitscherlich, Bertalanffy, Schumacher, Korf, Weibull and Richards have been utilized to characterize the diameter structure of forest stands (Gadow and Hui, 1998; Ishikawa, 1998; Zhang and Duan, 2003; Duan *et al.*, 2003; Duan *et al.*, 2004; Wang *et al.*, 2007). Of these, Richards and Weibull equations showed more flexibility than the others, and were respectively the first and the second most accurate (Zhang and Duan, 2004).

Today, the methods used to describe diameter distribution can be classified into parametric and nonparametric methods. The abovementioned functions and equations all belong to parametric methods. Nonparametric methods, like percentile prediction method (Borders *et al.*, 1987, Maltamo *et al.* 2000) and *k*-nearest neighbor estimation method (Tokola *et al.*, 1996; Maltamo and Kangas, 1998), do not rely on any predefined functional form and adapt to description of multimodal distributions. The disadvantage of nonparametric methods is that their high amount of required reference material is difficult to acquire and time-consuming (Haara *et al.*, 1997).

Doubtlessly, in parametric methods, the Weibull is the most commonly used probability density function for fitting tree diameter distributions. Since the three-parametric Weibull function was first derived by Weibull (1939), because of the relative simplicity of the expression formula and its flexibility in fitting a variety of shapes and degrees of skew, this function has proven to be a good distribution model. For the estimation of Weibull parameters, many different methods have been applied such as the moment method, maximum likelihood estimates method, percentiles method and nonlinear regression method (Dubey, 1967; Clutter *et al.*, 1983; Brooks and Borders, 1992; Lee and Hong, 2001; Zhang and Duan, 2003). With the introduction of advanced analysis software, the nonlinear regression method is increasingly presenting its superiority. The most prominent advantage of using this method is that distribution parameters can be accurately estimated simultaneously. However, for the three-parametric Weibull function, the iterated function is not easy to converge while using Weibull to fit the diameter distribution data and the correlativity between the parameters estimates and the whole stand characteristics becomes weak. Therefore, many studies have paid more attention to two-parametric Weibull distribution (Liu *et al.*, 2002; Chen, 2004). However, is there a function that hasn't the disadvantages of Weibull and still has its advantages such as the theoretical meaning of parameters and the high simulation precision?

The objectives of this study were to put forward a new distribution function, test the theoretical meanings of its parameters, and compare the properties of simulation and prediction for stands diameter distribution between the new function and the three-parametric Weibull distribution using the long-term repeated measurement data sets from chinese fir (*Cunninghamia lanceolata*) plantations in southern China.

2
MATERIALS AND METHODS

2.1
Data source

Data used in this study was same as previous section.

2.2
Computation of observed cumulative diameter distribution

The diameter classes applied were 2 cm wide. Diameter class, k, is defined as absolute scale (e.g., 1–2.9 cm for $k = 2$, 3–4.9 for $k = 4$, etc.), namely, diameter class k is the midpoint value of the absolute scale. The frequency of stems in diameter class k at stand i is given by:

$$F_{ki} = \frac{N_{ki}}{N_i}$$

where N_{ki} is the number of trees of diameter class k at stand i ($i = 1, 2, ..., 159$), and N_i is the total number of trees in stand i. The cumulative frequency of stems in diameter class k at stand i can be obtained by:

$$C_{ki} = F_{1i} + F_{2i} + \cdots + F_{(k-1)i} + F_{ki}$$

2.3
Methods

2.3.1
Model development

Table 1 shows the basic mathematical characteristics of Richards, Weibull and Logistic equations. In the expression of Weibull equations, a is the location parameter, b is the scale parameter, and c is the shape parameter. What, then, has caused the iterated function to not easily converge while employing SAS's (1991) nonlinear regression method to estimate the parameters of Weibull and, subsequently, for the correlativity between the parameter estimates and the whole stand characteristics to be weak? When the expression formula of the Weibull equation is analyzed, it is found the equation is meaningful only when

$$(x-a)/b \geqslant 0$$

namely, $x \geqslant a$. If $x < a$, Weibull equation is meaningless. Furthermore, it is difficult to give a suitable initial estimation for the location parameter (Newton *et al.* 2005), and the ultimate estimation of the location parameter cannot exceed the two neighboring diameter class of any given initial estimation, which can greatly increase the times of iteration. Obviously, it is the location of shape parameter which leads to the above-mentioned shortcomings of Weibull.

Table 1   The basic mathematical characteristics of Richards, Weibull and Logistic equations

Equations	Expression formula	Abscissa of inflection point	Ordinate of inflection point	Parameter range
Richards	$y=(1-Be^{-kx})^{\frac{1}{1-m}}$	$\frac{1}{k}\ln(\frac{B}{1-m})$	$m^{\frac{1}{1-m}}$	$k,\ m>0$
Weibull	$y=1-\exp[-((x-a)/b)^c]$	$b(1-1/c)^{1/c}+a$	$1-\exp(1/c-1)$	$b,\ c>0$
Logistic	$y=1/(1+e^{s-tx})$	s/t	0.5	$s,\ t>0$

Six kinds of theoretical growth equations have been put forward and applied to describe stand diameter distribution, and Richards equation was found to have very high precision and be suitable to fitting the sigmoid curve (Zhang and Duan, 2003). In the beginning, the curve is concave up, while in later life it becomes convex (Richards, 1959; Zeide, 1989; 1993). Therefore, on the basis of prior study, further analysis is needed to determine the mathematical characteristics of Richards. While fitting distribution data, the parameter B of Richards is < 0, and parameter m is > 1. As a result, the following new expression formula of Richards function in Table 3 is derived:

$$y = (1 + \exp(-(x - \ln(-B)/k)k^{-1}))^{1/(1-m)} \tag{1}$$

If $q = \ln(-B)/k$, $p = k^{-1}$, $r = 1/(1-m)$, Eq. (1) becomes

$$y = (1 + \exp(-(x-q)/p))^r \tag{2}$$

where: $p > 0$, $q > 0$, $r < 0$.

Undoubtedly, Eq. (2) will still have high simulation precision, and it is obvious and important that the parameters of Eq. (2) may have the same theoretical meaning as three– parametric Weibull function. Namely, parameter q may be the location parameter, parameter p may be the scale parameter, and parameter r may be the shape parameter. Note, whether the parameter q of Eq. (2) is $> x$ or not, problems that the equation has no meaning or parameters have difficulty to converge will not appear. We call Eq. (2) "R distribution". The probability density function of R distribution for a random variable x is

$$f(x) = -r/p \exp(-(x-q)/p)(1 + \exp(-(x-q)/p))^{r-1} \tag{3}$$

Eq. (2) and Eq. (3) have the advantage of a simple expression formula. Unlike Logistic equation which has a fixed inflection point ($= 0.5$), Eq. (2) has a floating inflection point, the abscissa and ordinate of inflection point of Eq. (2) are respectively given by

$$x = p\ln(-r) + q,$$
$$y = ((r-1)/r)^r.$$

Accordingly, R distribution has a good application prospect in the field of diameter distribution. Our database, including 150 cumulative diameter distributions, was used to fit the R distribution and Weibull equation, then the theoretical meaning of parameters of R distribution was analyzed by discussing the correlativity between the parameters estimates and the whole stand characteristics.

2.3.2

Model Evaluation

Parameter estimates for p ($\hat{p}$), q ($\hat{q}$), r ($\hat{r}$) were obtained by employing nonlinear regression method (NRN), parameter estimates for a ($\hat{a}$), b ($\hat{b}$) and c ($\hat{c}$) were obtained by employing nonlinear regression method (NRN) and maximum likelihood estimates method (MLE). Because the location parameter a of the three-parametric Weibull function was often viewed as the minimum observed diameter or its multiple (Newton *et al.*, 2005), parameter a was defined as the lower limit of the minimum diameter class when MLE was adopted. Parameter prediction method (PPM) and parameter recovery method (PRM) were used to build stand-level diameter distribution models (Hyink and Moser, 1983; Clutter *et al.*, 1983; Maltamo, 1997; Newton *et al.*, 2004; Duan *et al.*, 2004). Some parameters of R distribution and Weibull were regressed against stand-level attributes which included stand age, site index, planting density, average height, dominant height and quadratic mean DBH, some parameters were derived from the moments of the diameter distribution, which were themselves estimated from stand-level variables.

For R distribution, when PPM and PRM are simultaneously adopted to predict diameter distributions of stands used for model testing, based on preliminary graphical and correlation analyses, the parameter prediction equations for estimates for $\hat{p}$, $\hat{q}$ and $\hat{r}$ are given by Eq. (4), Eq. (5) and Eq. (6), respectively.

$$\hat{p} = f(x_1, x_2, x_3, x_4, x_5, x_6) \tag{4}$$

$$\hat{q} = f(x_1, x_2, x_3, x_4, x_5, x_6) \tag{5}$$

$$\hat{r} = -\exp(\frac{\hat{I}_x - \hat{q}}{\hat{p}}) \tag{6}$$

where $x_1, x_2, x_3, x_4, x_5, x_6$ are the stand-level variables, and $\hat{I}_x$ is the estimate of abscissa of inflection point of stand diameter distribution, which can be derived by

$$\hat{I}_x = f(x_1, x_2, x_3, x_4, x_5, x_6). \tag{7}$$

When only PRM is the adopted method, besides Eq. (6), Eq. (8) and Eq. (9) can be used to recover the parameters.

$$0.333 = (1 + \exp(-(\hat{D}_{0.333} - \hat{q}) / \hat{p}))^{\hat{r}} \tag{8}$$

$$0.9 = (1 + \exp(-(\hat{D}_{0.9} - \hat{q}) / \hat{p}))^{\hat{r}} \tag{9}$$

where $\hat{D}_{0.333}$ and $\hat{D}_{0.9}$ are the diameter at the percentile 0.333 and 0.9 on the distribution curve. Like $\hat{I}_x$, $\hat{D}_{0.333}$ and $\hat{D}_{0.9}$ can be predicted by the same formula as Eq. (7).

For the three-parametric Weibull function, the PPM and PRM are simultaneously adopted to predict distribution parameters. Parameters $\hat{a}$ and $\hat{b}$ can be estimated as parameters $\hat{p}$ and $\hat{q}$ of R distribution. Parameter $\hat{c}$ can be solved from the cumulative distribution function of Weibull by Eq. (10).

$$0.5 = 1 - \exp[-((\hat{D}_{0.5} - \hat{a})/\hat{b})^{\hat{c}}] \tag{10}$$

The reason that the 0.5 percentile was adopted is that this percentile was near the inflection point of the distribution curve (Zhang and Duan, 2003). The prediction of $\hat{D}_{0.5}$ can be achieved by using the same method as $\hat{D}_{0.333}$ and $\hat{D}_{0.9}$ of R distribution.

To further test the simulation properties of R distribution and Weibull, another database comprised of 159 diameter frequency distributions was used to test the models.

2.2.3
Comparison of the models

The application effect of R distribution and three-parametric Weibull function was examined by comparing the residual sum of square (*RSS*) and coefficient of determination (R^2). The residual sum of square and coefficient of determination were respectively calculated as

$$RSS = \sum_{k=1}^{n} (obs_k - est_k)^2 ,$$

$$R^2 = 1 - \frac{\sum_{k=1}^{n} (obs_k - est_k)^2}{\sum_{k=1}^{n} (obs_k - \overline{obs_k})^2} ,$$

where obs_k and est_k are the observed and predicted diameter frequency for diameter class k, and n is the number of diameter classes in a sample stand.

We used the Kolmogorov–Smirnov test to test the goodness of fit of distribution functions to the observations of diameter distribution.

3
RESULTS AND DISCUSSION

3.1
Modelling results of R distribution and three – parametric Weibull function

Table 2 and Table 3 show the mathematical characteristics of parameters and statistics for R distribution and the three-parametric Weibull function derived from the 150 plot measurements. For R distribution, the value of parameter $\hat{r}$ is < 0, which is identical to the theoretical distribution range shown in Eq. (2). Although the precision of the two models are both high, R distribution presents a more accurate simulation than the three-parametric Weibull function and has good convergence. For the three-parametric Weibull function, the precision of nonlinear regression method is far higher than maximum likelihood estimates method.

Table 2   The mathematical characteristics of parameters and statistics for R distribution derived from the 150 plot measurements

Equations	Parameter estimation Methods[1]	$\hat{p}$	$\hat{q}$	$\hat{r}$	R^2	The sum of *RSS*
R distribution	NRM	0.52~2.57	3.39~18.32	−6.83~−0.30	0.9918~1	0.1913

① NRM refer to nonlinear regression method.

Table 3   The mathematical characteristics of parameters and statistics for three-parametric Weibull function derived from the 150 plot measurements

Equations	Parameter estimation Methods[1]	$\hat{a}$	$\hat{b}$	$\hat{c}$	The sum of *RSS*	The average of R^2
Three- parametric Weibull function	NRM	0~12.00	4.53~17.65	1.93~8.59	0.2069	0.9988
	MLE	1.00~11.00	4.46~11.53	2.17~4.83	0.2814	0.9982

① NRM and MLM refer to nonlinear regression method and maximum likelihood estimates method, respectively.

3.2
Theoretical meaning of parameters of R distribution

The modelling accuracy and biological meanings of parameters are the two most important indexes used to judge whether a function is suitable to modelling diameter distributions and the two indexes are complementary. It is known that R distribution has high modelling precision. However, do the parameters of R distribution have good biological interpretation? This question can be answered by discussing the relationship between parameters of R distribution and the basic stand-level variables such as stand age, stand density, site index and quadratic mean DBH.

3.2.1
Theoretical meaning of parameters p of R distribution

Fig. 1 shows the relationship of parameter p of R distribution to stand age and quadratic mean DBH. Parameter p increased with increasing stand age and quadratic mean DBH. The relationship of parameter p and stand age and quadratic mean DBH were well approximated by the brief second polynomial. The resultant parameter prediction equation for predicting p is given by Eq. (11).

$$\hat{p} = 0.0012t^2 + 0.0502t + 0.4567 \tag{11}$$

where t refers to stand age. The result of analysis of variance showed that Parameter p had significant relativity with stand age at the 0.0001 significance level. The coefficients of determination (R^2) of the second polynomial between parameter p and stand age, planting density, site index and quadratic mean DBH were respectively 0.7369, 0.0235, 0.0093 and 0.3185. Their positive or negative relativities can reasonably interpret the theoretical meaning of parameter p as a scale parameter of diameter distribution. Therefore, parameter p can be considered the scale parameter of R distribution.

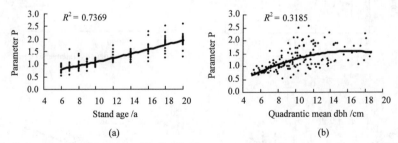

Fig. 1 Relationship of parameter p of R distribution to stand age (a) and quadratic mean dbh (b)

3.2.2
The theoretical meaning of parameters q of R distribution

The relationship of parameter q of R distribution to stand age, stand density, site index and quadratic mean DBH is illustrated in Fig. 2. Parameter q increased with increasing stand age, site index and quadratic mean DBH, while it decreased with increasing stand density. The coefficients of determination (R^2) of the second polynomial between parameter q and stand age, stand density, site index and quadratic mean DBH were respectively 0.2477, 0.5843, 0.3011 and 0.7886. It is obvious that quadratic mean DBH has the biggest effect on parameter q among these stand variables. The resultant parameter prediction equation for predicting q is given by Eq. (12).

$$\hat{q} = -0.0019D_g^{\,2} + 0.9355D_g - 0.1322 \tag{12}$$

where D_g refers to quadratic mean DBH. The coefficients of Eq. (12) were significant at the 0.0001 significance level. From Fig. 2 it can be seen that the positive or negative relativities of parameter q and the four stand variables can reasonably interpret the theoretical meaning of parameter q as a location parameter of diameter distribution. Accordingly, parameter q can be seen as the location parameter of R distribution.

In previous studies, Duan *et al.* (2003) discovered Richards function was suitable for modelling diameter distribution, but did not realize the underlying relationship between parameter B and k in Richards function. They thought parameter B had poor theoretical interpretation. For R distribution, parameter q, composed of parameters B and k, obviously has good biological meaning, and proved easy to converge. This might lead to the use of R distribution as a new diameter distribution.

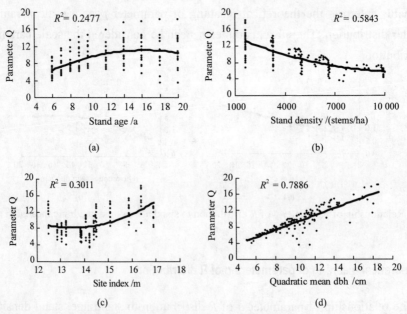

Fig. 2 Relationship of parameter q of R distribution to stand age (a), stand density (b), site index (c) and quadratic mean dbh (d)

3.2.3
Theoretical Meaning of Parameters r of R Distribution

Fig. 3 shows the relationship of parameter r of R distribution to stand age and quadratic mean DBH. Parameter r decreased with increasing stand age and quadratic mean DBH. The result of analysis of variance showed that Parameter r had significant relativity with stand age and quadratic mean DBH at the 0.01 significance level. The coefficients of determination (R^2) of the second polynomial between parameter r and stand age and quadratic mean DBH were 0.0562 and 0.0706, respectively. Although the R^2 of parameter r and the stand variables are relatively small, the value of $((r-1)/r)^r$, being the ordinate of inflection point of R distribution, is decided by parameter r, and which affects the modelling precision of R distribution. Therefore, parameter r can be considered the shape parameter of R distribution.

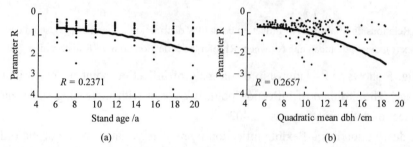

(a)   (b)

Fig. 3   Relationship of parameter r of R distribution to stand age (a) and quadratic mean dbh (b)

3.3
Relationship of inflection point of R distribution to three-parametric Weibull function

As shown in Fig. 4, the abscissa of inflection point of R distribution increased with increasing stand age, site index and quadratic mean DBH, and decreased with increasing stand density. The coefficient of determination (R^2) of the second polynomial between abscissa of inflection point and stand age, stand density, site index and quadratic mean DBH were 0.3454, 0.6180, 0.3197 and 0.9649, respectively. The deep relationship between the abscissa of inflection point and quadratic mean DBH can be described by Eq. (13).

$$p\ln(-r)+q = 0.0039D_g^2 +0.8782D_g -0.3067 \qquad (13)$$

where D_g refers to quadratic mean DBH.

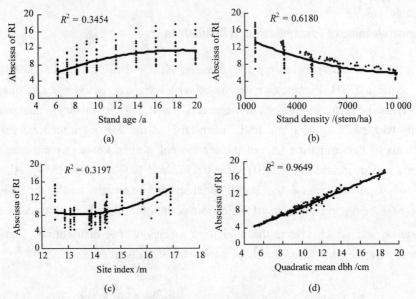

Fig. 4 Relationship of abscissa of inflection point of R distribution to stand age (a), stand density (b), site index (c), quadratic mean dbh (d) where RI refers to inflection point of R distribution

Fig. 5 shows the relationship of ordinate of inflection point of R distribution to stand age. The ordinate of inflection point decreased with increasing stand age. The coefficient of determination was 0.2402.

R distribution has a flexible inflection point. The variation range of the ordinates of inflection points is 0.3787~0.6436, and 91.33 percent of them distribute in the range of 0.4~0.6. Therefore, we can conclude that the main distribution range of inflection points for the cumulative diameter distribution of stands was 0.4~0.6.

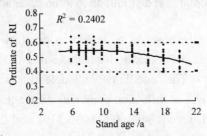

Fig. 5 Relationship of ordinate of inflection point of R distribution to stand age where RI refers to inflection point of R distribution

Fig. 6 shows the relationship of the inflection point of R distribution to the three-parametric Weibull function. It was surprising that the abscissas of inflection points of two distributions had very high relativity. The coefficient of determination (R^2) came up to 0.9947. The abscissa and ordinate of inflection point of R distribution

A new high-performance diameter distribution function for unthinned chinese fir (*Cunninghamia lanceolata*)
Plantations in southern China

75

increased with increasing that of the three-parametric Weibull function, which indicated that different distribution functions may have some underlying relationship.

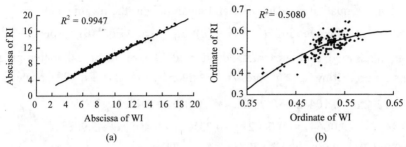

(a)   (b)

Fig. 6 Relationship of the abscissa (a) and ordinate (b) of inflection point of R distribution to three-parametric Weibull function where RI refers to inflection point of R distribution and WI refers to inflection point of three-parametric Weibull function

3.4

Evaluation

3.4.1

Functions for the estimation of distribution parameters

Data from 159 evaluation subplots provide an opportunity to analyze and compare the accuracy of the R distribution and three-parametric Weibull function. Stepwise regression analysis was applied to build the relationship between the parameters of two distributions and the stand-level variables composed of stand age, planting density, site index and so on at a 0.5 risk level. When nonlinear regression method were adopted, the resultant parameter prediction equations for predicting $\hat{p}$, $\hat{q}$, $\hat{r}$, $\hat{D}_{0.333}$, $\hat{I}_x$, $\hat{D}_{0.9}$, $\hat{a}$, $\hat{b}$, $\hat{c}$ and $\hat{D}_{0.5}$ are given by Eq. (14)~Eq. (23), respectively.

$$\hat{p} = -0.0338x_1 + 0.0631x_2 + 0.1019x_3 + 1.79 \times 10^{-5}x_4 - 0.5963 \tag{14}$$

$$\hat{q} = 0.4089x_1 - 0.2372x_2 - 0.4116x_3 - 0.0002x_4 + 0.7116x_5 + 0.2590x_6 + 4.5089 \tag{15}$$

$$\hat{r} = -0.0958x_3 - 0.0002x_4 - 0.3899x_5 + 0.3209x_6 + 2.04410 \tag{16}$$

$$\hat{D}_{0.333} = 0.4840x_5^{1.2016} \tag{17}$$

$$\hat{I}_x = 0.7940x_5^{1.0818} \tag{18}$$

$$\hat{D}_{0.9} = 1.2464x_5^{0.9690} \tag{19}$$

$$\hat{a} = -0.8613x_1 - 0.1626x_2 + 0.1521x_3 + 0.0004x_4 + 1.2081x_5 - 3.3789 \tag{20}$$

$$\hat{b} = 0.9723x_1 + 0.1286x_2 - 0.2324x_3 - 0.0004x_4 - 0.1999x_5 + 3.2160 \tag{21}$$

$$\hat{c} = 0.3315x_1 - 0.1574x_3 - 0.0002x_4 + 0.1441x_5 - 0.3081x_6 \tag{22}$$

$$\hat{D}_{0.5} = 0.0065x_5{}^2 + 0.8411x_5 - 0.4060 \tag{23}$$

Where $x_1, x_2, x_3, x_4, x_5, x_6$ is, respectively, dominant height, stand age, site index, planting density, quadratic mean DBH and mean height, the meanings of $\hat{I}_x$, $\hat{D}_{0.333}$, $\hat{D}_{0.9}$ and $\hat{D}_{0.5}$ can be seen in Eq. (6), Eq. (8), Eq. (9) and Eq. (10), respectively. When maximum likelihood estimates method adopted, the resultant parameter prediction equations for predicting $\hat{a}$, $\hat{b}$ and $\hat{c}$ are given by Eq. (24)~Eq. (27), respectively.

$$\hat{a} = -0.1202x_1 - 0.1044x_2 + 0.0002x_4 + 1.3106x_5 - 0.4907x_6 - 4.5917 \tag{24}$$
$$\hat{b} = 0.2468x_1 - 0.0664x_3 - 0.0002x_4 - 0.2318x_5 + 0.4059x_6 + 5.9888 \tag{25}$$
$$\hat{c} = -0.0654x_3 - 0.0001x_4 + 4.6787 \tag{26}$$
$$\hat{D}_{0.5} = 0.0078x_5{}^2 + 0.8097x_5 + 0.6644 \tag{27}$$

The coefficients of determination of equations from Eq. (14)~Eq. (27) were 0.7534, 0.8418, 0.0943, 0.9778, 0.9649, 0.9835, 0.5181, 0.5316, 0.4614, 0.9881, 0.8296, 0.5635, 0.4378 and 0.9884, respectively. Obviously, parameter $\hat{r}$ of R distribution was not adaptive to be directly predicted by stand variables, which could be indirectly obtained through Eq. (6) or Eq. (13). For parameter $\hat{a}$, $\hat{b}$ and $\hat{c}$, the coefficients of determination of second degree polynomials between the other parameter and above-mentioned stand variable were all smaller than those of Eq. (20), Eq. (21), Eq. (22), Eq. (24), and Eq. (25), respectively. Therefore, the five equations were adopted to predict the unknown diameter distributions.

Note that for the three-parametric Weibull function, regardless of whether the nonlinear regression method or maximum likelihood estimates method is used, $\hat{c}$ always has significant relativity with planting density and stand age at the 0.0001 significance level. Based on the abovementioned parameter prediction equations that have a high coefficient of determination, parameters of distribution models can be evaluated by introducing the related stand-level variables into these equations.

3.4.2
Goodness-of-fit for estimating diameter distribution

The diameter distributions were predicted with two functions, i.e., the R distribution and three-parametric Weibull function. In these calculations, two fitting methods (nonlinear regression method and maximum likelihood estimates method) and two parameter estimation methods (PRM and the combination of PPM and PRM) were used.

It was encouraging that R distribution was found to have lower RSS and higher non-rejection rate than the three-parametric Weibull function (Table. 4). Fig. 7 shows the distribution of the residual sum of square (*RSS*) against quadratic mean DBH, from which we can directly compare the prediction effects of the five methods. Method A has the highest precision among the five methods, which shows *R* distribution can accurately estimate diameter distribution of most future stands using the combination of PPM and PRM under the condition that only two stand-level variables are known (Table. 4). For method A, the result of the Kolmogorov-Smirnov test showed the null hypothesis that the observed and fitted distributions that are the same cannot be rejected for 128 out of 159 stands (80.50%). However, in view of the practical application of distribution models to stand management, method B, based on *R* distribution, would be a better option because of its dependence on stand variables related to the stand density and site quality and because its non-rejection rate reached 73.58%. Methods B and D used the same parameter recovery method and numbers of stand-level variables and had a nearly equal non-rejection rate, which showed *R* distribution had a distribution function equally as good as three-parametric Weibull function. Furthermore, because the iterated function of *R* distribution was easier to converge than three-parametric Weibull function when using nonlinear regression method to predict parameters, *R* distribution would have a wide application prospect.

For chinese fir plantations, the non-rejection rate of unthinned stands and thinned stands did not have obvious differences when methods A, B, C and D were adopted to predict the diameter distributions of future stands (Table. 4).

Additionally, for the three-parametric Weibull function, the nonlinear regression method is a more effective approach than the maximum likelihood estimates method in the estimation system of stand diameter distribution (Table. 4).

Table 4　The statistics of different evaluation methods for *R* distribution and the three-parametric Weibull function derived from the 159 plot measurements used for goodness-of-fit tests

Equations	Codes	Methods[①]	Related equations	Numbers of variables	The sum of *RSS*	Non-rejection rate/%		
						Un-thinned stands	Thinned stands	Total
R distribution	Method A	PPM and PRM	(11), (12), (13)	2	3.0920	80.95	80.21	80.50
	Method B　NRM		(13), (14), (15)	6	5.7097	68.25	77.08	73.58
	Method C	PRM	(6), (8), (9), (17), (18), (19)	1	3.5058	82.54	78.13	79.87
Weibull	Method D　NRM	PPM and PRM	(10), (20), (21), (23)	6	6.9981	73.02	71.88	72.33
	Method E　MLM		(10), (24), (25), (27)	6	14.2322	6.35	19.79	15.09

① NRM and MLM refer to nonlinear regression method and maximum likelihood estimates method, respectively.

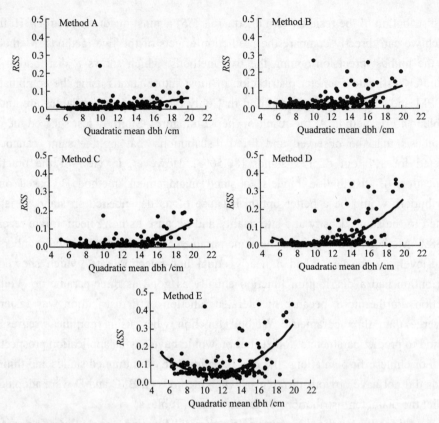

Fig. 7 The distribution of the residual sum of square (*RSS*) against quadratic mean dbh. Method A, Method B, Method C, Method D, Method E are codes in Table 4

4
Conclusions

Based on analysis of the disadvantages of the three-parametric Weibull function, this study develops a promising distribution function (*R* distribution), which is a new and essential exploration in the study of parametric methods (Kangas and Maltamo, 2000). We conclude that: ① *R* distribution has a more accurate simulation than the three-parametric Weibull function while modelling diameter distributions of chinese fir plantations; ② the parameters *p*, *q* and *r* of *R* distribution proved to be its scale, location and shape parameters, and have a deep relationship with stand-level variables; this means the parameters of *R* distribution have good biological interpretation; ③ the main distribution range of inflection points for the cumulative diameter distribution of chinese fir plantations was 0.4~0.6; ④ the goodness-of-fit test showed the diameter distributions of unknown stands can be accurately estimated by applying R distribution and with regards to modelling precision and biological interpretation, method B may be the most suitable choice due to its good convergence, high precision and included multiple stand variables.

References

Bailey R L, Dell T R. 1973. Quantifying diameter distribution with the Weibull function. For Sci, 19: 97~104

Borders B E, Surter R A, Bailey R L, *et al.* 1987. Percentile– based distributions characterize forest stand tables. For Sci, 33: 570~576

Brooks J R, Borders B E. 1992. Predicting diameter distributions for site-prepared loblolly and slash pine plantations. South J Appl For, 16: 130~133

Burgess D, Robinson C, Wetzel S. 2005. Eastern white pine response to release 30 years after partial harvesting in pine mixed wood forests. For Ecol Manage, 209: 117~129

Burkhart H E, Strub M R. 1974. A model for simulation of planted loblolly pine stands. pp. 128~135 in Growth models for tree and stand simulation, Stockholm, Sweden: Fries J (ed.) Royal Coll Of For Res Notes No. 30

Chen W J. 2004. Tree size distribution functions of four boreal forest types for biomass mapping. For sci, 50: 436~449

Clutter J L, Fortson J C, Pienaar L V, *et al.* 1983. Timber management: A quantitative approach. John Wiley and Sons, New York, USA

Duan A G., He C Y, Zhang J G., *et al.* 2004. Studies on dynamic prediction of stand diameter structure of Chinese fir plantation. Sci Sil Sin, 40: 32~38

Duan A G, Zhang J G., Tong S Z. 2003. Application of six growth equations on stands diameter structure of Chinese fir Plantation. Sci Sil Sin, 16: 423~429

Dubey S D. 1967. Some percentile estimators for Weibull parameters. Technometrics, 9:119~129

Gadow K V, Hui G Y. 1998. Modelling forest development. Kluwer Academic Press

Gove G H, Pati G P. 1998. Modelling the basal area-size distribution of forest stands: a compatible approach. For Sci, 44: 285~297

Haara A, Maltamo M, Tokola T. 1997. The *k*-nearest-neighbour method for estimating basal-area diameter distribution. Scand J For Res, 12: 200~208

Hafley W L, Schreuder H T. 1977. Statistical distributions for fitting diameter and height data in even-aged stands. Can J For Res, 4: 481~487

Hyink D M, Moser J W. 1983. A generalized framework for projecting forest yield and stand structure using diameter distributions. For Sci, 29: 85~95

Ishikawa Y. 1998. Analysis of the diameter distribution using the Richards distribution function (III): Relationship between mean diameter or diameter variance and parameter m or k of uniform and even –aged stands. J Plann, 31: 15~18

Kangas A, Maltamo M. 2000. Calibrating predicted diameter distribution with additional information. For Sci, 46: 390~396

Kilkki P, Paivinen R. 1986. Weibull function in the estimation of the basal area dbh-distribution. Silva Fenn, 20: 149~156

Lee Y J, Hong S H. 2001. Weibull diameter distribution yield prediction system for loblolly pine plantations. J Kor For Sci, 90: 176~183

Little S N. 1983. Weibull diameter distributions for mixed stands of western conifers. Can J For Res, 13: 85~88

Liu C M, Zhang L J, Davis C J. 2002. A finite mixture model for characterizing the diameter distributions of mixed-species forest stands. For Sci, 48: 653~661

Maltamo M. 1997. Comparing basal-area diameter distributions estimated by tree species and for the entire growing stock in a mixed stand. Silva Fenn, 31: 53~65

Maltamo M, Kangas A. 1998. Methods based on *k*-nearest neighbor regression in the prediction of basal area diameter distribution. Can J For Res, 28: 1107~1115

Maltamo M, Kangas A, Uuttera J, *et al*. 2000. Comparison of percentile based prediction methods and the Weibull distribution in describing the diameter distribution of heterogeneous Scots pine stands. For Ecol Manage, 133: 263~274

Newton P E, Lei Y, Zhang S Y. 2004. A parameter recovery model for estimating black spruce diameter distributions within the context of a stand density management diagram. For Chron, 80: 349~358

Newton P F, Lei Y, Zhang S Y. 2005. Stand-level diameter distribution yield model for black spruce plantations. For Eco Manage, 209: 181~192

Richards F J. 1959. A flexible growth function for empirical use. J Exp Bot, 10: 290~300

SAS. 1991. SAS/STAT user's guide, version 6.03. Inc Cary Nc

Schreuder H T, Swank W T. 1974. Coniferous stands characterized with the Weibull distribution. Can J For Res, 4: 518~523

Tokola T, Pitkanen J, Partinen S, *et al*. 1996. Point accuracy of a non-parametric method in estimation of forest characteristics with different satellite materials. Int J Remote Sens, 17: 2333~2351

Weibull W. 1939. A statistical theory of the strength of materials. Handlingar. 151: Ingeniörs Vetenskaps Akademien

Wang M L, Ramesh N I, Rennolls K. 2007. The Richit–Richards family of distributions and its use in forestry. Can J For Res, 37: 2052~2062

Zhang J G., Duan A G. 2003. Application of theoretical growth equations to simulating stands diameter structure. Sci Sil Sin, 39: 55~61

Zhang J G., Duan A G. 2004. Study on theoretical growth equation and diameter structure model. Beijing: Publishing House of Science

Zeide B. 1989. Accuracy of equations describing diameter growth. Can J For Res, 19: 1283~1286

Zeide B. 1993. Analysis of growth equations. For Sci, 39: 594~616

CHAPTER SIX:
Application of fuzzy functions in stand diameter distributions of chinese fir (*Cunninghamia lanceolata*) plantations

Abstract   Six fuzzy distribution functions were introduced to model diameter distribution of chinese fir plantations. Logistic, Gompertz, and Korf functions were also introduced for comparison purposes. Using the inflection point of their cumulative distribution functions (CDF), we compared their abilities of fitting the diameter distributions of the chinese fir stands with different ages and planting densities. Based on the statistical criterion of the standard error of estimate (*S.E.E.*), the order of the nine functions from high to low in fitting precision was: Fuzzy–Γ_5, Logistic, Fuzzy–Γ_3, Fuzzy–Γ_4, Fuzzy–C, Fuzzy–Γ_2, Gompertz, Korf, Fuzzy–Γ_1. Stand age and planting density had different effects on fitting precision of each CDF. Fuzzy–Γ_5, Fuzzy–Γ_3 and Logistic had stable and good fitting properties in terms of quality of fit to the variety of sample distributions. The Fuzzy–Γ_5 had the most consistent performance. Parameters of Fuzzy–Γ_3 were highly correlated with age and density of stands. The study showed that fuzzy functions were able to be used for modelling the diameter distribution of the stands with different ages and planting densities.

Key words   Fuzzy function; Diameter distribution model; Inflection point; Plantation

1
Introduction

Stand diameter structure is the most important and basic characteristics of forest stand. A diameter-class distribution model is commonly used to provide information on the frequency distribution of tree diameters at breast height (DBH) (Kangas and Maltamo, 2000; Liu *et al.*, 2004). Over the last 30 years, two methods (i.e., parametric and non-parametric) have been applied to model stand structures (Maltamo and Kangas, 1998). For parametric approaches, many theoretical probability density functions (PDF) have been used to characterize diameter distributions of forest stands, such as normal, log-normal, gamma, Johnson's S_B, beta, and Weibull (e.g., Bailey and Dell, 1973; Burkhart and Strub, 1974; Hafley and Schreuder, 1977; Little, 1983; Kilkki and Paivinen, 1986; Davis and Johnson, 1987; Kilkki *et al.*, 1989; Zeide, 1993; Kangas and Maltamo, 2000; Li *et al.*, 2002; Liu *et al.*, 2002). Additionally, standard logistic distribution function has been used to describing stand diameter cumulative distribution, based on the synthesis that cumulative diameter frequency increment is positively related to cumulative frequency and constrained by the biggest cumulative frequency (Gadow and Hui, 1998). Cao and Burkhart (1984) used a parameter recovery method with a segmented cumulative distribution to model diameter frequency data. Most recently, a logit-logistic distribution function has been introduced to model tree diameter distribution of chinese fir plantations (Rennolls and Wang, 2005). For non-parametric approaches which are independent on any distribution function, k-nearest-neighbor estimation method (Haara *et al.*, 1997; Maltamo and Kangas, 1998), Kernel estimation method (Dressler and Burk, 1989), and percentile-based distribution method (Border *et al.*, 1987) have been developed to characterize multimodal distribution. Those distribution-free methods have very strong flexibility, but are sophisticated for application (Liu *et al.*, 2002).

Since fuzzy sets theory was introduced by Zadeh (1965), fuzzy analysis methods have been widely applied in many fields (Arasan *et al.*, 1996; Zimmermann, 1996; Kivinen and Uusitalo, 2002; Zhang *et al.*, 2004). However, there has been no application of fuzzy distribution functions to describe stand diameter structures to date. In addition, according to the mathematical characteristics of Fuzzy functions, such as fuzzy membership value [0,1] which corresponds to distribution interval of a stand diameter cumulative distribution function (CDF), the differences in precision of modelling diameter distributions between Fuzzy functions can be well explained. Therefore, fuzzy distribution functions are introduced to model stand diameter structure in this study. Five common fuzzy distributions and a generalized fuzzy distribution were applied to model stand diameter distributions of chinese fir plantations. For comparison purposes, the well-known logistic function and two theoretical growth equations (i.e., Korf and Gompertz) were also included along with the six fuzzy functions to reveal the essential reasons for differences in modelling precision among different distribution functions.

In this study, we attempted to assess the flexibility of the fuzzy distribution functions for modelling stand diameter distributions of chinese fir plantations. The objectives were ① to compare mathematical quality and properties of nine functions in modelling diameter distributions. ② to assess the goodness of fit of the nine functions; ③ to evaluate relationships between parameters of fuzzy functions and stand characteristics. This study can improve modelling techniques of stands diameter structure and provide useful information on management of *Cunninghamia lanceolata* plantations.

2
Data and Methods

2.1
Data

Chinese fir (*Cunninghamia lanceolata* (Lamb.) Hook) is one of the most important reforestation and commercial species widely distributed in southern China. The species is highly valued for lumber and other products. Trial plots for chinese fir stands were located in a subtropical climate region in Jiangxi province, China. The altitude is 114°33′ E, the latitude is 27°34′ N. The elevation is 250 m. Soil is developed from sand-shale roch. Its color is yellow brown. Mean annual temperature, rainfall, and evaporation are 16.8 °C, 1656 mm, and 1503 mm, respectively.

The chinese fir (*Cunninghamia lanceolata*) plantations were established in 1981. Initial planting density was limited within an optimum range according to managerial purpose. In this study, all five initial densities of 1667, 3333, 5000, 6667, and 10 000 stems/ha in this region were chosen. For each initial density, random block design was used with 3 replications. Therefore, 15 plots with the area of 0.06 ha for each were selected to cover all planting densities. All trees in those plots marked for continuous measurement. Tree diameter at breast height (DBH) was measured after tree height reached 1.3 m. All plots were measured every year from 6- to 10-year-old of stand, and every 2 years after 10-year-old. Therefore, a total of 10 measurements for each plot were completed in 1999. A total of 150 diameter frequency distribution measurements were obtained and used in this study. Self-thinning occurred in some stands over the experimental period, and all stands were not thinned. The basic information was described in Table 1.

Table 1   Description of the data used for fitting the models

Planting density /(stems/ha)	Stands density /(stems/ha)	Age/a	Site index/m	DBH/cm		Height/m	
				Mean	Range	Mean	Range
1667(A)	1633~1667	6~20	12.52~16.42	14.13	7.90~18.35	10.69	5.50~15.50
3333(B)	3200~3333	6~20	14.52~16.92	11.14	6.59~14.07	9.79	5.10~15.2
5000(C)	4267~5000	6~20	14.07~14.47	9.33	5.59~12.27	8.96	4.65~13.70
6667(D)	5450~6667	6~20	12.88~13.25	8.14	5.16~10.89	8.11	4.60~12.60
10 000(E)	5783~10 000	6~20	13.85~14.23	7.84	4.97~10.75	8.19	4.40~13.20

2.2

Five fuzzy distribution functions

After stands were measured tree by tree, the number of trees and relative frequency in each 2 cm-interval DBH class were calculated. Then a cumulative percentage distribution series that is smaller than or equal to some diameter class was obtained. The cumulative percentage distribution ranged from 0 to 1. The basic feature of the DBH cumulative distribution of a stand is described in Fig. 1.

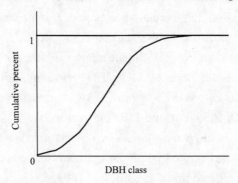

Fig. 1   The basic figure of stands diameter cumulative distribution

Since the DBH cumulative distribution presents non-linear characteristics (Fig. 1), 5 typical fuzzy membership functions such as Γ-typed, normal type, and Cauchy distribution were selected. These functions are all non-linear and S-shaped. In addition, inclined-big types of above-mentioned distribution forms were selected because the distribution series presented increasing trend. When the distribution interval is real number set (R), the membership function is called Fuzzy distribution. For simplicity and convenience, five Fuzzy distribution functions were marked by Fuzzy-Γ_1、Fuzzy-Γ_2、Fuzzy-Γ_3、Fuzzy-Γ_4, and Fuzzy-C, respectively. They can be described as follows:

(1) Fuzzy-Γ_1(Inclined-bigness type of Γ distribution)

$$\mu_{(x)} = \begin{cases} 0 & (x \leqslant a) \\ 1 - e^{-k(x-a)} & (x > a) \end{cases}$$

(2) Fuzzy-Γ_2(Inclined-bigness type of normal distribution)

$$\mu_{(x)} = \begin{cases} 0 & (x \leqslant a) \\ 1 - e^{-k(x-a)^2} & (x > a) \end{cases}$$

(3) Fuzzy-Γ_3

$$\mu_{(x)} = \begin{cases} 0 & (x \leqslant a) \\ 1 - e^{-k(x-a)^3} & (x > a) \end{cases}$$

(4) Fuzzy-Γ_4

$$\mu_{(x)} = \begin{cases} 0 & (x \leqslant a) \\ 1 - e^{-k(x-a)^4} & (x > a) \end{cases}$$

(5) Fuzzy-C(Fuzzy-C distribution)

$$\mu_{(x)} = \begin{cases} 0 & (x \leqslant a) \\ 1/(1 + k(x-a)^{-b}) & (x > a) \end{cases}$$

where $a > 0$, $b > 0$, and $k > 0$. Fig. 2 describe the basic feature of these five distributions.

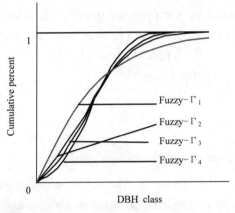

Fig. 2   The basic figures of four Fuzzy distributions

2.3
Three growth equations (Logistic, Korf, and Gompertz)

In order to compare characteristics of Fuzzy distribution function, three theoretical growth equations including Logistic, Korf and Gompertz were used. Their mathematical expressions are described in Table 2. When parameter K of each equation is equal to 1, the value range of each equation is [0, 1], so, these equations can be applied to model cumulative diameter distribution of a stand (Duan *et al.*, 2003). For Korf equation, it is the first time to be applied on stands diameter structure.

Table 2   Expression of formula, inflection point, parameter range for Gompertz, Logistic and Korf functions

Equation	Expression of formula	Inflection point	Parameter range
Gompertz	$y = K\exp(-e^{a-bx})$	$1/e$	$K, a, b>0$
Logistic	$y = K/(1+e^{p-qx})$	$1/2$	$K, p, q>0$
Korf	$y = K\exp(-b/x^{c})$	$\exp(-1-1/c)$	$K, b, c>0$

2.4
Parameter estimation method

All Fuzzy functions were fit to diameter data of each plot using the NLIN procedure of SAS with the Gauss-Newton iteration method (SAS Institute, 1999). To ensure the stability of parameter estimates, the models were refitted several times with the initial values estimated by the previous fitting. Validation statistics used in the performance comparison included the coefficient of determination (R^2) and the standard error of estimate (S.E.E.) (SAS Institute, 1999).

The *S.E.E.* was computed as follows:

$$S.E.E = \sqrt{\dfrac{\sum\limits_{i=1}^{m}(y_i - \hat{y}_i)^2}{n-2}}$$

where y_i and $\hat{y}_i$ are the observed and estimated number of trees in DBH class i. And m is the number of DBH classes. The *S.E.E.* provides an indicator of typical misfits of a model due to no cancellation between positive and negative values. The smaller the *S.E.E.*, the higher the precision of the model. In order to compare the mathematical characteristics of the nine functions, the value (or interval) of the inflection point of each function was obtained through the calculation of two-order derivative.

3
Results and Discussion

3.1
Five Fuzzy distribution functions

The parameters and fit statistics of five Fuzzy distribution functions are presented in Table 3. Each parameter (k, a, and b) of five Fuzzy distribution functions had a distribution range. Generally, the values of parameters k and a from Fuzzy-Γ_1 to Fuzzy-Γ_4 gradually decreased. Except Fuzzy-Γ_1, the four other distributions had relatively high precision in terms of R^2 values (greater then 0.97) (Table 3). It indicated that the four distribution functions had better fitting properties for stand diameter cumulative distribution. The maximum R^2 of Fuzzy-Γ_1 was 0.9713, which was less than the minimum R^2 (0.9727) of the other four distributions (Table 3). Fuzzy-Γ_3 had a minimum R^2 of 0.9877 and a maximum R^2 of 1.0000 (Table 3). For the *S.E.E.* statistics, The Fuzzy-Γ_3 had the lowest value. The order of five Fuzzy distributions from lowest to highest *S.E.E.* value was Fuzzy-Γ_3, Fuzzy-Γ_4, Fuzzy-C, Fuzzy-Γ_2, and Fuzzy-Γ_1 (Table 3). Based on the R^2 and *S.E.E.*, it seemed that Fuzzy-Γ_1 function without the inflection point had worse goodness of fit than those with the inflection point. Additionally, Fuzzy-Γ_3 and Fuzzy-Γ_4 with inflection point of around 0.5 fit better for stand diameter cumulative distribution than Fuzzy-Γ_2 and Fuzzy-C with inflection point of far away 0.5 (Table 3).

Table 3   Estimated regression coefficients, determination coefficient (R^2), and *S.E.E.* for different Fuzzy distribution functions[①]

Equation	Parameter			Inflection point	Fit statistics	
	Range of k	Range of a	Range of b		Range of R^2	S.E.E.
Fuzzy-Γ_1	0.0849~0.4186	1.7914~12.4408		None	0.7539~0.9713	0.1586(5)
Fuzzy-Γ_2	0.0114~0.3135	1.1409~11.6427		0.3935	0.9727~0.9999	0.0402(4)
Fuzzy-Γ_3	0.0008~0.0166	0~9.5397		0.4866	0.9877~1.0000	0.0210(1)
Fuzzy-Γ_4	0.0001~0.0025	0~7.3719		0.5276	0.9765~1.0000	0.0268(2)
Fuzzy-C	0.6276~0.8245	0~4.6800	4.5071~11.3865	0.6945~0.7280	0.9811~0.9995	0.0375(3)

① *S.E.E.*, standard error of estimate. The *S.E.E.* value in the Table was mean of all *S.E.E.* values of 150 samples.

Since Fuzzy-Γ_3 had the best performance in terms of R^2 and *S.E.E.*, this function was selected to establish the relationship between function parameters and stand characteristics as the parameter prediction method (PPM) (Liu *et al.*, 2004). The results are showed in Fig.3. It was obvious that parameters k and a decreased with increased stand age and stand density (Fig.3). Stand density means the number of trees per hectare at measurement time. After comparative analysis, relationship between parameter k and age (A; years) can finally be expressed by power function: $k = 0.1584A^{-1.6503}$ with a coefficient of determination of 0.90. The relationship between parameter a and density (D; stems/ha) was described in polynomial form: $a = 10.3670 - 0.0025D + 1 \times 10^{-7}D^2$ with a coefficient of determination of 0.92. Evidently, parameters k and a had a very close relationship with age and density, respectively.

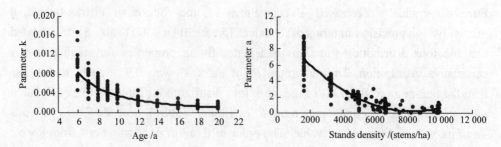

Fig. 3   The relationship between parameter k of Fuzzy-Γ_3 and stand age and the relationship between parameter a Fuzzy-Γ_3 and stand density (stems/ha)

The ultimate aim of modelling diameter distribution using the variety of the sample distributions is to predict structure of future stands. It would be useful for prediction methods to be scientific, reliable and simple. For Fuzzy-Γ_3, its fitting precision was highest among all the Fuzzy distributions, and its parameters were highly correlated with stand characteristics (i.e., stand age and stand density). Therefore, given both future stand age and current stand density, the future diameter distribution of the un-thinned stand can be estimated effectively with PPM with Fuzzy-Γ_3 distribution function.

3.2
A generalized Fuzzy distribution function

Fuzzy-Γ_1,-Γ_2-Γ_3, and-Γ_4 have the very similar mathematical expressions. Only difference among them is the power index of independent variables. However, it is this power index that determines the inflection point of every function. As shown in Table 3, the four fuzzy functions with different inflection points had obvious difference in the precision in terms of the fit statistics of *S.E.E.* and R^2. Accordingly, a generalized Fuzzy distribution function can be obtained after introducing a parameter c. It can be described as follows:

$$\mu_{(x)} = \begin{cases} 0 & (x \leqslant a) \\ 1 - e^{-k(x-a)^c} & (x > a) \end{cases}$$

While parameter $c>1$, the generalized Fuzzy distribution has a varied inflection point. It is expected to be more flexible for fitting diameter distributions. We call it a generalized Γ-typed distribution, marked by Fuzzy-Γ_5.

The fit statistics of Fuzzy-Γ_5 are presented in Table 4. Based on the values of R^2

and *S.E.E.*, Fuzzy-Γ_5 had the higher precision than the above-mentioned five distributions such as Fuzzy-Γ_3. Since the value of parameter c was greater than 1, Fuzzy-Γ_5 distribution had an inflection point. It indicated that the diameter cumulative distribution from the chinese fir plantations was a S-shaped distribution with first down convex and then up convex.

Table 4   Estimated regression coefficients, determination coefficient (R^2), and *S.E.E.* for Fuzzy-Γ_5 distribution function[①]

Equation	Parameter			Fit statistics	
	Range of *k*	Range of *a*	Range of *c*	Range of R^2	*S.E.E.*
Fuzzy-Γ_5	6.0428E-10~0.0362	0~12.0000	1.9304~8.5945	0.9877~1.0000	0.0144

① *S.E.E.*, standard error of estimate. The *S.E.E.* value in the Table was mean of all *S.E.E.* values of 150 samples.

In order to further understand the variation patterns of Fuzzy-Γ_5' inflection point, the relationship of its inflection point with stand variables (i.e., stand age, stand density, and site index) was studied. The determination coefficients of regression formula of inflection point with stand age, planting density, stand density, site index were 0.4308, 0.5676, 0.5023, and 0.3267, respectively. All the determination coefficients but the last one were significant at the probability level of 0.0001. It indicated that stand age and stand density had greatest effects on inflection point, whereas site index had the least. Since the infection point affected the difference in stand diameter distributions, it can be implied that that stand diameter distribution was mainly affected by stand age and density. The variation of inflection point with stand age, planting density, stand density, and stand age for each planting density is presented in Fig. 4. From Fig. 4, Fuzzy-Γ_5's inflection point gradually decreased with the increase of stand age and planting (initial) density. When planting density is fixed, inflection point decreased with stands density. This trend was more obvious when planting density is 10 000 stems/ha (Fig.4). The reason might be that after self-thinning took place, stand density decreased with age which made the inflection point of the stand diameter distribution decrease.   In Fig. 4, A, B, C, D, and E stand for five different densities. Inflection point obviously decreased with age, given an initial density. Given a stand age, inflection points of stands with high planting density are generally smaller than those of stands with low planting density. The results of two-way ANOVA showed that stand age and planting densities significantly affected the values of infection points.

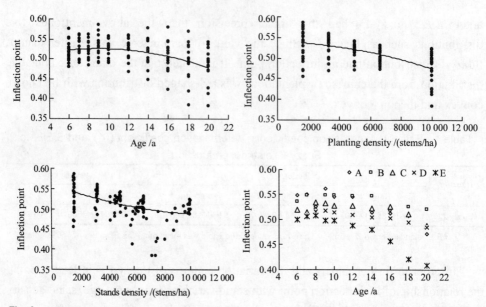

Fig. 4 Inflection point of Fuzzy-Γ_5's versus stand age, planting density (stems/ha), stand density, and stand age for five planting densities (A, B, C, D, and E). A, B, C, D, and E stand for 1667, 3333, 5000, 6000, and 10 000 stems/ha, respectively

3.3
Comparison of Fuzzy distributions and theoretical growth equations

The inflection points and *S.E.E.* statistics of three growth equations along with all six fuzzy functions are presented in Table 5. Based on *S.E.E.* statistics, the order of nine equations from high fitting precision to low fitting precision was: Fuzzy-Γ_5, Logistic, Fuzzy-Γ_3, Fuzzy-Γ_4, Fuzzy-C, Fuzzy-Γ_2, Gompertz, Korf, and Fuzzy-Γ_1 (Table 5). Except Fuzzy-Γ_1, all Fuzzy distribution functions, especially the generalized Fuzzy-Γ_5, displayed relatively high fitting precision.

Table 5   Range of inflection point and precision of nine different functions[①]

Equation	Fuzzy-Γ_1	Korf	Gompertz	Fuzzy-Γ_2	Fuzzy-Γ_3	Logistic	Fuzzy-Γ_4	Fuzzy-Γ_5	Fuzzy-C
Inflection point	None	0.2666 ~0.3292	0.3679	0.3935	0.4866	0.5000	0.5276	0.3824 ~0.5867	0.6945 ~0.7280
Precision (*S.E.E.*)	0.1586	0.0588	0.0403	0.0402	0.0210	0.0192	0.0268	0.0144	0.0375

① *S.E.E.*, standard error of estimate. The *S.E.E.* value in the Table was mean of all *S.E.E.* values of 150 samples.

Inflection point indicated the place where the biggest variation occurred in the curve of diameter cumulative distribution. While modelling diameter data sets, the value of inflection points of Fuzzy distribution functions may produce important effects on goodness of fit. From Table 5, Fuzzy-Γ_1 had no inflection point whereas all the other five distributions had an inflection point. In particular, the inflection point of Fuzzy-Γ_5, Korf and Gompertz had changeable intervals. From Table 5, the functions with the highest precision had a flexible inflection point. This maybe indicated that the inflection point of diameter cumulative percentage distributions was not a fixed value, but has a changeable range. The interval of inflection point of Fuzzy-Γ_5 distribution is 0.3824~0.5867 (Table 5), and 98 percent of inflection values belonged to the range of [0.4, 0.6]. It indicated that the main range of inflection points of stand diameter cumulative distribution is 0.4~0.6. In addition, the precision of Fuzzy-Γ_3, Logistic, and Fuzzy-Γ_4 distribution functions whose inflection points were close to 0.5 were relatively high. The results showed that inflection point of diameter cumulative distributions from the chinese fir plantations also had a main inflexible interval (0.4~0.6) with a central distribution point (0.5 or so). When the inflection point of a function such as Fuzzy-Γ_5, Fuzzy-Γ_3, and Logistic was in the main interval, its precision is relatively high. The closer to the central point (0.5) the inflection of point of a function, the higher the precision of the function was.

3.4
Effects of stands variables on precision of the distribution functions

Through above analyses, it was known that stand age and stand density had a great impact on the inflection point of a diameter cumulative distribution, and the size of inflection point of Fuzzy functions had a close relationship with the fitting precision. The differences in the precision among different distribution functions for five different planting densities are presented in Table 6. From Table 6, the precision of every distribution function was not fixed under different planting densities. Fuzzy-Γ_5 and Fuzzy-Γ_1 had highest and lowest precision, respectively. The results showed that effects of planting densities on the precision of distribution functions with different inflection points were different. For different planting densities, the orders of precision of the nine distribution functions were different in terms of the *S.E.E.* value. Generally, Fuzzy-Γ_5, Fuzzy-Γ_4, Logistic, and Fuzzy-Γ_3 distribution functions have relatively higher precision for fitting the diameter distributions of stands with different planting densities.

Fuzzy-Γ_5 distribution was always the best one for each planting density. The main reason was that its inflection point can vary reasonably with the change of specific stand diameter distributions. In terms of *S.E.E.*, Fuzzy-Γ_4 was the second best for three planting densities of A, B, C, whereas it had poor precisions for the stands with high planting densities of D and E. It indicated that Fuzzy-Γ_4 had good simulation properties for relatively low-density stands. This was because the inflection point of Fuzzy-Γ_4 is above 0.5 and the inflection point of the diameter cumulative distributions decreased to below 0.5 with the increase of planting density. On the contrary, Fuzzy-Γ_3 function had better fitting precision for relatively high-density stands as its inflection point was below 0.5. Since Logistic equation had the central value (0.5) of the inflection point, it had relatively stable and high precision. Fuzzy-C distribution performed relatively better for low density stands than for high density stands, whereas Fuzzy-Γ_2 and Gompertz distributions seemed to perform better for the high density stands than for the low density stands. The precision of Korf equation for all the five densities seemed the same. Although Fuzzy-Γ_1 distribution has no inflection point, it was relatively suitable for modelling stands with high density (Table 6).

Table 6   Precision of nine different functions for five planting densities

Planting density[①]	Equation								
	Fuzzy-Γ_1	Korf	Gompertz	Fuzzy-Γ_2	Fuzzy-Γ_3	Logistic	Fuzzy-Γ_4	Fuzzy-Γ_5	Fuzzy-C
A	0.1989(9)	0.0469(7)	0.0364(6)	0.0577(8)	0.0250(4)	0.0209(3)	0.0197(2)	0.0159(1)	0.0278(5)
B	0.1754(9)	0.0578(8)	0.0437(6)	0.0476(7)	0.0241(4)	0.0195(3)	0.0186(2)	0.0155(1)	0.0362(5)
C	0.1554(9)	0.0661(8)	0.0450(7)	0.0385(5)	0.0226(4)	0.0218(3)	0.0209(2)	0.0163(1)	0.0447(6)
D	0.1449(9)	0.0640(8)	0.0414(7)	0.0325(4)	0.0174(3)	0.0167(2)	0.0349(5)	0.0130(1)	0.0412(6)
E	0.1185(9)	0.0593(8)	0.0350(5)	0.0248(4)	0.0160(2)	0.0173(3)	0.0400(7)	0.0115(1)	0.0373(6)

① A, B, C, D, E stands for five different planting densities, which are 1667,3333,5000,6000 and 10 000 stems/ha, respectively. Precision in this Table was expressed by the average *S.E.E.* of 30 samples. The number in the parentheses was ranking based on the precision.

The effects of stand age on the precision of all the distributions but Fuzzy-Γ_1 are showed in Fig. 5. Stand age had different effects on the precision of distribution functions. Fuzzy-Γ_5, Logistic, and Fuzzy-Γ_3 had relatively high precision at any stand age. It indicated that the three functions were flexible for fitting stands at any stand age. The precision of Fuzzy-Γ_2, Gompertz, and Korf distributions gradually increased with increased stand age. From Fig. 5, Fuzzy-Γ_2 had higher precision for high-aged stands of planting density of E (10 000 stems/ha) than both Logistic and Fuzzy-Γ_3 functions. The main reason for this result was that their inflection points were in the left side of central point of inflection point of diameter cumulative distributions of those stands and the inflection point of the diameter cumulative distributions gradually closed to the inflection point of these three functions with the development of those stands. Therefore, the three functions were relatively more suitable for fitting high-aged stands. Fuzzy-C distribution showed no clear trend of precision with stand age. In general, it had slightly higher precision for fitting high-aged stands. Fuzzy-Γ_4 has similar precisions for different stand ages for any planting density. The results of two-way analysis of variance showed that stand age had a significant effect on precision of every distribution at probability level of 0.05 and differences in precision among the nine different functions were significant at the probability level of 0.05.

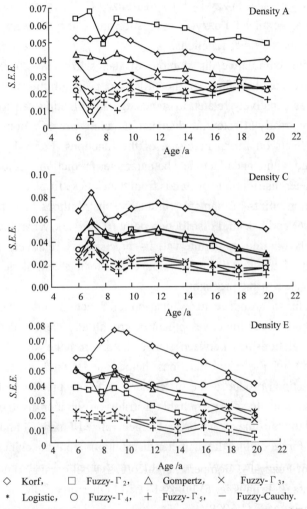

Fig. 5 Precision of eight functions versus stand age. Planting density A, C, and E were 1667, 5000, 10 000 stems/ha, respectively. The *S.E.E.* in this Figure was an average value of 30 samples

4

Conclusion

Six fuzzy distribution functions were introduced to model diameter distributions of chinese fir plantation. Due to the mathematical properties of different Fuzzy distributions, the differences in precision of their fitting the stand diameter distributions significantly existed. The following conclusions can be drawn as follows:

(1) Based on the *S.E.E.* criterion, functions ordered on precision from high to low were: Fuzzy-Γ_5, Logistic, Fuzzy-Γ_3, Fuzzy-Γ_4, Fuzzy-C, Fuzzy-Γ_2, Gompertz, Korf, and Fuzzy-Γ_1. The generalized Fuzzy-Γ_5, Logistic, and Fuzzy-Γ_3 were more consistent performers than the six other functions.

(2) Diameter cumulative distributions of stands from the chinese fir plantation were a S-shaped curve. Values of the inflection point of the diameter cumulative distributions was negatively related to stands age and planting density. Stand age and planting density greatly affected the diameter cumulative distributions. Also, stand age has different effects on fitting precision of the functions. Fuzzy-Γ_3'parameters were highly correlated with stands factors. The parameter prediction method was developed to predict diameter distributions of stands from the chinese fir plantation.

(3) Inflection points of diameter cumulative distributions have a main inflexible interval (0.4~0.6) and a central distribution point (0.5 or so). When the inflection point of a function lay in the main interval, its precision is relatively high. When the inflection point of the function had value closer to the central point, the function generally had higher fitting precision.

It was useful to introduce fuzzy distribution functions into characterizing stand diameter distributions for the development of growth and yield modelling techniques. Analyzing the relationships between stands factors and the key characteristic (i.e., inflection point) of the nine functions helped understand the reasons why the distribution functions produced the differences in fitting precision. The results have important implications to select a suitable distribution function for the specific stands. To summarize, the two fuzzy functions, the generalized Fuzzy-Γ_5 and Fuzzy-Γ_3, were able to be used for modelling the diameter distributions from the chinese fir plantations and provided potential alternatives for modelling diameter distributions of other types of forest stands such as natural or thinned stands.

References

Arasan V T, Wermuth M, Srinivas B S. 1996. Modelling of Stratified Urban Trip Distribution. Journal of Transportation Engineering, 122: 342~349

Bailey R L, Dell T R. 1973. Quantifying diameter distributions with the Weibull function. For Sci, 19: 97~104

Borders B E, Souter R A, Bailey R L, *et al.* 1987. Percentile-based distributions characterize forest stand tables. For Sci, 33: 570~576

Burkhart H E, Strub M R. 1974. A model for simulation of planted loblolly pine stands. In: Growth models for tree and stand simulation. Edited by J. Fries. Royal College of Forestry, Stockholm

Sweden, pp. 128~135

Cao Q V, Burkhart H E. 1984. A segmented distribution approach for modelling diameter frequency data. For Sci, 30: 129~137

Davis L S, Johnson K N. 1987. Forest Management (3rd Edition). New York: McGraw-hill

Dressler T D, Burk T E. 1989. A test of nonparametric smoothing of diameter distributions. Scand J For Res, 4:407~415

Duan A G, Zhang J G, Tong S Z. 2003. Application of six growth equations on stands diameter structure of Chinese fir Plantation. Forest Research, 16: 423~429

Gadow K V, Hui G Y. 1998. Modelling Forest Development[M]. Germany: CUVILLIER ERLAG Goettingen

Haara A, Maltamo M, Tokola T. 1997. The k-nearest-neighbor method for estimating basal area diameter distribution. Scand J For Res, 12: 200~208

Hafley W L, Schreuder H T. 1977. Statistical distributions for fitting diameter and height data in even-aged stands. Can J For Res, 4: 481~487

Kangas A, Maltamo M. 2000. Calibrating Predicted Diameter Distribution with Additional Information. For Sci, 46: 390~396

Kilkki P, Paivinen R. 1986. Weibull function in the estimation of the basal area dbh-distribution. Silva Fennica, 20: 149~156

Kilkki P, Maltamo M, Mykkanen R, *et al.* 1989. Use of the Weibull function in estimating the basal area dbh-distribution. Silva Fennica, 23: 311~318

Kivinen V P, Uusitalo J. 2002. Applying Fuzzy Logic to Tree Bucking Control. For Sci, 48: 673~684

Little S N. 1983.   Weibull diameter distributions for mixed stands of western conifers. Can J For Res, 13: 85~88

Liu C, Zhang S Y, Lei Y, *et al.* 2004. Evaluation of three methods for predicting diameter distributions of black spruce (*Picea mariana*) plantations in central Canada Can J For Res, 34: 2424~2434

Liu C, Zhang L, Davis C J, *et al.* 2002. A finite mixture model for characterizing the diameter distribution of mixed-species forest stands. For Sci, 48: 653~661

Maltamo, M. and Kangas, A. 1998. Methods based on k-nearest neighbor regression in estimation of basal area diameter distribution. Can. J. For. Res. 28:1107~1115

Rennolls K, Wang M. 2005. A new parameterization of Johnson's SB distribution with application to fitting forest tree diameter data. Can J For Res, 35: 575~579

SAS. 1999. SAS/STAT users guide. Version 8. SAS Institute Inc., Cary, N.C.

Zadeh L A. 1965. Fuzzy sets. Information and Control. 8: 338~357

Zeide B. 1993. Analysis of growth equations. For Sci, 39: 594~616

Zhang L, Liu C L, Davis C J, *et al.* 2004. Fuzzy classification of ecological habitats from FIA data. For Sci, 50: 117~127

Zimmermann H J. 1996. Fuzzy Set Theory – and Its Applications. Kluwer Academic Publishers, Boston, Dordrecht, London

CHAPTER SEVEN:
Testing the self-thinning rule in chinese fir (*Cunninghamia lanceolata*) plantations

Abstract   As yet, no comprehensive analysis in plant population ecology explains whether the self-thinning exponent remains constant or is variable. The objective of this study was to quantify the maximum average stem volume [V (dm^3)] and density [N (stems/ha)] relationship of chinese fir stands based on the determination of self-thinning onset. The study had 5 initial density levels (2 m × 3 m, 2 m × 1.5 m, 2 m × 1 m, 1 m×1.5 m   and 1 m × 1 m) and 3 replications for each, thus a total of 15 plots. Each plot was measured 16 times between 1983 and 2006. Subsets of the data were constructed and consisted of 0%~67%, 2%~67%, 5%~67%, 10%~67%, 15%~67%, 20%~67%, 23%~67%, 25%~67% and 30%~67% mortality intervals. Ordinary least squares (OLS) and reduced major axis (RMA) regression techniques were used to obtain parametric parameter estimates for each mortality interval subset. Results indicated that the RMA method combined with jackknife estimation (RMA + jackknife) was the most appropriate regression method. The self-thinning exponent for a mortality interval of 2%–67% sufficiently represented the maximum attainable volume-density relationship for chinese fir based on a determination of the onset of self-thinning. Self-thinning exponents systematically changed with different mortality intervals, and −1.5 was a transitory value in the course of self-thinning that gradually changed according to the maximum volume-density line due to dynamics of crown size distribution. We also conclude that self-thinning may occur when the ratio between crown length and tree height (CL/TH) in closed stands approaches 0.4.

1
Introduction

As a stand of trees grows, the demands each tree places on resources and growing space increases. If resources are no longer adequate for all stand components then there is intense competition between trees for resources. This leads to density-dependent mortality, or self-thinning. The self-thinning law, also known as the 3/2 power law of self-thinning (Yoda *et al.*, 1963), describes the relationship between mean plant weight (*w*) and plant density (N) during the development of overcrowded, even-aged stands as follows:

$$\ln w = k + \beta_{wN} \ln N \tag{1}$$

Where β_{wN} is the slope of self-thinning line close to $-3/2$ regardless of species, age, or site conditions and *k* is a constant which varies with species. In forestry, for practical reasons stem volume (*V*) is usually used as a substitute for biomass (Drew and

Flewelling, 1977, 1979; Smith and Hann, 1986; Smith, 1989; Newton and Smith, 1990; Bégin *et al.*, 2001; Ogawa and Hagihara., 2003; Newton, 2006). Thus Equation (1) is represented:

$$\ln V = k + \beta_{VN} \ln N \tag{2}$$

Some authors suggest that it is reasonable for the relationship between stand density (N) and diameter of stems (or quadratic mean diameter) (D) to be used to express the self-thinning model (Zeide, 1987; Inoue and Nishizono, 2004). The equation for this is described as follows:

$$\ln N = k + \beta_{ND} \ln D \tag{3}$$

According to Inoue and Nishizono, (2004) the gradient of self-thinning was -1.7991 for cypress and -1.3011 for pine. Renieke (1933), however, found β_{ND} to be -1.605.

Both of these are higher than the self thinning gradient calculated using Euclidian geometry in Yoda's 3/2 power law: -2.

Yoda's law has been studied many times in both forestry and agriculture since its inception (e.g., White and Harper, 1970; Bazzaz and Harper, 1976; Gorham, 1979; White, 1981; Westoby, 1977, 1984; Cousens and Hutchings, 1983; Weller, 1987a, 1987b; Zeide, 1985, 1987; Li *et al.*, 1999; Roderick and Barnes, 2004; Ogawa, 2005; Torres, 2001; Ogawa and Hagihara, 2003). At first it was widely accepted (White and Harper, 1970; Gorham, 1979; Westoby, 1984), then controversy over its generality developed (e.g., Weller, 1987a, 1987b, 1990, 1991; Zeide, 1985, 1987,1991; Lonsdale, 1990; Morris, 2002; Pretzsch and Biber, 2005; Pretzsch, 2006). The main focus of arguments for and against each model are detailed in the following sections (1.1 and 1.2).

1.1
Model (1): β_{wN} or β_{VN} or β_{ND} is $-3/2$

In 1963, when Yoda *et al.* formulated the 3/2 power law they assumed that plants are simple Euclidian objects and all plant scale isometrically to each other. Therefore the relationship between mean plant weight (w) and plant diameter (D) is:

$$w \propto D^3 \tag{4}$$

and the relationship between plant diameter (D) and occupied growing areas (s) is:

$$s \propto D^2 \tag{5}$$

As average growing areas (*s*) is the inverse of plant density N ($s \propto 1/N$), then Eq 5 can be written as $N \propto D^{-2}$, therefore, we get $w \propto N^{-3/2}$.

There are mixed opinions about the consistency of the −3/2 exponent; while some researchers support it (White and Harpeer, 1970; Westoby, 1977, 1984) other recent studies have questioned its consistency (Mohler *et al.*, 1978; Li *et al.*, 2000; Pretzsch, 2002; Osawa, 1995;Kikuzawa, 1999; Del *et al.*, 2001; Yang and Titus, 2002). For example, Mohler *et al.* (1978) suggested that the self-thinning exponent of plants varied considerably: from −0.95 to −1.30 in balsam fir (*Abies balsamea*) and from −0.81 to −1.90 in pin cherry (*Prunus pensylvanica*).

Recently West *et al.* (1997,1999) and Enquist *et al.*(1998) posited a scaling law for plants and animals which considers plants as fractal objects and postulates the generality of quarter-power scaling. Using their model they predicted β_{wN} to be −4/3, β_{ND} to be −2, and plant weight (*w*) and plant diameter (*D*) scale as $w \propto D^{8/3}$ ($\beta_{wD} =$ 8/3). They then extended their conclusions to include animals, plants, cells and mitochondria (Franco and Kelly, 1998; Enquist and Niklas, 2001). The generality of their research, however, provoked Whitefield (2001), Kozlowski and Konarewski (2004,2005), and Li *et al.* (2005) to question it. After numerical and empirical scrutiny they criticized the model as neither mathematically correct, nor biological relevant or universal.

Li *et al.*(2000) used ecological field theory and statistical mechanics to establish a model which relates plant mass (*w*) to plant density (*N*) by a power-law equation with an exponent of $-2/\eta$ (with η representing biomass accumulation). Thus, if biomass accumulation of a plant is three-dimensional (as it is for most tall plants), the slope of self-thinning is −2/3 . For plants with two-dimensional growth (ground-cover plants), the value of $-2/\eta$ becomes −1; however, if we let η equal 8/3, the value of $-2/\eta$ could be −4/3. Therefore they concluded that the self-thinning exponents varied from −3/2 to −1. A similar conclusion was arrived at by Osawa *et al.* (1995).

1.2
Model (2)The effects of site conditions and initial stand density on β_{WN} or β_{VN} or β_{ND}

Yoda *et al.* (1963) investigated all populations of *Erigeron canadensis* grown at a range of soil fertilities, and made a conclusion that, when their growth was plotted, they all thinned along a line of common slope and intercept point irrespective of soil fertility. However, this claim of a consistent the self-thinning ratio across differing growth conditions has been questioned (Zeide, 1985, 1987; Morris, 2002; Berger and

Hanno, 2003). Zeide (1985) analyzed slopes of four southern pine species (*Pinus* spp.) in different growing conditions and concluded that the gradient of the self-thinning line varied with site condition. Morris (2002) argued that the slope of self-thinning line was flatter at a lower fertility level than that at a higher fertility level. Bi *et al*. (2000) introduced a modified expression of the self-thinning rule, $B=KS^bN^a$, where B is stand biomass per unit area, N is stand density, S is relative site index, and K, a, and b are parameters. Results show that a was not significantly different from −0.5 at the 95% confidence level, yet b was significantly different from 0 at the 95% confidence level.

Eric and Thomas (2000) found stand history has a large impact on the level of the self-thinning line. Stands with initially high density exhibited lower self-thinning lines than stands with lower density. They also found site index chiefly affected the rate at which stand dynamics progress: higher quality sites progressed through stand development at faster rates than did sites with lower quality.

Chinese fir (*Cunninghamia lanceolata*) is naturally distributed in south China, and is the main silvicultural tree in this region. chinese fir (which is a relatively fast growing tree with good quality timber) is wildly used in industry. However, few studies about self-thinning have been made on this species. Such knowledge is of fundamental value in understanding the ecology of the chinese fir and its management. Therefore, the main purposes of this study are: ① to establish self-thinning relationships between V and N, N and D, V and D, respectively; ② to analyze the affection of site conditions and initial stand density on the self-thinning and ③ to evaluate the time required for the self-thinning process. To verify our results we compared our findings from two study sites.

2
Materials and methods

2.1
Site description and plant material

This study was made on two sites. One is on a 26-year-old chinese fir (*Cunninghamia lanceolata*) stand in the Weimin Forestry Center, Shaowu city of Fujian province. This plantation was situated on an east-facing 25~35° slope. Fifteen plots of 20m×30m in area were established in 1982. The second site was located in Nianzhu Forestry Center, Fenyi county of Jiangxi province. It also has 15 plots of 20m×30m, established in 1981.

Fifteen plots in two sites were all grouped into five density classes. Class A plots were 2m×3m, class B 2m×1.5m, class C 2m×1m, class D 1m×1.5m, and class E 1m×1m. Each density class was represented by three sample plots. The 15 plots represent a range of site indices: from 12 to 22 in Fujian sites, and from 14 to 18 in Jiangxi site. Due to damage from a heavy snowfall only 10 plots from Jiangxi site were included in the results. Summaries for the two sites are given below in Table 1.

Table 1   Summaries for Fujian site and Jiangxi site

Site	Plots		Initial density/0.06hm^2	Site index[①]/m
	A	A_1	100	16
		A_2	100	20
		A_3	100	22
	B	B_1	200	14
		B_2	200	20
		B_3	200	18
Fujian site	C	C_1	300	16
		C_2	300	20
		C_3	300	18
	D	D_1	400	14
		D_2	400	20
		D_3	400	14
	E	E_1	600	12
		E_2	600	20
		E_3	600	12
	A	A_1	100	18
		A_2	100	18
		A_3	100	16
	B	B_1	200	16
		B_2	200	16
		B_3	200	16
Jiangxi site	C	C_1	300	14
		C_2	300	16
		C_3	300	16
	D	D_1	400	14
		D_2	400	14
		D_3	400	14
	E	E_1	600	14
		E_2	600	16
		E_3	600	16

① site index indicates the average height of dominant trees at 20 years old.

2.2
Method

Yoda *et al.* originally proposed Eq.(1) (page 96) of the relationship between w and N or V and N in fully stocked pure stands during the self-thinning process. To select appropriate data points, we use data with a mortality rate of above 10% to estimate the self-thinning line. The reasons for this are, firstly, that any stands with a mortality rate of above 10% should be undergoing the self-thinning process and experiencing density-related mortality of late successional species (Fang *et al.*, 1991; Fang, 1992). Secondly, Solomon and Zhang (2002) have suggested that plots composed of late successional species with a relative density index higher than 0.7 should be selected as the most fully-stocked plots for model development, thus the relative density of all plots selected for use in this study was higher than 0.9. Thirdly, by selecting a mortality rate of 10% a sufficient number of plots were able to be included in the study.

There are two regression methods used to estimate the self-thinning line: one is ordinary least square regression (OLS) and the other is reduced major axis regression (*RMA*). *RMA* is a more objective method than OLS because OLS relies on an unsubstantiated assumption that the standard error has no variance (Zeide, 1987, Pretzsch, 2006; Kmenta, 1986, cited in Solomon and Zhang, 2002). The *RMA* slope coefficient is $\beta_{RMA}=\beta/|r_{yx}|$, where r_{yx} is the Pearson correlation coefficients between y and x. Sackville *et al.*(1995) showed that slope estimates of all algorithms converge with an increasing R^2 value. Therefore, the differences between OLS and *RMA* methods had no noteworthy effect on the final results of this study. Therefore, in this study we used *RMA* to estimate coefficients when R^2 was less than 0.95, and used OLS when R^2 was greater than 0.95.

Seventy-one datasets were selected for estimating the self-thinning line based on the above methods. In order to analyze the effect of site conditions and initial stand density on the slope of self-thinning, we introduced a dummy variable. The equations are as follows:

$$Y=a+b_1I_1+b_2I_2+b_3I_3+b_4I_1x+b_5I_2 x +b_6I_3 x +b_7x \tag{6}$$

$$Y=c+d_1I_4+d_2I_5+d_3I_6+d_4I_4x+d_5I_5 x +d_6I_6 x +d_7x \tag{7}$$

Where Y is $\ln V$; x is $\ln N$; a, b_1, b_2, b_3, b_4, b_5, b_6 , b_7 , d_1, d_2, d_3, d_4, d_5, d_6 and d_7 are parameters; I_1, I_2, I_3, I_4, I_5 and I_6 are dummy variables:

$$I_1 = \begin{cases} 1 & 200stems/0.06ha \\ 0 & others \end{cases}$$

$$I_2 = \begin{cases} 1 & 300 stems/0.06ha \\ 0 & others \end{cases}$$

$$I_3 = \begin{cases} 1 & 400 stems/0.06ha \\ 0 & others \end{cases}$$

$$I_4 = \begin{cases} 1 & \text{site index}:20 \\ 0 & others \end{cases}$$

$$I_5 = \begin{cases} 1 & \text{site index}:18 \\ 0 & others \end{cases}$$

$$I_6 = \begin{cases} 1 & \text{site index}:14 \\ 0 & others \end{cases}$$

Thus if $I_1=1$, I_2 and I_3 are both zero the equation represents the self-thinning line of a stand with a density at 200 stems/0.06 ha, the same case as I_2 and I_3. When I_1, I_2, I_3 are all zero, the equation shows the self-thinning line to be at a density of 600 stems/0.06 ha. If $I_4=1$ and I_5 and I_6 are both zero the equation represents the self-thinning line of a stand with a site index of 20. When I_4, I_5, I_6 are all zero, the equation shows the self-thinning line of the stand with a site index of 12. There are no stands with a site index of 16 and 22 in equation (7) because self-thinning didn't occur in these two classes of site.

3
Results

3.1
Parameters for the self-thinning line

Table 2 displayed the parameters of model LnV versus LnN, LnN versus LnD and LnV versus LnD (estimated using datasets with mortality above 10%). The parameter β_{VN} in Fujian plots was −1.502, with a 95% confidence limit of −1.616～−1.389. It varied around −3/2, (which did not match the predicted result of −4/3). The parameter β_{ND} was −1.913, (95% confidence limit of −2.043～−1.784), varied around −2, which also did not fit the prediction of −1.605. The parameter β_{VD} was 2.873, with a 95% confidence limit of 2.750～2.997. This was predicted to be 8/3 or three. It was not in this range, although it was close to three.

The results of the Jiangxi site were similar to those of the Fujian site. The parameter β_{VN} in Jiangxi plots was −1.503 with a 95% confidence limit of −1.651～

−1.237. β_{ND} was −1.889 with a 95% confidence limit of −2.103~−1.674, and β_{VD} was 2.839 with 95% confidence limit of 2.678 to 2.999.

Table 2　Results of the slope of the self-thinning line for the Ln*V* versus Ln*N*, Ln*N* versus Ln*D* and Ln*V* versus Ln*D* relationships in Fujian site and Jiangxi sites

Experiment Plots	Ln*V* versus Ln*N*		Ln*N* versus Ln*D*		Ln*V* versus Ln*D*	
	β_{VN} /95% CI	R^2	β_{ND} /95% CI	R^2	β_{VD} /95% CI	R^2
Fujian site	−1.502(−1.616 to −1.389)	0.931	−1.913(−2.043 to −1.784)	0.945	2.873(2.750 to 2.997)	0.978
Jiangxi site	−1.503(−1.651 to −1.237)	0.923	−1.889(−2.103 to −1.674)	0.947	2.839(2.678 to 2.999)	0.987

3.2
Self-thinning lines differ with initial density and site index

The parameters of equation (6) are shown in Table 3 below. The parameter b_7 is −1.569, with 95% confidence limit of −1.665~−1.473. The parameters b_1 b_2 b_3 b_4 b_5 b_6 were not significantly different from 0. This means that plots with an initial density of 200 stems/0.06 ha, 300 stems/0.06 ha, 400 stems/0.06 ha were not significantly different from plots with an initial density of 600 stems/0.06 ha. This supports the observation made in Fig. 1 (that stands with different initial densities tend to approach the same self thinning line). Fig. 2 is based on data from Jiangxi site, and shows the same trend as that from the Fujian site.

Table 3　Results of parameters in equation (6)

Parameters	Estimate	Standard error	t	P	R^2
a	11.000	0.832	13.210	0.0001	0.954
b_1	−3.937	5.911	−0.670	0.509	
b_2	−2.232	1.858	−1.200	0.236	
b_3	−0.323	2.027	−0.160	0.874	
b_4	0.483	0.748	0.650	0.522	
b_5	0.271	0.224	1.210	0.233	
b_6	0.053	0.237	0.233	0.823	
b_7	−1.569	0.096	−16.380	0.0001	

The results of parameters in equation (7) are similar to those above (Table 4). Parameter d_7 is −1.518, with a 95% confidence limit of −1.690~−1.364, it also varied around −1.5. Again the parameters d_1 d_2 d_3 d_4 d_5 d_6 are all not significantly different from 0. This demonstrates that plots with a site index of 14, 18 and 20 are not significant different from plots with a site index of 12.

Therefore, β_{VN} remained constant regardless of differences in site index and initial tree density (it always varied around -1.5)

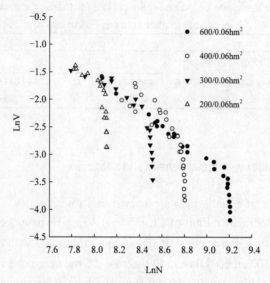

Fig. 1   Mean stem volume and density of trial plots over time (Fujian province)

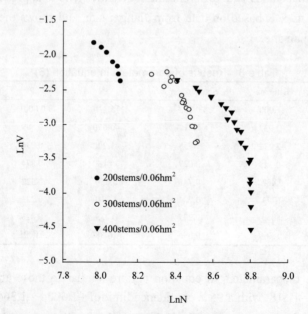

Fig. 2   Mean stem volume and density of trial plots over time (Jangxi province)

Table 4   Results of parameters in equation (7)

Parameters	Value	Standard error	t	P	R^2
c	10.541	1.513	6.97	0.0001	0.952
d_1	−0.971	1.661	−0.585	0.562	
d_2	−3.134	2.425	−1.292	0.203	
d_3	−3.476	2.614	−1.323	0.191	
d_4	0.132	0.191	0.691	0.494	
d_5	0.385	0.292	1.318	0.195	
d_6	0.415	0.303	1.370	0.179	
d_7	−1.518	0.172	−8.8	0.0001	

3.3
Time-trajectory of self-thinning line

Fig. 3 shows the trend over time of self-thinning, measured at 10-year intervals. The angle of the self-thinning slope β_{VN} tended to decrease with increasing stand age, approaching −3/2 towards the end of the study period.

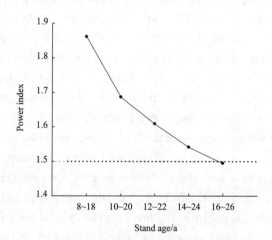

Fig. 3   Changes in power index between mean stem volume and stand density with increasing growth stage, showing the self-thinning slope β_{VN} approaching the self-thinning line of −3/2. The dotted line shows the self-thinning line of −3/2

We also selected the data with mortality rates above 0, 2%, 5%, 10% and 20% to estimate LnV versus LnN, LnN versus LnD and LnV versus LnD. Equations are shown in Table 5. Results for data with mortality rates above 2%, 5%, 10% and 20% found that the parameter β_{VN} was close to −1.5, parameter β_{ND} was close to −2, and for parameter β_{VD} there was a small change: from 2.840 to 2.929.

Table 5   Relationship between LnV versus LnN, LnN versus LnD during different periods

periods	LnV versus LnN			LnN versus LnD			LnV versus LnD		
	β_{VN}	k	R^2	β_{ND}	k	R^2	β_{VD}	k	R^2
Mortality rate 0%~68%	−1.771	12.574	0.817	−1.667	12.698	0.873	2.929	−9.855	0.984
Mortality rate 2%~68%	−1.554	10.838	0.895	−1.851	13.220	0.926	2.850	−9.635	0.981
Mortality rate 5%~68%	−1.539	10.760	0.928	−1.876	13.223	0.943	2.862	−9.655	0.982
Mortality rate 10%~68%	−1.502	10.333	0.931	−1.913	13.411	0.945	2.840	−9.598	0.978
Mortality rate 20%~68%	−1.487	10.454	0.899	−1.944	13.496	0.919	2.850	−9.628	0.972

4

Discussion

Perry (1994) assumed that the time-trajectory of V and N is characterized by three stages. During the early stage of stand development competition among trees is not severe enough to cause mortality, and average stem volume increases with no corresponding decrease in stand density. In this stage, the time-trajectory parallels the y-axis (stage 1). Eventually, the stand grows crowded enough that an increase in the average stem volume cannot occur unless some trees die, resulting in a reduction in stand density (stage 2). Following its initial curve, the time-trajectory asymptotically approaches and then follows closely along straight line, which means that a given increase in average stem volume is matched by a given decrease in stand density (stage 3) (Perry, 1994; cited in Ogawa and Hagihara, 2003). Therefore the V-N trajectory should gradually approach and eventually moves along the predicted self-thinning line at the third stage of stand development. If the data during first and second stage were selected for estimating the self-thinning line results would be quite different from those predicted by the model, thus the method of data selection is clearly very important. In this paper we use data with a mortality rate above 10% to estimate the self-thinning line. The data selected in this experiment is therefore in the third stage of stand development (Fig. 4). Thus the slope of the self-thinning in Equation 2 obtained from this method is close to −1.5. However, if regression included all data points with mortality above zero, the gradient estimated in Equation 2 is steeper than −3/2. This trend is also shown in Fig. 3 and table 6. The self-thinning slope tended to decrease with increasing stand age, finally approaching 3/2. All of these can be regarded as evidence that the method we used is appropriate.

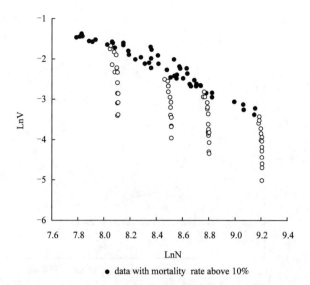

Fig. 4 Time-trajectory of mean stem volume V and density N and quadratic mean diameter (*D*) with increasing growth stage

The relationships between *V* and *N*, *N* and *D*, *V* and *D* during the process of self-thinning were formulated separately by Reineke (1933), Yoda *et al.*(1963) and Enquist *et al.*(1998) (Table 6). Each author had a separate theory and evidence to support it, however the coefficients obtained from their models were not the same. Reineke's stand density rule is an empirically invariant scaling law. Yoda *et al.*'s 3/2 power law is based on Euclidian geometry, and the WBE (West, Brown and Enquist) model is based on fractal geometry. The results of this study indicate that β_{VN} increases with increasing stand age(Fig. 3, Fig. 5), and β_{ND} is decreasing with increasing stand age (Fig. 6, Fig. 7) and that there is only a small change in β_{VD} (Fig. 8, Fig. 9): from 2.840 to 2.955.

Table 6   Self-thinning Parameters in different models

Parameters	Reinke's equation	3/2 power law	WBE's model
β_{VD}		3	8/3
β_{ND}	-1.605	-2	-2
β_{VN}		-3/2	-4/3

Between eight and 18 years 81.43% of datasets had a mortality rate above 0. Between 14 and 24 years 75% of datasets had a mortality rate above 5%, and between 16 and 26 years 78.33% of datasets had a mortality rate above 10%.

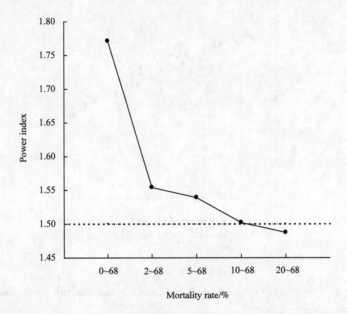

Fig. 5   Changes in the power index between mean stem volume and stand density over different time periods. The dotted line shows the self-thinning line of −3/2

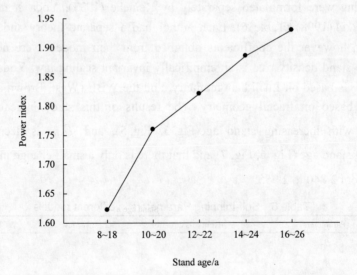

Fig. 6   Changes in power index between stand density (*N*) and quadratic mean diameter (*D*) with increasing growth stages

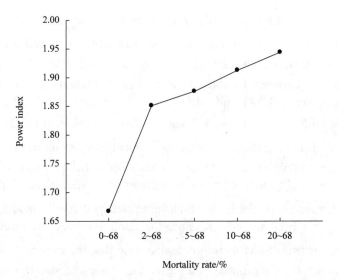

Fig. 7 Changes in power index between stand and quadratic mean diameter during different growth periods

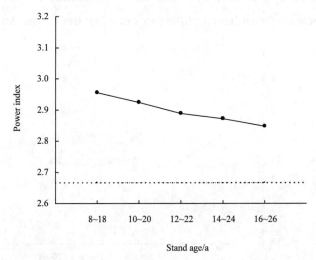

Fig. 8 Changes in power index between stand mean stem volume V and quadratic mean diameter (D) with increasing growth stage (The dotted lines show β_{VD} for WBE's model: $-8/3$)

During the period from 8 to 18 years (with most datasets where mortality was above 0% selected) β_{ND} was -1.667 and -1.622. These results are close to Reineke's constant: -1.605. During this stage, however, competition among trees is not severe, and thus there was little mortality (this period encompasses the first and second stages of growth discussed in the beginning of section 0). However, during the periods from 12 to 22 years, 14 to 24 years and 16 to 26 years, (when stand mortality rates selected were above 2%, 5%, 10% and 20%) β_{ND} were all under −1.8. Therefore, Reineke's stand density rule may be formulated using data which included unthinned stands (datasets which included stands with mortality less than 2%). When data from the period of growth between 16 and 26 years (with a mortality rate above 10%) was selected, β_{VN} were −1.502 and −1.494, which are close to the 3/2 power law's prediction of −1.5. β_{ND} was −1.913 and −1.930 also close to the 3/2 power law's prediction of −2. During this growth period competition among trees was severe and thus it belonged to the third stage of growth described at the beginning of section 4. As growth continues β_{VN} may continue to increase, and after a long lapse β_{VN} may become −4/3, which is similar to the results predicted by the WBE model. In this study, however, β_{VD} has been around 2.85 since the stand mortality rate reached above 2% (Fig. 9). The present results therefore demonstrate that the exponents of each of the three models are only appropriate during certain stages of stand growth, as during stages in which self-thinning occurred β_{VN} varied around −1.5, β_{ND} was closer to −2, and β_{VD} was 2.84. It is also clear that stands of chinese fir exhibited a similar self-thinning behavior regardless of differences in initial tree density and site index.

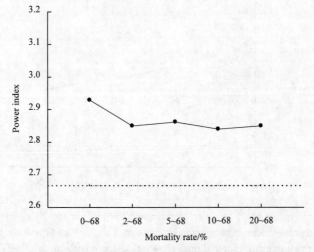

Fig. 9 Changes in the power index between mean stem volume and quadratic mean diameter during different growth periods (The dotted lines shows β_{VD} for WBE's model: −8/3.)

References

Bazzaz F A, Harper L J. 1976. Relationship between plant weight and numbers in mixed population of *sinapsis alba*(L.) and *Lepidium sativum*(L.). Appl Ecol, 13: 211~216

Berger U, Hanno H. 2003. The strength of competition among individual trees and the biomass-density trajectories of the cohort. Plant Ecology, 167: 89~96

Bégin E, Bégin J, Bélanger L, *et al*. 2001. Balsam fir self-thinning relationship and its constancy among different ecological regions. Canadian Journal of Forest Research, 31: 950~959

Bi H Q, Wan G, Turvey N D. 2000. Estimating the self-thinning boundary line as a density-dependent stochastic biomass frontier. Ecology, 81: 1477~1483

Cousens R, Hutchings M J. 1983. The relationship between density and mean frond weight in monospecific seaweed stands. Nature, 301: 240~241

Del R M, Montero G, Bravo F. 2001. Analysis of diameter-density relationships and self-thinning in non-thinned even-aged Scots pine stands. For Ecol Mana, 142: 79~87

Drew T J, Flewelling J W. 1977. Some recent Japanese theories of yield-density relationships and their application to Monterey pine plantations. For Sci, 23: 518~534

Drew T J, Flewelling J W. 1979. Stand density management: an alternative approach and its application to Douglas fir plantations. For Sci, 25: 518~532

Enquist B J, Brown J H, West G B. 1998. Allometric scaling of plant energetics and population density. Nature, 395: 163~165

Enquist B J, Niklas K J. 2001. Invariant scaling relations across tree-dominated communities. Nature, 410: 655~660

Eric C T, Thomas E B. 2000. Modelling self-thinning of unthinned Lake States red pine stands using nonlinear simulatneous differential equations. Can J For Res, 30: 1410~1418

Fang J Y, Kan M, Yamakura T. 1991. Relationships between population growth and population density in monocultures of *Larix leptolepis*. Acta Botanica Sinica, 33: 949~957

Fang J Y. 1992. self-thinning rule in plant population. Rual Eco–Environment, 2: 7~12

Franco M, Kelly C K. 1998. The interspecific mass–density relationship and plant geometry. Proceedings of the National Academy of Science of USA, 95: 7830~7835

Gorham E. 1979. Shoot height, weight and standing crop in relation to density of monospecific plant stands Nature, 279: 148~150

Hutchings M J. 1983. Ecology's law in search of a theory. New Scientist, 98: 765~767

Inoue A, Nishizono T. 2004. Allometric model of the Reineke equation for Japanese cypress (*Chamaecyparis obtuse*) and red pine (*Pinus densiflora*) stands. Journal of Forest Research, 9: 319~324

Kikuzawa K. 1999. Theoretical Relationships Between Mean Plant Size, Size Distribution and Self Thinning under One-sided Competition. Annals of Botany, 83: 11~18

Kmenta J. 1986. Elements of econometrics, 2nd Edition. Macmillan, New York, p.786

Kozlowski J, Konarzewski M. 2004. Is West, Brown and Enquist's model of allometric scaling mathematically correct and biologically relevant? Functional Ecology, 18: 283~289

Kozlowski J, Konarzewski M. 2005. West, Brown and Enquist's model of allometric scaling again: the same questions remain. Functional Ecology, 19: 739~743

Li B L, Wu H, Zou G. 2000. Self-thinning rule: a causal interpretation from ecological field theory. Ecological Modelling, 132: 167~173

Li H T, Han X G, Wu J G. 2005. Lack of Evidence for 3/4 Scaling of Metabolism in Terrestrial Plants. Journal of Integrative Plant Biology, 47: 1173~1183

Li X, Ogawa K, Hagihara A, *et al*. 1999. Self-thinning exponents based on the allometric model in Chinese pine *(Pinus tabulaeformis* Carr.) and Prince Rupprecht's larch (*Larix principis-rupprechtii* Mayr) stands. Forest Ecology Management, 117: 87~93

Lonsdale W. 1990. The self-thinning rule: dead or alive? Ecology, 71: 1373~1388

Mohler C L, Marks P L, Sprugel D G. 1978. Stand structure and allometry of tree during self-thinning of pure stand. Journal of Ecology, 68: 598~614

Morris E C. 2002. Self-thinning lines differ with fertility level. Ecological Research, 17: 7~28

Newton P E. 2006. Asymptotic size-density relationships within self-thinning black spruce and jack pine stand-types: parameter estimation and model reformulations. Forest ecology and management, 226: 49~59

Newton P E, Smith V G. 1990. Reformulated self-thinning exponents as applied to black spruce. Can J For Res, 20: 887~893

Osawa A. 1995. Inverse relationship of crown fractal dimension to self-thinning exponent of tree population: a hypothesis. Canadian Journal of Forest Research,. 25: 1608~1617

Ogawa K. 2005.Time-trajectory of mean phytomass and density during acourse of self-thinning in a sugi (*Cryptomeria japonica* D.Don) plantation. Forest Ecology and Management, 214: 104~110

Ogawa K, Hagihara A. 2003. Self-thinning and size variation in a sugi (*Cryptomeria japonica D. Don*) plantation, Forest Ecology and Management, 174: 413~421

Perry D A, 1994. Forest Ecosystems. The Johns Hopikins University Press, Baltimore, pp649.

Pretzsch H. 2002. A unified law of spatial allometry for woody and herbaceous plants. Plant Biology, 4: 159~166

Pretzsch H, Biber P. 2005. A re-evaluation of Reineke's rule and stand density index. Forest Science, 51: 304~320

Pretzsch H. 2006. Species-specific allometric scaling under self-thinning: evidence from long-term plots in forest stands. Oecologia, 146: 572~583

Reineke L H. 1933. Perfecting a stand-density index for even-aged forests. Journal of Agricultural Research, 46: 627~638

Roderick M L, Barnes B. 2004. Self-thinning of plant population from a dynamic viewpoint. Functional Ecology, 18: 197~203

Sackville H N, Matthew C, Lemaire G. 1995. In defence of the −3/2 boundary rule: a re-evaluation of self-thinning concepts and status. Annals Botany, 76: 569~577

Smith N J. 1989. A stand density control diagram for western red cedar(*Thuja plicata*). For Ecol Manag, 27: 235~244.

Smith N J, Hann D W. 1986. A growth model based on the self-thinning rule. Can J For Res, 16: 330~334

Solomon D S, Zhang L J. 2002. Maximum size–density relationships for mixed softwoods in the northeastern USA. Forest Ecology and Management, 155: 163~170

Torres J L. 2001. On the conceptual basis of the self-thinning rule. Oikos, 95: 544~548

Weller D E. 1987a. A reevaluation of the −3/2 power rule of plant self-thinning. Ecological Monographs, 57: 23~43

Weller D E. 1987b. Self-thinning exponent correlated with allometric measures of plant geometry. Ecology, 68: 813~821

Weller D E. 1990. Will the real self-thinning rule please stand up? A reply to Osawa and Sugita Ecology, 71: 1204~1207

Weller D E. 1991. The self-thinning rule: Dead or unsupported? A reply ro Lonsdale Ecology, 72: 747~750

Westoby M. 1977. Self-thinning driven by leaf area not by weight Nature, 265: 330~331

Westoby M. 1984. The self-thinning rule. Advances in Ecology Research, 14: 167~225

West G B, Brown J H, Enquist B J. 1997. A general model for the origin of allometric scaling laws in biology. Science, 276: 122~126

West G B, Brown J H, Enquist B J. 1999. A general model for the structure and allometry of plant vascular systems. Nature, 400: 664~667

White J. 1981. The allometric interpretation of self-thinning rule. Journal of Theoretical Biology, 89: 475~500

White J, Harpe J L. 1970. Correlated changes in plant size and number in plant populations. Journal of Ecology, 58: 467~485

Whitfield J. 2001. All creatures great and small. Nature, 413: 342~344

Yang Y, Titus S J. 2002. Maximum size-density relationship for constraining individual tree mortality functions. Forest Ecology and Management, 168: 259~273

Yoda K, Kira T, Ogawa H, Hozumi H. 1963. Self-thinning in overcrowded pure stand under cultivated and natural conditions. Joural of Biology of Osaka City University, 14: 107~129

Zeide B. 1985. Tolerance and self-tolerance of trees. Forest Ecology and Management, 13: 149~166

Zeide B. 1987. Analysis of the 3/2 power law of self-thinning. Forest Science, 33: 517~537

Zeide B. 1991. Self-thinning and stand density. For Sci, 37: 517~523

CHAPTER EIGHT:
Estimation of the self-thinning boundary line within even-aged chinese fir (*Cunninghamia lanceolata* (Lamb.) Hook.) stands: Onset of self-thinning

Abstract   Self-thinning rates were measured on permanent sample plots over 26 years on unthinned, even aged stands of chinese fir (*Cunninghamia lanceolata*) in Fujian and Jiangxi provinces, China. Data over a wide range of sites and initial densities was collected. The mortality method (with a mortality rate above 10%) was used to select data for estimating the self-thinning rate. Relationships between mean stem volume (V) and stand density (N), stand density (N) and quadratic mean diameter (D), and between mean stem volume(V) and quadratic mean diameter (D) were established ($\ln V = k + \beta_{VN} \ln N$, $\ln N = k + \beta_{ND} \ln D$, $\ln V = k + \beta_{VD} \ln D$). The value of β_{VN} was found to be -1.502 (95% CI: -1.616 to -1.389, and β_{ND} to be -1.913 (95% CI: -2.043 to -1.784), β_{VD} was 2.873 (95% CI: 2.750 to 2.997). β_{VN} remained constant regardless of changes in site index and initial tree density. Additionally, the values of β_{VN}, β_{ND} and β_{VD} were calculated at 10 year growth intervals. The value of β_{VN} increased with increasing stand age (reaching approximately -1.5 during stages of self-thinning), while β_{ND} decreased with increasing stand age, finally approaching -2. β_{VD} showed only a small change during the study period: from 2.848 to 2.955.

Key words   *Cunninghamia lanceolata* (Lamb.) Hook.; Stand density; Average stem volume; Onset of self-thinning; Crown closure

1
Introduction

The self-thinning rule describes the size–density dynamics of crowded, even-aged and single-species stands. Specifically, the average biomass per individual plant increases as the number of individual plants per area decreases. Ultimately, fewer but larger individual plants survive at the expense of the death of smaller individuals (Yoda *et al.*, 1963). In order to describe the density-dependent mortality process, self-thinning is normally used. Yoda *et al.* (1963) derived a self-thinning exponent, $-3/2$, based on Euclidian geometry. This was supported by many empirical data sets of mean plant size and plant density in forestry (e.g., Drew and Flewelling, 1977; Gorham, 1979; Long and Smith, 1984; Hamilton *et al.*, 1995; Jack and Long, 1996). Alternative values, such as $-4/3$, were obtained by West *et al.* (1997, 1999) and Enquist *et al.* (1998) based on fractal geometry. However, after numerical and empirical scrutiny, Torres *et al.* (2001) and Kozlowski and Konarzewski (2004) concluded that the $-4/3$ self-thinning exponent value is mathematically incorrect owing to biologically unjustified assumptions. Although there are still some cases deviating from −3/2 (e.g., Weller, 1987; Zeide, 1987; Osawa and Sugita, 1989; Osawa and Allen, 1993; Kikuzawa, 1999; Li *et al.*, 2000; Río *et al.*, 2001; Yang and Titus, 2002) and may vary within a certain range (e.g., Mohler *et al.*, 1978; Lonsdale, 1990; Roderick and Barnes, 2004), the self-thinning exponent −3/2 is still the more practical value.

Why has the debate primarily focused on whether the exponent of the self-thinning line is invariant or not? Lack of objectivity with arbitrary data point selection is one of the most important reasons in self-thinning line fittings (Zeide, 1987; Weller, 1989; Osawa and Allen, 1993; Bi and Turvey, 1997; Zhang *et al.*, 2005; Newton, 2006). In the data treatment, it is necessary to eliminate some data points with no density-dependent mortalities from the populations because the self-thinning line that illustrates the maximum biomass−density relationship only acts when the stands are sufficiently crowded. However, since there is usually no *a priori* estimate of the position of the self-thinning line, decisions to eliminate some data points must be made *a posteriori* (Westoby, 1984). The elimination of some data points before data fitting was practiced based on subjective criteria such as visual inspection of the positions of the data points (Yoda *et al.*, 1963; Drew and Flewelling, 1977), mortality in successive measurements (Westoby, 1984; Weller, 1987; Fang *et al.*, 1991), threshold stocking levels (Lonsdale, 1990; Solomon and Zhang, 2002) and degree of canopy closure (Xue *et al.*, 1999; Zeide, 1987) in some cases. However, such criteria cannot ensure all data points selected and used for the data fitting are representative of the maximum stand biomass at varying densities. Therefore, inclusion of some unreliable data points in the fitting results in slopes and intercepts that cannot correctly describe the true stand biomass−density dynamics (Bi *et al.*, 2000).

Data point selection based on the onset of self-thinning plays a very important role in determining the self-thinning exponent. Simultaneously, parameter estimation techniques (e.g., ordinary least squares (OLS), reduced major axis (RMA), and reduced major axis combined with jackknife parameter estimates (RMA + jackknife)) afford opportunities to improve the quantitative understanding of the density-dependent upper boundary line of stand biomass within even-aged stands undergoing self-thinning (Newton, 2006). Thus, one objective in this study was to choose a range of mortality rate classes based on the amount of self-thinning, fit the size−density relationships, and then select the most reliable exponent.

In this paper, we focus on the onset of self-thinning to estimate objectively the self-thinning line based on Yoda's self-thinning rule using OLS, RMA, and RMA+ jackknife parameter estimation techniques. Because chinese fir (*Cunninghamia lanceolata* (Lamb.) Hook.) is one of the most important commercial tree species in southern China with 9.21 million ha planted in pure or mixed stands (Lei, 2005), knowledge of self-thinning in relation to the stand density at which natural mortality rapidly increases is useful for determination of optimal thinning regimes.

2

Materials and Methods

2.1

Experimental sites and measurements

The chinese fir stands located in Shaowu County (27°20′N, 117°29′E), Fujian province, in southern China were established in 1982. The plots were planted in a random block arrangement with the following tree spacings: 2 m × 3 m (1667 stems/ha), 2 m × 1.5 (3333 stems/ha), 2 m × 1 m (5000 stems/ha), 1 m × 1.5 m (6667 stems/ha) and 1 m × 1 m (10 000 stems/ha). Each spacing level was replicated three times. Each plot comprised an area of 20 m × 30 m and a buffer zone consisting of similarly treated trees surrounded each plot. The data for three plots with a planting density of 2 m × 3 m, one plot with a density of 2 m × 1.5 m and one plot with a density of 2 m × 1 m were excluded since their mortality rates did not exceed 5% (stems/ha). Thus, the data for 10 plots out of the 15 total plots were used in this study. The trees in all of the plots were numbered, and measurements were conducted after the tree height reached 1.3 m. Sampling was performed in each winter from 1983 to 1990 and then every other year until 2006. The measurements comprised the total tree height (m), diameter at breast height (cm), crown width within and between rows (m) and height to the base of the lowest live branch (m). The stem volume (dm³) was estimated using the experimental formulae developed by Liu and Tong (1980) for chinese fir. The reduction in number of trees was recorded in two categories: intrinsic mortality (trees that died through natural processes) and harvest mortality (trees that were removed via harvesting). A summary of the statistics for the plots is presented in Table 1.

Table 1   Summary of the stand attributes of the chinese fir stands

Stand attribute	Mean	S.D.[①]	Minimum	Maximum
Age/a	16	6	2	26
Density/(stems/ha)	5783	2216	2516	10 000
Quadratic mean diameter/cm	10.77	3.10	5.48	17.54
Diameter at breast height/cm	10.98	4.02	6.23	11.24
Live crown ratio[②]	0.30	0.06	0.25	0.67
Average stem volume/dm³	0.07	0.05	0.01	0.32

① S.D.: standard deviation.

② Live crown length/total tree height ratio.

2.2

Data selection and parameter estimation

Crucial to the relationship between average stem volume and stand density within self-thinning populations is determination of the onset of self-thinning. The procedure comprises four basic steps. The first step is to select data from plots for which the mortality exceeds 5% as described by Fang *et al.* (1991). In this study, the data points of 10 plots were selected and those of five plots were excluded owing to their low mortality (<5%). The second step is to identify the onset of self-thinning. In order to analyze the problem conveniently, we arbitrarily defined seven mortality values for the onset of self-thinning, i.e. 0%, 5%, 10%, 15%, 20%, 25% and 30%. It was found that density-dependent factors initially had less impact on the self-thinning trajectory than density-independent factors, but with increasing mortality rate became dominant and density-independent factors made no contribution. Although the same fitting data were included in different mortality rate classes in this process, the unreliable observations, which resulted from the density-independent factors, were eliminated. Then we used parameter estimation methods to test which mortality rate is the nearest to the onset of self-thinning. The third step is to evaluate the corresponding self-thinning exponents using the data from these seven sample data subsets together with two additional data subsets created based on the following findings. By examining the data, we considered that the onset of self-thinning should be reached before the stand mortality rate reaches 5%. To examine this more precisely, we evaluated 1%~67%, 2%~67%, 3%~67% and 4%~67% mortality rate classes. We found that the onset of self-thinning starts as the stand mortality reaches 2%. Therefore, in the analysis we added 2% mortality to the mortality rate classes. In addition, the slope of the 15%~67% mortality rate class had almost the same value as that of the 20%~67% mortality rate class, which was obviously different from that of the 25%~67%. We then added a 23%~67% mortality rate class to the data subset to reflect the steepness of the slope trend. Overall, we had nine sample data subsets with 0%~67%, 2%~67%, 5%~67%, 10%~67%, 15%~67%, 20%~67%, 23%~67%, 25%~67% and 30%~67% mortality rates for analysis. The last step is to estimate the results gained from the third step to determine the onset of self-thinning. The criteria consisted of: ① assessing the magnitude of standard errors (S.E.) with the parameter estimation and identifying the most appropriate regression techniques and, given this, ② determining the onset of self-thinning based on whether the parameter confidence interval calculated for a specific mortality rate class includes the parameter estimators calculated by its entire latter mortality rate classes (Bégin *et al.*, 2001; Solomon and Zhang, 2002).

The parameter estimation was performed using traditional models (e.g., Drew and Flewelling, 1979; Long and Smith, 1984; Smith and Hann, 1986; Bégin *et al.*, 2001; Ogawa and Hagihara, 2003; Newton, 2006). Yoda *et al.* (1963) proposed an experimental function between average biomass (*w*) and the number of surviving individuals (*N*). White (1981) showed that there is a close isometric relationship between the stem volume (*V*) and *w*. In self-thinning studies, within forest stands, *V* is usually used to represent biomass for practical reasons. Lonsdale (1990) indicated that the volume–density plot reduces the variability of self-thinning lines. The logarithmic specification of the self-thinning rule takes the form:

$$\log V_i = k_i - a_i \log N_i + \varepsilon \tag{1}$$

where V_i is the average stem volume (dm^3), N_i is the number of surviving individuals, k_i is a species-specific constant and a_i is the slope of the self-thinning line, specific to the i th mortality rate class subset, regardless of species, age or site conditions, and ε is an error term.

The intercept and slope coefficients of each mortality rate class subset are often estimated by parameterization methods such as OLS and RMA (e.g., Solomon and Zhang, 2002; Niklas *et al.*, 2003; Inoue *et al.*, 2004; Pretzsch and Biber, 2005; Zhang *et al.*, 2005; Newton, 2006; Pretzsch, 2006). In this study we used RMA + jackknife, which is a non-parametric procedure and allows reduction of the bias in the estimation of the population value and its associated S.E. In order to compare the results obtained from different estimation methods, we also used the OLS and RMA methods and presented all the parameters and regression statistics obtained from them. Computations for OLS were carried out in SAS (SAS Institute Inc., 1999) whereas the RMA parametric and jackknife parameter estimates were obtained using RMA Regression Software (Bohonak, 2004) employing 500 bootstrap replicates.

3
Results

The subsets with a range of mortality rate classes were employed to determine the onset of self-thinning and analyze its self-thinning trajectory. Table 2 shows the parameter estimates and associated S.E. for each regression method and estimation procedure using each mortality rate class subset. The self-thinning exponents derived from the OLS method varied over a narrow range from −1.574 to −1.394 among the nine mortality rate classes with intercepts between 9.561 and 10.909. When the assumed onset of self-thinning increased from 0% to 2%, 5%, 10%, 15% and 20%, the slope value decreased from −1.574 to −1.494, −1.473, −1.450, −1.423, and −1.394, respectively, which implied that the self-thinning line gradually becomes flatter. The slope value for the 20%~67% mortality rate class was the lowest and the self-thinning line became steeper with increasing mortality rate (see the 23%~67%, 25%~67% and 30%~67% mortality rate classes in Table 2). The slopes were U-shaped with increasing mortality rate. The estimators obtained with the RMA and RMA + jackknife regression techniques ranged from −1.771 to −1.480 and −1.769 to −1.477, respectively, with intercepts between 10.283 and 12.571 and between 10.256 and 12.558, respectively. Similarly, the slope values exhibited a U-shape and the lowest slope was in the 15%~67% mortality rate class (Table 2).

Table 2　Parameter estimates for the maximum volume–density line using the OLS and RMA regression methods in self-thinning of the chinese fir stands

Mortality	Sample size	Regression method	r^2 [1]	Slope			Intercept	
				Estimation	S.E.(S) [2]	95%CI [3]	Estimation	S.E.(I) [4]
0%~67%	83	OLS	0.810	−1.574	0.085	−1.744,−1.405	10.909	0.724
		RMA	0.817	−1.771	0.084	−1.938,−1.603	12.571	0.717
		RMA+Jackknife	0.818	−1.769	0.074	−1.921,−1.640	12.558	0.627
2%~67%	66	OLS	0.910	−1.494	0.058	−1.612,−1.376	10.345	0.499
		RMA	0.895	−1.554	0.063	−1.680,−1.428	10.838	0.533
		RMA+Jackknife	0.897	−1.553	0.045	−1.656,−1.475	10.828	0.393
5%~67%	59	OLS	0.922	−1.473	0.056	−1.587,−1.359	10.199	0.481
		RMA	0.928	−1.540	0.055	−1.649,−1.430	10.755	0.463
		RMA+Jackknife	0.929	−1.537	0.045	−1.638,−1.463	10.733	0.392
10%~67%	51	OLS	0.925	−1.450	0.059	−1.569,−1.330	10.026	0.501
		RMA	0.931	−1.501	0.056	−1.615,−1.388	10.458	0.477
		RMA+Jackknife	0.932	−1.499	0.050	−1.615,−1.421	10.439	0.430
15%~67%	43	OLS	0.903	−1.423	0.073	−1.572,−1.274	9.809	0.618
		RMA	0.904	−1.480	0.071	−1.625,−1.336	10.283	0.600
		RMA+Jackknife	0.906	−1.477	0.061	−1.622,−1.367	10.256	0.519
20%~67%	37	OLS	0.886	−1.394	0.085	−1.568,−1.220	9.561	0.713
		RMA	0.899	−1.487	0.080	−1.649,−1.325	10.333	0.667
		RMA+Jackknife	0.901	−1.485	0.066	−1.622,−1.357	10.311	0.564
23%~67%	33	OLS	0.873	−1.525	0.113	−1.758,−1.291	10.657	0.954
		RMA	0.878	−1.581	0.106	−1.798,−1.363	11.115	0.889
		RMA+Jackknife	0.878	−1.570	0.105	−1.804,−1.422	11.022	0.899
25%~67%	28	OLS	0.889	−1.550	0.105	−1.768,−1.331	10.852	0.895
		RMA	0.898	−1.549	0.099	−1.793,−1.384	11.170	0.832
		RMA+Jackknife	0.898	−1.578	0.101	−1.820,−1.423	11.075	0.870
30%~67%	25	OLS	0.892	−1.619	0.112	−1.759,−1.290	10.640	0.949
		RMA	0.895	−1.614	0.110	−1.856,−1.400	11.507	0.925
		RMA+Jackknife	0.893	−1.613	0.121	−1.886,−1.460	11.385	1.040

① Correlation Coefficient

②④ S.E.(S) and S.E.(I) are standard errors associated with the slope and intercept estimate, respectively.

③ 95% confidence intervals

The S.E. is of crucial importance here because it represents the reliability of estimation for the observations. The S.E. of the slopes estimated using the OLS method was all larger than those estimated using the RMA method (Table 2). Therefore, the RMA method was considered the most appropriate of the parameter estimation methods employed to fit the self-thinning line.

Next the onset of self-thinning was investigated by evaluating the confidence interval (CI) that bounds the exponent estimate. The 95% confidence interval was computed for each coefficient. Among the nine mortality rate classes, only the 0%~67% mortality rate class had a self-thinning exponent with a CI that did not include −1.5. It was reasonable to conclude that individual tree mortality at the initial stand development stage is caused by reduced vigor owing to limited resources. Mortality-independent factors could have resulted in reduction in the number of individual trees. It was also found that the CI of the slope estimated in the 0%~67% mortality rate class did not include the entire latter estimators. However, the slope of the next mortality rate class (2%~67%) and its subsequent estimates not only contained −1.5 but also its entire latter estimates. This suggests that the onset of self-thinning starts when mortality equals 2%.

The self-thinning exponents obtained with RMA regression and RMA + jackknife were extremely similar (Table 2) and showed similar trends as mortality increased. Jackknife estimation was performed on the basis of the distribution of slopes and intercepts of the observed data set with resampling, allowing us to reduce the S.E. of a sample average. Thus the line fitted using the RMA + jackknife procedure having a slope of −1.553 (Fig. 1-(b)) can adequately represent the maximum volume-density relationship within the even-aged chinese fir stands (Fig.2).

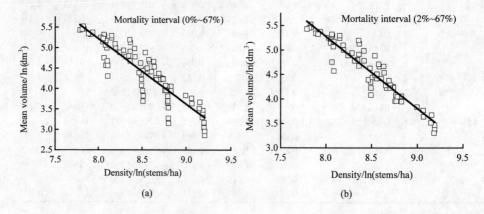

(a)   (b)

Estimation of the self-thinning boundary line within even-aged chinese fir (*Cunninghamia lanceolata* (Lamb.) Hook.) stands: Onset of self-thinning

121

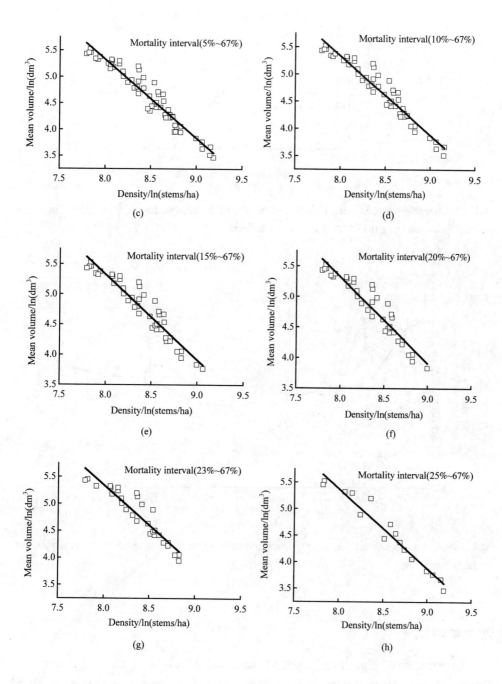

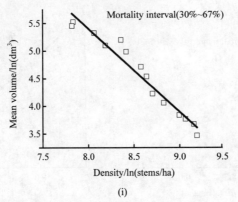

(i)

Fig.1   Relationship between mean volume and density of the chinese fir stands with nine mortality intervals estimated using the RMA + jackknife technique

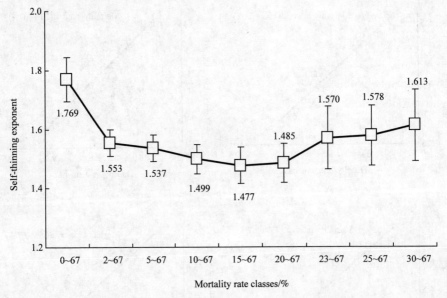

Fig.2   RMA + jackknife technique confidence intervals for the self-thinning exponent across the mortality rate classes

4
Discussion

The patterns of growth and death of individual trees leads to changes in tree size distribution (e.g., average stem volume) during stand development (Mohler *et al.*, 1978; Ogawa and Hagihara, 2003). Therefore, the self-thinning line varies with the stand growth stage. In this study, we found that the trajectory of self-thinning becomes

Estimation of the self-thinning boundary line within even-aged chinese fir (*Cunninghamia lanceolata* (Lamb.) Hook.) stands: Onset of self-thinning

123

U-shaped with increasing mortality rate, and it is therefore possible to describe the trajectory of self-thinning stands through the following three stages.

During the early stage of stand development, competition among trees is not severe enough to cause mortality, and average stem volume increases with no corresponding decrease in the stand density. This results in little size variation among the individual trees. The crown dimensions (horizontal and vertical) increase with full incident light intensity and other abiotic resources (e.g., precipitation and soil nutrients) (stage 1). As a result, the self-thinning line on a log–log coordinate is approximately parallel to the *y*-axis.

With growth the trees become larger, the stand becomes dense and a further increase in average stem volume results in increased tree mortality. At this time, the beginning of competitive interactions coincides more or less with canopy closure. The growth rate for an individual tree is reduced relative to its potential in the absence of intraspecific competition. The self-thinning line on a log–log coordinate now begins to curve towards the left, denoting a reduction in stand density (stage 2). At this stage, the crown closure is at its maximum, the growth rate of an individual tree is reduced relative to its potential, and intraspecific competition accelerates the size differentiation among individuals in the population (Zeide, 1987). In our present study, the slope of the self-thinning line (−1.769) was steeper than predicted (−1.5) (Fig. 1- (a)). As competition-induced mortality progresses, the increased severity in competition makes the individual trees, especially those of subordinate crown classes with limited availability to light, more susceptible to direct agents of mortality (Givnish, 1986; Xue *et al.*, 1999). The live-crowns of the chinese fir trees receded upward with canopy closure, and the ratio of live crown length to tree height (CL/TH) decreased to 0.3089 at the 2% stand mortality rate when self-thinning occurs (Fig. 3). Long (1985) found that the CL/TH ratio is below 0.4 in Douglas fir (*Pseudotsuga menziesii* var. *glauca*) and Lodgepole pine (*Pinus contorta*) stands at a 50% stand mortality rate with occurrence of self-thinning. Therefore, it is expected that self-thinning occurrences may eventually coincide with a certain CL/TH ratio. During this time interval, there is little gain in volume for the chinese fir stands because the stand suffers sharp mortality due to competition. This feature results in gradual flattening of the slopes in the plot, indicating that an increase in the average stem volume matches the corresponding decrease in stand density (stage 3). When the mortality sequentially increases from 2% to 5%, 10%, 15% and 67%, the slope accordingly flattens to −1.553, −1.537, −1.499 and −1.477, respectively (Fig.1- (b), Fig.1- (c), Fig.1- (d), Fig.1- (e)).

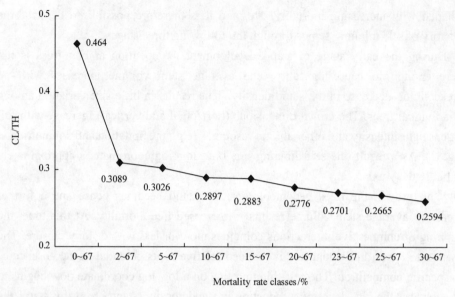

Fig. 3   Relationship between the crown length/total tree height ratio and mortality rate classes

However, as the forest canopy becomes more open as the stands grow, small gaps in the canopy, which are typically a result of the death of the smaller, suppressed trees, are rapidly reclaimed by the stand as the crowns of residual trees expand. This leads to a gradual increase in relative growth rates of the average stem volume. At this time, an increasingly large percentage of the small and suppressed trees die, and the stand is now composed mainly of the surviving larger-sized trees. In other words, the slope changes following the accumulation of average stem volume with little mortality occurring over the next time interval. This occurs when mortality exceeds 20% and the slope becomes steeper. For the chinese fir stands, self-thinning slopes are increased from -1.485, -1.570 and -1.578 to -1.613, which correspond to the accumulative mortality rates of 20%, 23%, 25% and 30%, respectively (Fig.1- (f), Fig.1- (g), Fig.1- (h), Fig.1- (i)).

Bi *et al*. (2000) demonstrated the use of a method with stochastic frontier functions free from selecting data points for fitting self-thinning lines for even-aged *Pinus radiata* stands. However, the constant slope obtained by these authors may not reflect a competition-induced self-thinning trajectory because during the course of self-thinning, crown expansion affects not only the rate of average stem volume growth but also the stem number. Therefore, the self-thinning exponents cannot systematically vary with different mortality rate classes and instead remain constant or fluctuate around a constant value. Because of this, we have no reason to believe that the slope attained at different mortality stages would remain fixed for a long time. Rather, -1.5 is a transitory value in the course of self-thinning as the maximum $V - N$ line gradually changes due to the crown size dynamics.

5
Conclusions

In this study, we quantify the maximum average stem volume (V; dm^3) and density (N; stems/ha) relationship of chinese fir stands based on determination of the onset of self-thinning. We performed two steps to confirm the relationship. First, we established that the RMA technique is the most appropriate regression technique, as shown from comparison of S.E. estimated using the OLS and RMA techniques. Given the results from the RMA, we found that the mortality rate class of 2%~67% is sufficient to represent the onset of self-thinning since its estimation interval includes the entire latter estimators. When mortality equals 2%, we obtained a self-thinning line with a slope of −1.553 using the RMA + jackknife procedure. From the onset of self-thinning, we found that the self-thinning line varies with the stand growth stage and the trajectory of self-thinning becomes U-shaped with increasing mortality. In addition, the maximum volume–density trajectory had a close relationship with the canopy size distribution. The ratio of live crown length to tree height (CL/TH) decreased rapidly from a 0% to 2% mortality rate. When the chinese fir stand enters the self-thinning stage, the CL/TH value reaches 0.3 and thereafter declines gradually.

References

Bégin E, Bégin J, Bélanger L, *et al*. 2001. Balsam fir self-thinning relationship and its constancy among different ecological regions. Can J For Res, 31: 950~959

Bi H, Turvey N D. 1997. A method of selecting data points for fitting the maximum biomass-density line for stand undergoing self-thinning. Austral Ecology, 22: 356~359

Bi H, Wan G, Turvey N D. 2000. Estimating the self-thinning boundary line as a density-dependent stochastic biomass frontier. Ecology, 81: 1477~1483

Bohonak A J. 2004. RMA: Software for reduced major axis regression (V. 1.17), San Diego State University. http://www.bio.sdsu.edu/pub/andy/rma.html; last accessed Sep, 3, 2004

Drew T J, Flewelling J W. 1977. Some recent Japanese theories of yield-density relationships and their application to monterrey pine plantations. For Sci, 23: 517~534

Drew T J, Flewelling J W. 1979. Stand density management: an alternative approach and its application to Doulas-fir plantations. For Sci, 25(3): 518~532

Enquist B J, Brown J H, West G B. 1998. Allometric scaling of plant energetics and population density. Nature, 395: 163~165

Fang J, Kan M, Yamakura T. 1991. Relationships between population growth and population density in monocultures of Larix Leptolepis [in Chinese]. Acta Botanica Sincia, 33(12): 949~957

Givnish T J. 1986. Biomechanical constraints on self-thinning in plant populations. Journal of Theoretical Biology, 119: 139~146

Gorham E. 1979. Shoot height, weight and standing crop in relation to density in monospecific plant stands. Nature, 279: 148~150

Hamilton N R, Matthew C, Lemaire G. 1995. In defence of the −3/2 boundary rule: a re-evaluation of self-thinning concepts and status. Annals of Botany, 76: 569~577

Inoue A, Miyake M, Nishizono T. 2004. Allometric model of the reineke equation for Japanese cypress (*Chamaecyparis obtuse*) and red pine (*Pinus densiflora*) stands. J. For Res, 9: 319 ~ 324

Jack S B, Long J N. 1996. Linkages between silviculture and ecology: an analysis of density management diagrams. For Ecol Manag, 86: 205~220

Kikuzawa K. 1999. Theoretical relationships between mean plant size, size distribution and self thinning under one-sided competition. Annals of Botany, 83: 11~18

Kozlowski J, Konarzewski M. 2004. Is West, Brown and Enquist's model of allometric scaling mathematically correct and biologically relevant? Functional Ecology, 18: 283~289

Lei J. 2005. Forest Resource in China [in Chinese]. Beijing, China: China Forestry Publishing House, p172

Li B L, Wu H, Zou G, 2000. Self-thinning rule: a causal interpretation from ecological field theory. Ecol Model, 132: 167~173

Liu J, Tong S. 1980. Studies on the stand density control diagram for Cunninghamia Lanceolata[in Chinese]. Scientia Silvae Sinicae, 4: 241~251

Lonsdale W M. 1990. The self-thinning rule: dead or alive? Ecology, 71: 1373~1388

Long J N. 1985. A practical approach to density management. The forestry Chroncle, 61: 23~27

Long J N, Smith F W. 1984. Relation between size and density in developing stands: a description and possible mechanisms. For Ecol Manag, 7: 191~206

Mohler C L, Marks P L, Sprugel D G. 1978. Stand structure and allometry of trees during self-thinning of pure stands. The Journal of Ecology, 66: 599~614

Newton P F. 2006. Asymptotic size–density relationships within self-thinning black spruce and jack pine stand-types: Parameter estimation and model reformulations. For Ecol Manag, 226: 49~59

Niklas K J, Midgley J J, Enquist B J. 2003. A general model for mass-growth-density relations across tree-dominated communities. Evolutionary Ecology Research, 5: 459 ~ 468

Osawa A, Allen R B. 1993. Allometric theory explains self-thinning relationships of mountain beech and red pine. Ecology, 74: 1020~1032

Osawa A, Sugita S. 1989. The self-thinning rule: another interpretation of weller's results. Ecology, 70: 279~283

Ogawa K, Hagihara A. 2003. Self-thinning and size variation in a sugi (*Cryptomeria japonica D. Don*) plantation. For Ecol Manag, 174: 413~421

Pretzsch H, Biber P. 2005. A re-evaluation of reineke's rule and stand density index. For Sci, 51: 304~320

Pretzsch H. 2006. Species-specific allometric scaling under self-thinning: evidence from long-term plots in forest stands. Oecologia, 146: 572 ~583

Río M, Montero G, Bravo F. 2001. Analysis of diameter-density relationships and self-thinning in non-thinned even-aged Scots pine stands. For Ecol Manag, 142: 79~87

Roderick M L, Barnes B. 2004. Self-thinning of plant populations from a dynamic viewpoint. Functional Ecology, 18: 197~203

SAS. 1999. SAS/STAT User's guide, Version 8 [computer manual]. SAS Institute Inc., Cary, N.C., USA

Smith N J, Hann D W. 1986. A growth model based on the self-thinning rule. Can J For Res, 16: 330~334

Solomon D S, Zhang L. 2002. Maximum size-density relationship for mixed softwoods in the northeastern USA. For Ecol Manag, 155: 163~170

Torres J, Sosa V J, Eguihua M, *et al*. 2001. On the conceptual basis of the self-thinning rule. Oikos, 95: 544~548

Weller D E. 1987. A reevaluation of the −3/2 power rule of plant self-thinning. Ecological Monographs, 57: 23~43

Weller D E. 1989. The interspecific size-density relationship among crowded plant stands and its implications for the −3/2 power rule of self-thinning. The American Naturalist, 133: 20~41

West G B, Brown J H, Enquist B J. 1997. A general model for the origin of allometric scaling laws in biology. Science, 276: 122~126

West G B, Brown J H, Enquist B J. 1999. A general model for the structure and allometry of plant vascular systems. Nature, 400: 664~667

Westoby M. 1984. The self-thinning rule. Advance in Ecological Research, 14: 167~225

White J. 1981. The allometric interpretation of the self-thinning rule. Journal of Theoretical Biology, 89: 475~500

Xue L, Ogawa K, Hagihara A, *et al*. 1999. Self-thinning exponents based on the allometric model in Chinese pine (*Pinus tabulaeformis Carr.*) and Prince Rupprecht's larch (*Larix principis-rupprechtii Mayr*) stands. For Ecol Manag, 117: 87~93

Yang Y, Titus S J. 2002. Maximum size-density relationship for constraining individual tree mortality functions. For Ecol Manag, 168: 259~273

Yoda K, Kira T, Ogawa H, *et al*. 1963. Self-thinning in overcrowded pure stand under cultivated and natural conditions. Journal of Biology of Osaka City University, 14: 107~129

Zeide B. 1987. Analysis of the 3/2 power law of self-thinning. For Sci, 33: 517~537

Zhang L, Bi H, Gove J H, *et al*. 2005. A comparison of alternative methods for estimating the self-thinning boundary line. Can J For Res, 35: 1507~1514

CHAPTER NINE:
A comparison of methods for estimating the self-thinning boundary line: selecting data points and fitting coefficients

Abstract   The self-thinning boundary line represents the upper boundary of possible yield-density combinations in crowded stands. The aim of this study was to elucidate how to objectively select data points and the most appropriate regression method for estimating the self-thinning boundary line. Alternative methods for selecting data points and fitting coefficients were compared. Methods for selecting data points included visualized inspection, mortality criterion, the equal intervals method, and the relative density method. Fitting coefficients tested included ordinary least squares regression, the reduced major axis method, quantile regression, and the stochastic frontier function. Data from an even-aged chinese fir (*Cunninghamia lanceolata* (Lamb.) Hook) stand were used. Visualized inspection was subjective. The mortality criterion could precisely determine the onset of self-thinning if density independent mortality was not included. The equal intervals method may reduce the effects of density independent mortality and the selected data points may adequately reflect stand self-thinning dynamics. The relative density method can also avoid the influence of density independent mortality and ensure stand density threshold value. Stand self-thinning span is a limiting factor for both the equal interval and relative density methods. The slope and intercept estimates used in ordinary least squares regression and reduced major axis regression differed from the stand self-thinning upper boundary line. Both the quantile regression technique and stochastic frontier function produced a self-thinning boundary line as for each of these methods analyses could be performed without significant departures from the real self thinning line through selection of an appropriate quantile value.

Key words   *Cunninghamia lanceolata* (Lamb.) Hook; coefficient fitting; data point selection; regression analysis; self-thinning boundary line

1

Introduction

The self-thinning rule describes a crowded, even-aged, single-species stand in which the biomass per individual plant increases as the number of individual plants per area decreases; fewer larger individual plants survive at the cost of smaller individuals that die (Yoda *et al.*, 1963). The slopes of many reported self-thinning lines are around −3/2 (or −1/2), including data from monospecific populations ranging in size from small herbs to large trees (Weller, 1987).

Historically, there have been many attempts to define the upper boundary of possible yield-density combinations in crowded stands (Yoda *et al.*, 1963; Mohler *et al.*, 1978; White, 1981; Fang *et al.*, 1991; Enquist *et al.*, 1998; Li *et al.*, 2000; Roderick and Barnes, 2004), determining maximum size-density rules. However, the mechanisms underlying variation in the slope of the maximum size-density rule are poorly understood. Explaining these mechanisms can strengthen plant population ecology theory and provide valuable information and guidelines for silvicultural treatments (e.g., thinning) and harvesting practices.

Yoda et al. (1963) expressed the relationship for self-thinning stands by relating mean plant weight (W) to number of trees per unit area (N) on a log scale as follows:

$$\log W = \log c - k \log N \tag{1}$$

Where $\log c$ is a constant which varies with species, but only within narrow logarithmic limits from 3.5 to 4.4 (White, 1985), while the slope parameter k of the self-thinning boundary line on double logarithmic scaled graph is apparently constant regardless of species, age, and site quality (Jack and Long, 1996). The self-thinning trajectory on the log-log coordinates travels along a straight line of −3/2 slope, so is called '−3/2 power law' or 'self-thinning rule'. The self-thinning rule has been observed to apply for many species ranging from mosses to large trees, including herbaceous plants, and thus it has been considered one of the most important principles in plant population ecology (Long and Smith, 1984; Zeide, 1987; Jack and Long, 1996). However, the controversy about the theoretically discrepancy and empirical imprecision of the self-thinning rule has been more intense. The debate has primarily focused on ① acknowledging that slope of the self-thinning boundary line is a constant, but may differ from −3/2 (or −1/2) (Weller, 1987; Zeide, 1987; Osawa and Sugita, 1989; Osawa and Allen, 1993; Kikuzawa, 1999; Li et al., 2000; Río et al., 2001; Yang and Titus, 2002) and ② recognizing that the slope of the self-thinning boundary line is not a constant ,but varies at a certain interval (Mohler et al., 1978; Lonsdale, 1990; Roderick and Barnes, 2004). A long-standing concern centers on the best methods for selection of data points and fitting coefficients in self-thinning boundary equations (Weller, 1989; Bi and Turvey, 1997; Bi et al., 2000). For example, the erroneous inclusion of data points from stands of mean density (number of plants per unit area) that have not yet begun to thin will flatten the estimated slope of the line from −3/2 toward −1, while inclusion of data points from stands of high density that have not yet begun to thin will steepen the slope of the line (Westoby, 1984; Zhang et al., 2005). Over the last four decades researchers have applied different methods for selecting appropriate data points for estimation of the maximum size-density relationship. A common method is to purposefully select data points that lie close to an arbitrarily visualized upper boundary based on some criteria (Yoda et al., 1963;

Westoby, 1984; Osawa and Sugita, 1989; Osawa and Allen, 1993; Wilson *et al.*, 1999). This method subjectively eliminates data points from populations that are believed to be not undergoing density-dependent mortality. As many authors have pointed out, this method is arbitrary and subjective. To improve objectivity, Fang *et al.* (1991) proposed using the mortality criterion. This method uses the plant mortality rate to indicate the onset of self thinning. For example, once the plant population reaches substantial mortality (say, 20%), self-thinning is considered to have begun (Westoby, 1984; Fang *et al.*, 1991). Data above this mortality rate are selected and can reflect the real self-thinning trajectory. However, this method can mistakenly include data points from stands affected by density-independent factors, such as pathogens, forest wind or snow damage or forest fire, which have not yet reached the target level of density dependent mortality. These data are likely to provide results different from the real self-thinning trajectory. Bi and Turvey (1997) developed the equal intervals method with log-log coordinates. The method involves the division of a cluster of data points into a specified number of intervals. From each interval, the point with the maximum stand size is selected to contribute to the fitting trajectory. From these estimates, one can be chosen to represent the maximum size-density line. Newton (2006) used the equal intervals method to quantify maximum size-density relationship for black spruce (*Picea mariana* (Mill.) B.S.P.) and jack pine (*Pinus banksiana* Lamb.) stands and demonstrated that this selection method can be employed to determine a stand's real self-thinning trajectory. In comparison with the visualized inspection and mortality criterion methods, the equal intervals method has two advantages: ① it is less subjective than visualized data point selection and ② since the maximum biomass for each interval was selected, the potential effect of density-independent mortality is reduced. Nonetheless, the limitation of the equal intervals method is that when the self-thinning data point is invariant the number of data points selected and the number of equal intervals is constrained. In a recent study, Solomon and Zhang (2002) assumed a theoretical value for the slope coefficient of the maximum size-density line (i.e.-1.5 for the $\log V - \log N$ relationship, where V is mean tree volume, N is in number of plants per area). The intercept coefficient was calculated as $a = \log V + 1.5 \log N$, using the stand with the largest relative density (RD) (Drew and Flewelling, 1979). Once determined, the equation was used to compute maximum stand density (N_{max}) for N of a given stand. The RD was calculated as N/N_{max} for each stand, where N is current stand density. In theory stands with higher RD (say, RD$\geqslant$0.7) should have been undergoing self-thinning and experiencing density-related mortality. Therefore, it is reasonable to select plots with an RD larger than a predetermined threshold value to fit the maximum size-density relationship. However, the concern with the RD method is that the calculation of RD for each plot is based on a theoretical constant for the slope coefficient (say, -1.5). Thus, the central tendency of this subset of the plots has been predetermined or influenced by the theoretical slope constant.

There are several regression methods for estimation of the two coefficients of the maximum size-density line, including ① arbitrarily hand fitting a line above an upper boundary of data points (Yoda *et al.*, 1963; Drew and Flewelling, 1979); ② fitting an ordinary least square regression (OLS); ③ using reduced major axis regression (RMA) (Mohler *et al.*, 1978); ④ applied quantile regression (QR) (Cade *et al.*, 1999); ⑤ the stochastic frontier production function (SFF).

OLS is generally acknowledged to be the best method for estimating the conditional mean of one random variable given a fixed value for another. However, estimation of the two coefficients of the maximum size-density line OLS is inappropriate, since the primary interest is the values of the equation parameters themselves, which are used to describe the functional relationship between two random variables (Zhang *et al.*, 2005). In addition, the method defines an "average" size-density line rather than a "biological" maximum size-density line. In theory, the maximum size-density line should be the upper boundary line of the selected data points (Weller, 1987; Osawa and Sugita, 1989).

Mohler *et al.* (1978) introduced the use of reduced major axis (RMA) to estimate the regression coefficients for *Prunus pensylvanica* L. and *Abies balsamea* (L.) Mill. between $\log W$ and $\log N$. This method can overcome the scale dependence of the major axis regression technique by standardizing the variables W and N before the scaling exponent is computed (LaBarbera, 1989). RMA can be summarized as follows (Solomon and Zhang, 2002): Assume a linear regression model $y = \alpha + \beta x$, where y and x are dependent and independent variables, respectively, α and β are OLS regression coefficients. The RMA slope coefficient is $\beta_{RMA} = \beta / |r_{yx}|$, where r_{yx} is Pearson's correlation coefficient between y and x. The standard error (SE) of β_{RMA} is equal to the SE of β. The RMA intercept coefficient is $\alpha_{RMA} = \bar{y} - \beta_{RMA}\bar{x}$, and the SE of α_{RMA} is equal to the SE of α. The SE values are essential for constructing confidence intervals for the coefficients. Therefore, the slope from RMA is smaller than that from OLS, but the intercept for RMA is larger than that for OLS. However, both OLS and RMA have the same fitting principle, that is, the two coefficients are based on the sum of the squares of the residuals.

Cade *et al.* (1999) applied quantile regression (QR) to account for unmeasured ecological factors by estimating changes near the upper extremes of data distributions. The QR method of Koenker and Bassett (1978) is generally used to estimate the variance-covariance matrix of the coefficients and generate estimates of regression coefficient standard errors:

$$\min\left[\sum_{\{i|y_i \geqslant x_{ij}\beta\}}\theta\left|y_i - \sum_{j=0}^{p} x'_{ij}\beta_j\right| + \sum_{\{i|y_i < x_i\beta_j x_{ij}\}}(1-\theta)\left|y_i - \sum_{j=0}^{p} x_{ij}\beta_j\right|\right] \tag{2}$$

Where the θ th quantile ($0 \leqslant \theta \leqslant 1$) of a random variable y is defined as the smallest real value of y, such that the probability of obtaining any smaller value is greater than or equal to θ. y_i is an $i \times 1$ vector of dependent responses, x_i is an $i \times 1$ vector of independent responses, β is a $p \times 1$ vector of unknown regression coefficients. θ represents the ratio of the number of fitted data to the whole observed data. In least absolute values regression, the QR regression model is fitted by minimizing the sum of the absolute values of the residuals rather than the sum of the squares of the residuals as in OLS regression models. QR regression models based on least absolute values criteria are resistant to extreme outlying values in the y direction such that the model fit is unaffected by changes in y values, as long as the signs of the residuals are maintained. Moreover, QR regression models minimizing the sum of absolute deviations are particularly appropriate for estimating nonparametric measures of location (Koenker and Bassett, 1978). However, the selection of quantile values is based on the researchers' subjective criteria, so the fitted parameters of the QR technique will differ with quantile selection (Scharf *et al.*, 1998).

Bi et al. (2000) and Bi (2001) adopted a stochastic frontier production function (SFF) to estimate the self-thinning line for an even-aged *Pinus radiate* stand. They concluded that if all data points were selected in a non-subjective manner an efficient estimation of the self-thinning upper boundary was made. Over the past three decades, the SFF technique has been used extensively in the analysis of the maximum production efficiency in economics and management science in the form:

$$Y_i = AX_1^{\beta_1}X_2^{\beta_2}...X_k^{\beta_k}e^{v_i}e^{-\mu_i} \tag{3}$$

Where Y_i is the i th observed value of the dependent variable which is called output in econometrics, X'_i s are independent variables, A and β_k s are parameters, e^{v_i} and $e^{-\mu_i}$ are two error components. The distribution of v_i is assumed to be normal with a zero mean and constant variance σ_v^2 and μ_i is assumed to be the absolute value of a normally distributed variable with zero mean and constant σ_u^2 such that $0 \leqslant \mu_i \leqslant \infty$ and $0 \leqslant e^{-\mu_i} \leqslant 1$. In logarithmic form, the model becomes:

$$y_i = \alpha + \beta x_i + \varepsilon_i \tag{4}$$

Where $y_i = \log Y_i$, $\alpha = \log A$, x_i is the i th vector of log-transformed independent variables and β is a vector of parameters. The error term, $\varepsilon_i = v_i - \mu_i$, is a compound random variable with two components and each is assumed to be independently and identically distributed across observations. Bi et al (2000) pointed out that $e^{-\mu_i}$ represented site occupancy. Before full site occupancy, stands do not have to sacrifice individuals for further growth through competition induced mortality: $0 < e^{-\mu_i} < 1$. When the site is fully occupied, stands have accumulated the maximum attainable biomass at that stand density and further growth will incur mortality: $e^{-\mu_i} = 1$. v_i represents external factors during the stand self-thinning such as climatic variations, insect attacks, diseases, or other changes in the environment specific to each stand and time. The estimated value of the slope coefficient of the maximum size-density line will vary with the exact selection of data points and method of coefficient fitting employed.

Chinese fir is naturally distributed in southern China and is the main silvicultural tree in this region. chinese fir, which is a relatively fast growing tree with good timber quality, is wildly used in industry. However, there are few studies on the self-thinning of this species. Such knowledge would be of fundamental importance for understanding the ecology of the chinese fir and its management. Therefore, the main purpose of this study was to establish the optimal relationship between stand biomass and stand density through comparison of methods for selection of data points and fitting coefficients.

2
Material and Methods

2.1
Experimental sites and measurements

Chinese fir stands located in Shaowu County (27°20′N, 117°29′E), Fujian province in southern China was established in 1982. Plots were designed in a randomized block arrangement with five levels of tree spacing: 2 m × 3 m (1667 stems/ha), 2 m × 1.5 m (3333 stems/ha), 2 m × 1 m (5000 stems/ha), 1 m×1.5 m (6667 stems/ha) and 1 m × 1 m (10 000 stems/ha). Each level of spacing was replicated three times. Each of the 15 plots had an area of 20m × 30m, and a buffer consisting of two rows of trees surrounded each plot. Data points for 3 plots with planting density 2 m × 3 m, 1 plot with density 2 m × 1.5 m and 1 plot with density 2 m × 1 m were excluded since their mortality rate did not exceed 10%.   Thus, data from twelve plots were used for the purpose of this study. Trees in every plot were tallied, and measurements were conducted after tree height reached 1.3 m. Sampling was performed each winter from 1983 to 1990 and then every other year until 2006. Measurements included total tree height, diameter at breast height, crown width within and between rows and height to the base of lowest live branch. Stem volume was estimated from experimental formulae for chinese fir (Liu and Tong 1996). The reduction in the number of trees was recorded in two categories: died, and removed for unknown reasons.

Summary statistics for these plots are shown in Table 1.

Table 1   Descriptive statistics for plots

Plot	Planting density /(stems/ha)	Stand density in 2006 /(stems/ha)	Mean diameter of breast height/cm	SD	Minimum diameter of breast height/cm	Maximum diameter of breast height /cm
B_2	3333	2517	10.65	2.42	6.49	13.80
B_3	3333	2483	12.29	2.71	7.58	16.23
C_2	5000	3467	9.57	2.44	5.51	13.16
C_3	5000	2417	10.21	2.74	6.04	14.04
D_1	6667	3317	8.76	2.02	5.53	11.90
D_2	6667	4267	8.85	2.67	4.95	13.14
D_3	6667	3800	9.13	2.62	5.33	13.26
E_1	10 000	5117	8.39	2.01	5.55	11.70
E_2	10 000	3183	8.42	2.50	4.80	13.08
E_3	10 000	5217	8.75	2.71	5.10	13.11

2.2
Methods

The relationship between $\log D$ and $\log N$ were used for several reasons: ① the mean diameter at breast height (D) , the easiest tree dimension to measure exhibits a close relationship with tree mass and stand total basal area (Zeide, 1987); ② to avoid the introduction of bias into the analysis due to computing tree volume using a specific tabulated volume equation (Zhang *et al.*, 2005), and ③ since the higher precision in fitted parameters is obtained using $\log D \sim \log N$ compared to $\log W \sim \log N$ when a stand enters the self-thinning stage (Zeide, 1987). The regression model takes the form:

$$\log D = \beta_0 - \beta_1 \log N + \varepsilon \tag{5}$$

Where β_0 is intercept and β_1 is slope, both of them are regression coefficients to be estimated. ε is a model error term. The estimated regression coefficients β_0 and β_1 from regression model (5) were computed based on each of four different data points selection methods. ① Two data points close to a visualized upper boundary were purposefully selected and $\log D$ and $\log N$ were each computed separately and ② mean diameter at breast height and number of trees per unit area were computed for zero mortality, above 10% mortality and 20% mortality, separately. OLS was then applied to compute regression coefficients β_0 and β_1 using regression model (5). ③ With $\log D \sim \log N$ log-log coordinates, the observed data points were equally divided into five trees, 10 trees and 20 trees. The largest diameter at breast height was then selected and corresponding number of trees per unit area for each interval. The selected data points were used to compute regression coefficients β_0 and β_1 using regression model (5) and the OLS technique. ④ Plots with RD⩾0.7, RD⩾0.8 and RD⩾0.9 were used to fit regression model (5) using OLS technique. Lastly, all available plots were used to fit regression model (5) using the OLS, RMA, QR and SFF techniques. SAS (SAS Institute Inc, 1999) was employed for OLS, RMA and QR (regression quantile θ =0.99) analyses and LIMDEP 7.0 (Econometric Software Inc, 1998) was used for the SFF methods.

3
Results and Discussion

In the visualized inspection method the self-thinning line was placed across the upper boundary of available plots (Fig.1- (a)). The x and y coordinates of the top-most two plots ($\log D_1$ = 2.78, $\log N_1$ = 8.36, and $\log D_2$ = 2.65, $\log N_2$ = 8.58) were used to compute the β_0 and β_1 coefficients of regression model (5), resulting in $\log D = 7.63 - 0.58 \log N$.

The slope of self-thinning ($\beta_1 = -0.56$), which denotes when chinese fir plots began mortality, is steeper than the theoretical constant, -0.5. This is due to density-independent mortality, and thus the real self-thinning process is not reflected (Table 2). When data points were selected based on 10% and 20% mortality, the slopes of self-thinning were -0.51 and -0.49, both tending to -0.5. This reflects the effect of intraspecific competition leading to self-thinning and apparently excluded the density-independent effects when the stand mortality rate was above 10%. The self-thinning boundary lines for data points above 10% and 20% mortality selected for fitting the self-thinning line almost entirely overlapped (Fig. 1–(b)). However, these results differed from those found for 20% mortality by Westoby (1984) or 1/3 mortality by Fang *et al.* (1992) Nonetheless, this study shows that when density-independent mortality is not apparent, mortality criterion may reliably determine the onset of self-thinning.

The slopes and intercepts of the self-thinning line exhibited little difference when determined using either a 10 tree or 20 tree equal intervals method, but there was a significant difference between the 10 tree and 20 tree intervals with a 5 tree interval (Fig. 1-(c)). The self-thinning slopes became flatter when the sample size increased and tended towards −0.5. The number data points that can be selected based on a 5 tree sample size is greater than can be selected with a 10 tree or 20 tree sample size, but the fitting precision for all 3 was much the same with a coefficient of determination above 0.9 (Table 2). This is because data points selected using a 5 tree sample size include the data points selected using a 10 tree and 20 tree sample size. The equal intervals method was less subjective than the visualized inspection method. However, it often generates a small sample size for model fitting (Bi and Turvey, 1997) and the coefficient estimates may also vary depending on the number of size classes and the method of dividing size classes. More importantly, it is possible to include some plots at lower densities (i.e., at the left end of the $\log N$ axis) that have not reached the stage of self-thinning. Consequently, the slope coefficient of the self-thinning line based on this subset of the plots may be flatter than expected (Zhang *et al.*, 2005). Therefore, this method should only be employed once a stand has grown sufficiently crowded and when the effects of density-independent mortality are negligible.

Relative density (RD) denotes the ratio of the current stand density to that of the most fully-stocked stand (Drew and Flewelling, 1979). As RD increases the stand approximates the most fully-stocked stand. Solomon and Zhang (2002) proposed that stands with a relative density index higher than a certain threshold value should be undergoing self-thinning. Therefore, it is reasonable to select plots with RD larger than a predetermined threshold value to fit the maximum size-density relationship. In this study, 0.7, 0.8 and 0.9 were selected as threshold values for RD. Fig. 1–(d) illustrated that the self-thinning slope became flatter as the threshold increased and tended to −0.5 (Table 2). The slope of self-thinning for the 0.7 RD value was smaller than that for the 0.8 and 0.9 RD values. This was because stands with 0.7 RD did not yet approximate the most fully-stocked stands and density-independent factors were still apparent. As RD increases stands approximate the most fully-stocked and there is little different among the slopes of self-thinning for different RD values all tending towards the theoretical constant. This shows that it is reasonable to use higher threshold values for RD to calculate the stand self-thinning line.

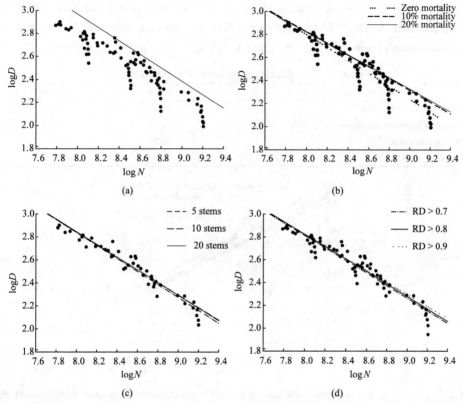

Fig. 1   Maximum stand density-mean diameter of breast height relationship for four regression methods (a) Visualized inspection. (b) Mortality criterion. (c) Equal intervals. (d) Relative density.

Table 2   Comparison of the selecting data points and fitting coefficients

Selecting data points and numbers (n)	Slope (SE)	Intercept (SE)	R^2
Mortality criterion			
Zero mortality (83)	−0.56 (0.046)	7.28 (0.612)	0.817
10% mortality (51)	−0.51 (0.037)	6.79 (0.435)	0.931
20% mortality (37)	−0.49 (0.029)	6.19 (0.367)	0.934
Equal intervals			
5 stems (43)	−0.62 (0.071)	7.91 (0.610)	0.917
10 stems (31)	−0.55 (0.069)	7.26 (0.583)	0.922
20 stems (19)	−0.54 (0.089)	7.23 (0.762)	0.939
Relative density (RD)			
RD > 0.7 (71)	−0.58 (0.069)	7.14 (0.583)	0.883
RD > 0.8 (62)	−0.54 (0.056)	7.09 (0.472)	0.929
RD > 0.9 (57)	−0.53 (0.057)	6.70 (0.478)	0.900

One way to avoid the subjective selection of data points is to use all available plots and fit the self-thinning line using appropriate regression techniques. OLS, RMA, QR and SFF regression methods were compared. Table 3 shows the two regression coefficients for the OLS, RMA, QR and SFF regression methods. Fig. 2 illustrates the regression lines obtained by the OLS, RMA, QR and SFF regression methods.

Table 3　Regression coefficients of the four models

Regression technique	Slope	Intercept
Stochastic frontier function	−0.52	7.03
Ordinary least squares regression	−0.54	7.63
Reduced major axis	−0.57	7.39
Quantile regression	−0.52	7.05

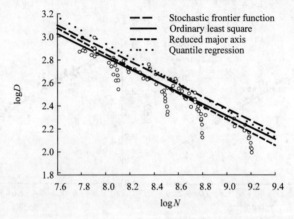

Fig. 2　Comparison of four fitting self-thinning boundary line methods. Stochastic frontier function, Ordinary least square, Reduced major axis, and Quantile regression

It is clear that the slope of self-thinning ($\beta_1 = -0.54$) from OLS differed from the theoretical slope value −0.5 and the self-thinning line represented a central tendency line across the range of the data. The two coefficients ($\beta_1 = -0.57$ and $\beta_0 = 7.39$) for RMA were recalculated based on Pearson's correlation coefficient between log D and log N, producing a slope greater than that described by OLS. OLS and RMA have been used to consider the most appropriate fitting methods for self-thinning lines. The results indicate that it is impossible to employ the same fitting method for plants with different growth characteristics and to reach the same conclusion. Thus, when selecting the fitting method for the self-thinning line it is important to understand the statistical constraints of the method and ensure that the regression results coincide with the biological growth trajectory for that species.

QR is capable of providing statistics and estimation for linear model fit for any part of a response distribution, including near the upper bounds, without imposing stringent assumptions on the error distribution. The slope of self-thinning ($\beta_1 = -0.52$) converges to -0.5, and can reflect chinese fir self-thinning process. In addition, as QR increases residual variation decreases. Two peaks occur with 10%~20% QR and 80%~85% QR. When QR tends to 100%, fitting is most precise (Fig.3), thus it is most appropriate to select QR values between 99%~100%.

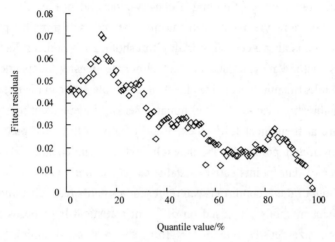

Fig. 3   Relationship between quantile value and fitted residuals

SFF and QR result in the same slope ($\beta_1 = -0.52$). Both SFF and QR methods forced all observations to be on or below a limiting boundary line, but produce a self-thinning line very different from the upper limiting boundary line of the OLS and RMA methods. The SFF technique specifies that the maximum output a producer can obtain is assumed to be determined both by the production function and by random external factors. Bi and Turvey (1997) and Bi *et al*. (2000) used this method for maximum stand biomass research. In their article, the SFF method describes the maximum size-density relationship by including site occupancy due to density-dependent growth and mortality within individual stands and the effects of external factors that take place at random over space and time on the frontier. Therefore, the result can show the self-thinning trajectory for chinese fir stands. In addition, the error term ε in the SFF method has an asymmetric and non-normal distribution with a negative mean. But a negative mean does not imply that all residuals are negative and allows a few residuals to be positive, especially when residuals absolute values, $\left|\sigma_v^2\right|$, is much larger than zero (Bi *et al*. 2000). However, the SFF method can yield an upper limiting boundary line only when the estimated σ_v^2 is small and close to zero.

4
Conclusions

Comparison of data point selection methods, including visualized inspection, mortality criterion, equal interval and RD, indicated that mortality criterion may indicate the occurrence of self-thinning if density-independent mortality is negligible. Nevertheless, maximum yield data can masque the real self-thinning process when stand mortality rate is above certain mortality threshold. Data points selected using the equal intervals method may reduce but not eliminate density-independent mortality factors, meanwhile, the number of size classes and sample size can restrict one another. Using a higher threshold value of RD eliminates density-independent mortality factors, when stands are at their most fully-stocked and results in the most precise fit. Thus, during selection of data points, we should exclude density-independent data and ensure that the number of data points satisfies statistical constraints. Only those data points which satisfy both of these conditions can represent a stand's real self-thinning process. Fitting coefficient methods are based on different statistical hypotheses and thus the fitted maximum size-density line differs from the real self-thinning process. The maximum size-density boundary of OLS and RMA crosses the middle of the observed data and this "average" maximum size-density line cannot represent the real self-thinning boundary line. QR regression models are resistant to extreme outlying values in the y direction so that fit is unaffected and residual variation is reduced. On the other hand, the QR technique can reflect marginal effects between independent and dependent variables. Therefore, QR regression can reliably reflect self-thinning trajectory. Nonetheless, incorrectly selecting the QR value can lead to fitted results very different from the real self-thinning trajectory. The fitted self-thinning line approximates to the maximum size-density line and fitted residuals decrease rapidly when QR increases from 85% to 100%. Therefore, it is optimal to select QR between 99% and 100%. SFF includes site occupancy and mortality-related external factors, and thus the fitted self-thinning line can be objective and exhibit an appropriate slope. However, SFF produces a self-thinning line lower than the upper limiting boundary line when the estimated residuals are larger than zero.

References

Bi H. 2001. The self-thinning surface. Forest Sci, 47: 361~370

Bi H, Turvey N D. 1997. A method of selecting data points for fitting the maximum biomass-density line for stand undergoing self-thinning. Aust J Ecol, 22: 356~359

Bi H, Wan G, Turvey N D. 2000. Estimating the self-thinning boundary line as a density-dependent stochastic biomass frontier. Ecology, 81: 1477~1483

Cade B S, Terrell J W, Schroeder R L. 1999. Estimating effects of limiting factors with regression quantiles. Ecology, 80: 311~323

Drew T J, Flewelling J W. 1979. Stand density management: an alternative approach and its application to Douglas-fir plantations. Forest Sci, 25: 518~532

Econometric S, 1998. LIMDEP 7.0 User's Manual (computer manual). New York: Econometric Software Plainview

Enquist B J, Brown J H, West G B. 1998. Allometric scaling of plant energetics and population density. Nature, 395: 163~165

Fang J Y. 1992. Self-thinning rule in plant population. Rural Eco Env, 2: 7~12

Fang J Y, Jian C, Yamakura T. 1991. Relationships between population growth and population density in monocultures of Larix leptolepis. Acta Bot Sin, 33: 949~957

Jack S B, Long J N. 1996. Linkages between silviculture and ecology: an analysis of density management diagrams. Forest Ecol Manag, 86: 205~220

Kikuzawa K. 1999. Theoretical relationships between mean plant size, size distribution and self thinning under one-sided competition. Ann Bot–London, 83: 11~18

Koenker R, Bassett G. 1978. Regression quantiles. Econometrica, 46: 33~50

LaBarbera M. 1989. Analyzing body size as factor in ecology and evolution. Annual Rev Ecol Syst, 20: 97~117

Li B, Wu H, Zou G. 2000. Self-thinning rule: a causal interpretation from ecological field theory. Ecol Model, 132: 167~173

Londsdale W. 1990. The self-thinning rule: dead or alive? Ecology, 71: 1373~1388

Long J N, Smith F W. 1984. Relation between size and density in developing stands: a description and possible mechanisms. Forest Ecol Manag, 7: 191~206

Mohler C, Marks P, Sprugel D G. 1978. Stand structure and allometry of trees during self-thinning of pure stands. J Ecol, 66: 599~614

Newton P F. 2006. Asymptotic size-density relationships within self-thinning black spruce and jack pine stand-types: parameter estimation and model reformulations. Forest Ecol Manag, 226: 49~59

Osawa A, Allen R B. 1993. Allometric theory explains self-thinning relationships of mountain beech and red pine. Ecology, 74: 1020~1032

Osawa A, Sugita S. 1989. The self-thinning rule: another interpretation of Weller's results. Ecology, 70: 279~283

Río M, Montero G, Bravo F. 2001. Analysis of diameter-density relationships and self-thinning in non-thinned even-aged Scots pine stands. Forest Ecol. Manag., 142: 79~87.

Roderick M L, Barnes B. 2004. Self-thinning of plant populations from a dynamic viewpoint. Funct Ecol, 18: 197~203

SAS. 1999. SAS/STAT User's Guide, version 8 (computer manual). SAS Institute Inc., Cary, New York, USA

Scharf F S, Juanes F, Sutherland M. 1998. Inferring ecological relationships from the edges of scatter diagrams: comparison of regression techniques. Ecology, 79: 448~460

Solomon D S, Zhang L. 2002. Maximum size-density relationships for mixed softwoods in the northeastern USA. Forest Ecol Manag, 155: 163~170

Weller D E. 1987. A reevaluation of the −3/2 power rule of plant self-thinning. Ecol Monogr, 57: 23~43

Weller D E. 1989. The interspecific size-density relationship among crowded plant stands and its implications for the −3/2 power rule of self-thinning. Am Nat, 133: 20~41

Westoby M. 1984. The self-thinning rule. Adv Ecol Res, 14: 167~225

White J. 1981. The allometric interpretation of the self-thinning rule. J Theor Biol, 89: 475~500

White J. 1985. The thinning rule and its application to mixtures of plant populations. In studies on plant demography. London: Edited by J. White. Academic Press, pp. 291~309

Wilson D S, Seymour R S, Maguire D A. 1999. Density management diagram for Northeastern red spruce and balsam fir forests. N J Appl Forest, 16: 48~56

Yang Y, Titus S J. 2002. Maximum size-density relationship for constraining individual tree mortality functions. Forest Ecol Manag, 168: 259~273

Yoda K, Kira T, Ogawa H. 1963. Self-thinning in overcrowded pure stand under cultivated and natural conditions. J Biol Osaka City Univ, 14: 107~129

Zeide B. 1987. Analysis of the 3/2 power law of self-thinning. Forest Sci, 33: 517~537

Zhang L, Bi H, Gove J H, *et al*. 2005. A comparison of alternative methods for estimating the self-thinning boundary line. Can J Forest Res, 35: 1507~1514